Twenty-Four Dead Men . . .

One for every year of Larry Lynmouth's life! No wonder Crooked Horn buzzed with excitement when Larry walked up to the bank door—and knocked!

He went straight to the president's desk and took out a wallet. Three armed men watched him as he counted out sixty-two bank notes of five hundred dollars each.

"That's just a present to help the old bank along."

President Baynes counted the money stupefied. Thirty-one thousand dollars! Four years ago a desperado, single-handed, had walked into that bank in the middle of the afternoon, and walked out again with thirty-one thousand dollars in hard cash.

"Stop him!" cried Baynes. But Lynmouth was already gone.

Max Brand

THE OUTLAW

PUBLISHED BY POCKET BOOKS NEW YORK

POCKET BOOKS, a Simon & Schuster division of
GULF & WESTERN CORPORATION
1230 Avenue of the Americas, New York, N.Y. 10020

ISBN: 0-671-83416-9

First Pocket Books printing June, 1951

15   14   13   12   11   10   9   8   7

POCKET and colophon are trademarks of Simon & Schuster.

Printed in the U.S.A.

CONTENTS

THE OUTLAW

I

TO HELP THE BANK

NORTHWEST of Crooked Horn, where the most prosperous ranches were located, ran a little wabbling line of telephone poles. Over this line, from ten miles away, came the news on this bright spring morning.

As soon as the word arrived in Crooked Horn, it spread to the limits of the little town like the proverbial ripple around the fallen stone.

The presidents and chief officers of each of the two banks ran out from their buildings and returned with armed men, who were placed in positions of advantage inside and outside the buildings.

Deputy Sheriff Neilan took his post with two assistants at the post office.

Isaac Stein, the owner of the pawnshop and jewelry store, went in frantic haste for his two nephews, who were placed behind the counter with double-barreled riot guns in their hands. Also, he ran out and hailed two passers-by. They were closed in the back room, where there was nothing worth stealing, but through the entrance to which they could fire into the front chamber. They, also, were equipped with riot guns.

Up and down the main street of Crooked Horn there were six saloons, and three stores, besides the hotel. From the hotel, the stores, and the saloons, came hastening men carrying sacks of cash and notes from cash drawers and registers. These sums of money were hastily deposited at one or the other of the banks.

Two of the stores and three of the saloons closed down, locked doors, windows, and shutters, and the proprietors remained inside under arms, while outposts were placed in upper windows.

"Faro Pete" closed his layout, locked it, barred and

1

bolted it, and brought his cash to the Merchants' Loan & Trust. After that, he did not delay, but mounted his fastest horse and spurred out of town with a desperate face.

"Two-gun" Billy Lambert had no cash to deposit, but he also mounted his best horse, and, with both his guns, and a rifle besides, dashed from Crooked Horn, taking the river road.

Young Sam Townsend, recently notorious and famous for his battle with the Brintons on the lower Pecos, followed the two good examples which had just been set. Young Sam did not even wait to dress fully. Rising in an undershirt and a pair of trousers—he had been out late the night before at a quiet poker game—Sam went out of Crooked Horn lashing his horse at every jump.

The citizens, however, who could not pretend either to a stock of hard cash or to any great reputation as gamblers, crooks, or man-killers, appeared rather unconcerned. They merely made sure that their children and womenfolks were safely within doors. They themselves were to be seen at posts of vantage, such as the corners of the central plaza, or perhaps idling in their gardens—if they were particularly cautious men.

A telephone message was sent to Stephen's Crossing, to the south, that it might be well to get a posse of picked men ready to take horse. Another message reached First Chance, in the northern desert, to take similar precautions. County Sheriff Dan Peach was warned in a similar manner at his home, twenty miles away; and he announced that he was taking horse immediately to appear on the scene as soon as four strong legs could gallop the distance.

So Crooked Horn and the country round made what preparation could be made, and then waited, holding its breath. At the bridge, on the north road, young Joe Masters volunteered to take his post and signal from the top of the big cottonwood as soon as he was apprised of the danger coming down the road.

Doctor Crosswell, watching with glasses from the roof of his home, presently was able to see a white cloth waved from the top of the cottonwood, and in this manner he was able to know that the danger was, indeed, coming down the north road, and that it was close at hand.

He climbed down from the roof, and from an upper

window he shouted the tidings to the street, where it ran up and down like wildfire. Every soul in Crooked Horn knew in another instant, and the town held its breath even more.

Then, around the turn beyond the hotel, a single rider appeared. As he came closer, it could be seen that he was mounted on a cream-colored horse.

"It's him, and he's on Fortune!" went the word down the street.

Then the rider came still closer, and a dozen glasses made out his face in the distance.

"It's Larry Lynmouth himself, riding the mare, Fortune!"

Mouths gaped, and eyes widened. Women grew pale behind windows. Children stood tiptoe. Little girls trembled. Little boys shuddered with ecstatic joy.

Yet even to those who knew his face, even to those who had studied the familiar features a thousand times in a thousand newspaper photographs, it was a shock to see him as he actually was, in the flesh.

He was exactly twenty-four years old. He had been famous for almost half that time.

He was said to have killed twenty-four men, that is to say, a man a year. He had been arrested five times. He had broken away from his captors twice on the way to prison —once by the expedient of jumping out the window of a rapidly moving train and falling forty feet from the bridge it was crossing, into the water beneath. (This had been done with irons on hands and feet, so that for three months it had been considered certain that he lay dead in the mud of the river bottom.)

Three times, safely lodged behind bars, he had broken out. Once it was apparently by bribery. Once he had taken a jailer by the throat and forced the man to unlock the doors. Once he had worked a passage through three feet of solid masonry from a dark cell!

He had been hunted by private detectives, by public posses, by the most expert officers of the law, from Dawson to Panama, and from San Francisco to Halifax.

He was known to have "stuck up" at least six stages, and he was more than suspected of having a hand in three train robberies—one of them the spectacular holdup of the T. & L. train by a single man. Two bank robberies definitely were traced to his name, and twenty others were attributed to him.

But now Larry Lynmouth rode unharmed down the main street of Crooked Horn. Society stood on guard, but society dared not touch him without new provocation, for, a scant two weeks before, he had been cleared and pardoned for all crime by the proclamations of five governors within whose territories he had committed the deeds of which he had been accused, and for which he had been tried in the past.

Except for a new offense, there was no use in arresting him again, because it was so certain that no jury would convict him. For it was now hardly a month since the affair of the Ridley Dam, and all men remembered how he had ridden a hundred miles between dusk and dawn, and, by the aid of this same beautiful mare, Fortune, had come to the Ridley Dam in time to stop the dastards who had planned to blast the big structure to a ruin. Sheer blindly venomous sabotage on their part, regardless of the crowded homes which huddled unprotected in the valley below the dam.

For this reason, Crooked Horn was on guard and held its breath, but dared not lift its hand.

And for all these reasons Crooked Horn stared with amazement upon the real facts about Lynmouth, as they appeared in his physical presence.

Where were the wild rumors about him? Where were they to be lodged?

As for his gigantic strength, how could it be confined in a rather slender body, certainly not over, but under six feet in height?

As for his gaudy clothes, he was dressed neatly, to be sure, but not unlike any other cow-puncher. Unless one were to take note of the manner in which the mane and tail of the mare had been braided. There was some openwork of gold, in the Mexican style, glittering on his tall sombrero. That was all! No silver conchos, no gaudy blues and reds.

And then, finally, those tales of grim ferocity—who could give them a local habitation and a name in connection with such a handsome and open young face? His blue eyes, to be sure, rested on one with a glance as straight as a rifle barrel steady on its mark, but a faint, continual smile of good nature appeared on his lips.

All the way before him, people stared, mute. All the way behind him, down that street, a murmur of comment arose.

Dangerous as a snake?

Not a bit of it! Not if they could read faces, as they thanked Heaven they could!

He stopped where?

Straight in front of the First National!

A wild buzz of excitement swept through Crooked Horn.

Was it possible that he would walk in there among those heavily armed and prepared fighting men? Would he walk into that set trap and try to rob the place?

He could not do it, under a miracle. But then, miracles were a favorite diet of this young man. Crooked Horn—at least, the citizens who had no deposits in the First National —rather wished that the miracle could be attempted. And, if attempted, who could wish bad luck to so amiable a young man, who wore a smile upon his face?

The door of the bank was locked. But it was slowly opened when he knocked.

He went straight to the president's desk and took out a wallet. Three armed men watched him from the corners of the room as he counted out sixty-two bank notes of five hundred dollars each. He pushed these across to President Baynes.

"Are you opening an account, Larry?" asked the banker, amazed.

"No," said Larry Lynmouth. "That's just a present to help the old bank along."

President Baynes counted the money, stupefied. Thirty-one thousand dollars!

And then that sum shocked his mind into understanding. Four years ago a desperado, single-handed, had walked into that bank in the middle of the afternoon, and walked out again with thirty-one thousand dollars in hard cash.

He looked up, but Lynmouth was already gone.

"Stop him!" cried Baynes. "No, it's no use!"

"He's gone across to the Merchants' Loan & Trust," they told him.

"The Merchants' Loan & Trust? They've lost nothing! But—give me a drink, somebody. I'm ten years younger all in a minute, and I can't stand the shock!"

2

HONEST MONEY

STRAIGHT across to the Merchants' Loan & Trust Bank went Mr. Larry Lynmouth.

At the door, he was met by a man with a hand in each coat pocket, and in either hand there was a short-nosed bulldog revolver. The porter nodded, and pointed his weapons, as well as he could, at the midriff of the robber.

"Kind of a warm day, Mr. Lynmouth?"

"It's hot as the deuce," agreed Larry Lynmouth. "Where's President Oliver?"

"Right in here," said the other. "I'll take you in."

He walked behind Lynmouth. His jaw was hard set. The killing of Larry Lynmouth would be a famous deed, even if the shots came from behind.

"Looks bad for this bank," said Lynmouth, halting.

"What does?" asked the porter.

"All the boys must be packing their own flasks. I never saw so many bulging pockets. Yours, for instance?"

He turned to the porter. He was smiling, but the porter never had found a smile so hard to endure. He flushed; then he lost all his color, as though it had been covered with whitewash.

"Well—well—" he stammered.

"Never drink whisky when the thermometer climbs above ninety," said Larry Lynmouth. "But no doubt that's lemonade you have in each hand?"

The porter could have groaned, but he restrained himself. It was plain that the eye of Lynmouth had seen through his coat, as if with an X-ray. How many nights could he spend hereafter, untroubled by the nightmare?

He lost his ambition to kill an outlaw. He wished that he never had seen Larry Lynmouth. He wished that he never had seen Crooked Horn, even.

So he stepped ahead and rapped on the door of President William Oliver of the Merchants' Loan & Trust Bank. He opened the door.

"Mr. Larry Lynmouth to see you, Mr. Oliver," said he.

He blushed as he spoke. As if he had to announce the name when, for the last five minutes, the whisper of it had been enriching every nook and corner of the bank!

"Come in with Mr. Lynmouth," said President Oliver.

They went in together.

President Oliver had turned a little from his desk. In the drawer he had a good, old-fashioned, single-action revolver, which he had used in the days of his youth, and used well. The inside breast pocket of his coat was well filled, not by a wallet, but by a little two-shot pistol which could kill as well as a Colt—at ten paces. He understood all about that little pistol, too. He had practiced half an hour a day with it ever since he could remember. So President Oliver, though perhaps a trifle high in color, met the eye of the robber with a steady glance.

"Hello, Lynmouth," said he.

"You're Mr. Oliver?" said the young man.

There was something precise as well as graceful about him. His smile paused. His step paused. His whole attitude was one of pleasant suspense. President Oliver felt like a yokel.

"Yes, that's my name," said he.

Then he stood up and held out his hand, trying to cover up his breach of etiquette by saying:

"I forgot that I'm not so well known as you are, Lynmouth. How are you?"

His hand was taken in a firm, quick grasp.

After it, Lynmouth drew back just a shade. And Oliver almost smiled. It was so plain that this young man, no matter what his present good will, was not accustomed to shaking hands. To surrender that invincible and terrible right hand of his to the grasp of another must have been to him like blindfolding to a tight-wire performer.

He motioned to the chair at his right hand. It was bolted to the floor, to prevent overconfidental callers from hitching it too close. But Lynmouth, after a glance at it, shook his head.

Two windows and a door opened behind that chair. Could they have had anything to do with his reluctance to take it?

"I've been sitting half the day—the saddle," said he.

"You're one of these iron men," said the banker. "Well, stand if you please."

"Thanks," said Lynmouth.

He drifted to the other side of the desk. That put him on the president's left hand. An awkward position for a draw from an inside coat pocket. Oliver noted that, and said nothing. He summoned a smile, and resolutely maintained it; but his color was heightened.

How could Lynmouth know that behind each of the three doors opening to the room armed men now were posted, to say nothing of the two night watchmen who were on guard outside and underneath the window of the room?

Lynmouth was looking out that window.

"Good view, here," said he.

"Yes, of the mountains," said the banker.

"And of sombreros, too," said Lynmouth.

He was cool as metal. Plainly he had seen the heads of the two guards outside the window, and recognized the reason for their presence. And the color ebbed out of Oliver's face. But he was himself a very brave man. He felt that he had arranged this matter so well that, no matter what came to him, his assailant never could escape alive. On the spot he renounced all hope of ever matching young Larry Lynmouth. The fellow was too calm. His adroitness of hand, in some manner, gleamed in his blue eyes. Never had the banker seen eyes so blue, except in one person, whose name he could not at the moment bring to mind.

"Opening an account?" asked the banker.

"I'm collecting a note," said Lynmouth.

"Note?"

"Yes. To be exact, it is a check that I have."

"Very glad to see it."

He held out his hand. And into that hand was dropped a wrinkled check signed "Everett Morton." It was for twenty-eight thousand, eight hundred and seventy-four dollars.

The banker stared. That was the one account in the bank that every person in the place knew about. Even the janitor could have told how much was in the account of Everett Morton. It was for exactly that amount.

Nobody ever had seen Everett Morton. The account had been opened by mail and continued by mail. Everett Morton was a mystery, so far as the Merchants' Loan & Trust was concerned. A thirty-thousand-dollar mystery!

"I have a note for you, too."

Lynmouth dropped the note into the banker's hand. Like the check, it was travel-stained and pocket-wrinkled. It read:

MERCHANTS' LOAN & TRUST BANK,
Crooked Horn.

DEAR SIRS: With regret I am closing my account in your institution with a check made out to Mr. Larry Lynmouth, in payment of an old debt.

Yours very truly,
EVERETT MORTON

There was no need to consult any one.

Oliver himself was perfectly familiar with the handwriting of the mysterious Morton, and he could have sworn that this was correct. The check was right. The amount was exactly that of the account. All seemed regular.

And yet—just suppose that the check had been written at the point of a gun?

He hesitated. He colored. But suddenly he said:

"It's a big check, Lynmouth."

"Yes. It's a big check," agreed Lynmouth, and waited.

"Suppose I ask the nature of the debt? I mean to say —I must be careful, Lynmouth."

"I might have held him up for the check, you mean?"

"Well—of course I don't mean that—but—"

"You don't offend me, Mr. Oliver. The nature of the debt consisted of a series of loans."

"Ah? Loans?"

"Yes."

"Loans," said Oliver, and pulled at his tobacco-stained mustache. He was in a quandary. He wanted to be polite. But he was the most honest man in the world. Very simple to cash this check, but Oliver was, like many a banker—in spite of what part of the world may say—perfectly willing to die for the integrity of his institution. It was his. He had conceived it, made it, cherished it, nourished it through panics and droughts. He had turned the First National from a little boy to a big man. The Merchants' Loan & Trust was growing healthily. And how could he protect the mysterious interests of Everett Morton?

So he flushed deeper, and stirred in his chair.

"Mr. Lynmouth?"

"Yes, sir?"

How neat and crisp an answer, and phrased like a boy speaking to his respected elder!

"I haven't the right to ask. Yet, I can't help asking how you got this money?"

"Suppose I explain?"

"Then I should have to hand over this money to you."

"I'll tell you how I got it," said the robber. "Most of my money I've brought home at the end of a gun. I didn't fish for this in that manner, however. No, I got it in another way. I bought a five-year-old that was lame. I paid twenty-five dollars that I made by working a month at J. P. Ristall's ranch. He may remember. I bought that horse from him, and sold it for a hundred and fifty to Tom Mays, of Estobal. I took that hundred and fifty and played Chris Morgan's faro game in Phoenix. I walked out with twenty-two hundred, and loaned two thousand to Everett Morton. He made his first deposit here, at that time. With the extra two hundred, I grubstaked Lew Mason. Lew found the Prairie Dust Mine in the Mogollons, that time. My half went to fourteen thousand. I loaned twelve to Everett Morton, and he sent it in to deposit here. I soaked the other two thousand into Mexican beef that I fattened in the Big Bend, and cleaned up seven thousand clear! I gave six to Everett Morton. He banked it here, and I put—"

"Wait a moment. It seems that this is all honest money, Lynmouth."

The robber looked carefully about him. Then he said with a smile:

"I don't see any Bible about. Perhaps you'll take my word for it, Mr. Oliver?"

"Yes!" said Oliver suddenly. "I certainly shall."

3

BAD TIDINGS

IT WOULD not have been a hard story to have concocted. As for the names and dates, however, they could be verified, easily. And yet Oliver felt that they need not be verified. Something leaped in him, and told him that the boy was speaking the truth. He tapped on the desk with rapid fingers. Everett Morton must be protected, of course.

"You want to cash this now?" he asked.

"No. I want to open an account for this sum."

"Give me your check," said the banker. He took out a bank book and passed it across the desk. "Your checks will be good for this amount. Give me your check for this amount, and I open the account in your name. I believe you, my lad."

There was a knock at the door.

William Oliver turned toward it rather impatiently.

"Mr. Jay Cress calling, Mr. Oliver."

"Tell him I'm busy. And don't open that door again unless I tell you to."

"Cress?" said Lynmouth, as the door closed.

"Cress, the gambler," said the banker shortly.

"Cress, the gambler!" exclaimed the robber. "I took fifteen hundred from a fellow named Cress, one day. I'd just learned to stack the pack and run it up with one crimp in it."

"Cress? Mole in the middle of the forehead?"

"Yes. That's the man."

He leaned to the making of his check, and the banker stared at him. Those fingers were slender and smooth, and faintly marked by the seams of the gloves he had been wearing, gloves as delicately smooth as the skin of a fawn, nicely thinned. Such gloves would save the tactile delicacy of the fingers of a gambler, yet not interfere with a gun play to any extent.

And how easily this youth had confessed that he was himself a crooked gambler—the deepest detestation of William Oliver!

Yet the head was a noble one. Seeing it canted above the writing, the banker regarded it with care. He was almost a believer in phrenology, and he could see nothing wrong here. The bumps were in the right places, beyond doubt. A child could have guessed that, knowing nothing about phrenology. There were none of the signs of brutality in the lack of size behind the ears to balance the forward portion of the skull. The eyes, too, were big, widely separated. The nose was straight. The mouth was sensitive, though perhaps there was rather too much mobile strength in the upper lip, such as one sees so often in the upper lip of an actor.

Whatever the moral character of the robber, the banker felt that in him there were the possibilities of good. Far more than that, however, he was certain of strength. This was a machine capable of lifting great weights, and lifting them with speed. The young man looked to have the easy decision of a philosopher, and the handicraft of a gymnast. He was all in good balance, like a made-to-order shotgun.

Oliver took the check.

"Wait here a moment," said he, and left the room.

He took the slip of paper to his cashier.

"Lynmouth wants to open an account," said he. "With Morton's money."

He placed the other check and the note beside the check of the robber.

"Do you make anything of that?"

The cashier was a very old man. The rosy hue of his scalp shone through his white, sparse hair. He took a reading glass and leaned for two critical minutes above the three specimens. Then he looked up and folded the glass into its case.

"What do you expect me to find, Mr. Oliver?"

"Similarities!" barked the banker roughly. "Any similarities?"

"I should say," said the other, "that Morton is the well-trained left hand of Larry Lynmouth."

"You mean that there is no Morton at all?"

"I should say not. These letters have the same mind behind them. I imagine that they're merely the work of a right hand here, and a left hand there. Suppose you look at the up and down strokes—"

He produced the reading glass.

"I'd rather have your opinion than mine," said William Oliver.

He hesitated, and made a turn or two through the room. He was in a deep quandary, which he decided on a sudden impulse. With a snap of his fingers, he said:

"Enter this money for the account of Larry Lynmouth. I may be a fool. It may be stolen money. But I can't help believing at least part of the story which he's been telling me, and that this account is honest!"

He went back to his office, and there he found young Lynmouth standing exactly where he had been standing before, and in a characteristic pose. That is to say, his head was flung well back, and his hands were clasped behind him, and he had the expression of one contemplating a pleasant fancy.

"I've taken the account over in your name," said the banker. "The thing is finished. I hope that I can believe what you've told me about the honest money. I do believe it, in fact."

"Thank you," said the robber.

"And I can't help wondering," went on the banker, "if this means a change in your way of life?"

"I think it does," said Larry Lynmouth.

"And that you're going to settle down, young man?"

"Yes," said he. "I'm going to settle down. Marriage usually means that, sir."

"Yes, marriage usually means that. You are going to marry, Lynmouth?"

"Yes."

"It's a serious responsibility, my boy. It's the most serious step that a man can take. Not that I wish to advise you. I haven't the right. But I can't help wondering, Lynmouth, if you've made a proper choice—not simply some pretty face that you've run across here or there, not long enough to know her, but just enough to permit romance to grow. Now, you see, I've said a great deal more than I should. But every one takes a personal interest in you since the Ridley Dam affair."

"I understand," said the boy, "and I thank you for it. Of course, a man can't tell, but I think that you'd approve of the girl that I'm to marry."

"Would I? Would I?" said the banker dubiously. "Well, I hope so. If I ever see her—"

"Oh, you've seen her already, Mr. Oliver."

"Have I? Well, that explains your opening of your account here. You expect to settle down near here?"

"This is where she lives. I thought she'd be happier here."

"Perhaps, perhaps! A neighbor of mine, then?"

"Yes. She's in the town of Crooked Horn."

"Hm-m-m!" said the other broodingly. "I have it. It's the young McPherson girl. That wild, pretty young thing. It's a good, gay, romantic story, my lad—of how you took her to the dance. Well, I hope that she'll make you a good wife."

"She'll make a good wife, no doubt, but not for me."

"No? Then who— But I haven't a right to ask."

"Yes," said the robber, "you have a better right than any one. You really ought to know, as a matter of fact."

"What is my right, Lynmouth?"

"Well, you're her father, sir."

This lifted the banker from his chair. He did not move suddenly, but little by little the tidings raised him and stirred the hair upon his head. Then he let go with both hands, dropped back into the chair with a jarring impact.

"Kate!" said he, the name jolted out of him.

"Yes, sir," said Lynmouth.

He maintained the same attitude, but it was obvious that he was under a strain.

William Oliver looked at the three doors through which armed men might pour into the room, and wished, almost, that he could give the signal which would bring them in, shooting as they came. Then he stared back at the boy.

"You've not even seen Kate!" he said. "At least, not to my knowledge."

"Yes, I saw her."

"How many times?"

He listened in eager dread and pain. To think that his fair-faced daughter, Katherine, should have deceived him even with silence in such an affair as this!

Uneasy must he be who has a daughter!

"I saw her only once," said the robber.

"Good heavens!" breathed the astonished banker. "And she intends to marry you after one meeting?"

"So she says, sir."

"One meeting?"

"It was on the way home from that dance to which I took Alice McPherson."

The banker groaned. "This is a grim thing to me, young man," said he.

"We've been exchanging letters for a good long while, said the boy.

"And the girl could do that by subterfuge, without ever speaking a word to us?"

He spoke more in anger than in pain. There were two other younger daughters growing up after Katherine. He could only pray to Heaven that they would not follow in her footsteps. But she had been his favorite, his nearest and dearest of them all!

"Well," said the robber, "of course it seems bad. Perhaps in a way it was bad. But you can't expect me to condemn her for it? Promises aren't much good. All I can say is that if she can live down the disgrace of marrying an ex-outlaw, I'll hope to take good care of her."

Mr. Oliver did not answer. He sat with a blotched and livid face.

"Good-by, then," said Lynmouth.

"Good-by," whispered William Oliver.

He could not stir in his chair. He could only look straight before him, seeing the ruin and wreckage of his daughter's life. The door closed. The robber was gone, and poor William Oliver remained exactly where he had been sitting.

He began to feel very faint, so he opened the window and leaned out of it.

The two guards, below, looked up to him at once, and one of them muttered faintly:

"Is everything all right, chief?"

He looked down at them in profoundest gloom.

"Yes," said he. "Everything's all right."

He left the window and began to pace the room.

Everything was all right. The vault of the bank had not been touched. Not a hair of any one's head had been injured, but Mr. Oliver would rather have seen the whole surroundings strewn with wreckage than to have heard his last tidings.

4

DRY POWDER

OUTSIDE the bank, Larry Lynmouth found the gambler, Jay Cress, waiting for him.

"Hello, Larry," said he, coming up with extended hand. "I'm glad to see you."

"Yeah. You're fifteen hundred dollars' worth glad to see me, I suppose," said the robber.

"What's gone is gone. I'm not a short-sport, old-timer. How's things?"

He looked not a day older than when Lynmouth had last seen him. His lean, weather-dried face was not one to show the passage of time, and the same smile was making a cleft in either cheek and wrinkling his eyes.

"Things are fair," said Lynmouth, gathering his reins to mount.

Fortune turned her lovely head and nipped affectionately at his shoulder.

"Some day, when you're feeling like a game, I'll take you on, Lynmouth."

Larry Lynmouth turned away from his horse.

"You'll never rest till you have a shot at that fifteen hundred again," said he. "Well, I'll give you one chance, man. No cards. We'll spin a coin."

"Why, anything you please, Larry. Here you are. Call it!"

Into the hand of the other slipped a coin. It winked upward.

"Heads," said Lynmouth.

The coin spatted upon the flat palm of the gambler. Tails!

"I'll write you a check for it," said Lynmouth, undisturbed, "and take you into the bank while you cash it."

"Ah," said the gambler. "A moneyed man, these days, Larry?"

"Enough to pay you fifteen hundred."

"Come, come! I'm flush myself. I don't want your money, Larry. I'll toss you again, double or nothing."

Lynmouth laughed.

"Not a chance," said he. "I'm through with that business, old-timer. No more gambling."

"Come on, Larry. Three thousand on the turn of the coin. There's no chance for crookedness, there. You spin it and I'll call. It's like old days, seeing you!"

"Well, a last time."

The coin flicked upward, dissolved in sunshine, spatted on the flat hand of Lynmouth. He had lost again, and this time he frowned.

Six thousand out of twenty-eight thousand made a very appreciable difference. He had felt that for about thirty thousand dollars he could get himself fairly well started. But this was very difficult. Different, at least.

He heard the gambler saying:

"You don't like that, Larry? I tell you again, I don't want your money. I'm flush as can be. I ran into a sucker in El Paso, and he won't forget the day." He laughed, adding, "Double or nothing, again!"

"By George," muttered Lynmouth, "is it possible that

I'm such a fool? But I can't do it. At this rate, of course, you're sure to lose what you've fairly won."

"Come on, Larry. It's nothing to me. I want you to win it back. So here we go."

He spun the coin upward, and, in spite of himself, Lynmouth could not help calling:

"Heads!"

He had lost again!

Stunned, the street quaking before him, he stared at the face of the coin. Twelve thousand gone—nearly half of his little fortune. What good was the rest for the establishment of a home worthy of Kate Oliver, accustomed as she was to the best?

"Well, Larry, I'll give you a last shot at it, if you want; but you're getting into deep money, and the luck seems against you."

"I'll take the chance!" said Lynmouth harshly. "Here she is!"

He tossed.

He had lost again. There, in the space of a single minute, had gone flickering twenty-four thousand dollars. There remained to him only the chicken feed of his stake on which he was to have married and begun the new life.

Two thoughts flashed through his mind.

The first sent his eyes wavering across the street toward the face of the First National. The second made his glance narrow, like the gleam of metal, upon Jay Cress.

The latter appeared not to notice that murderous regard. He was saying gently:

"Well, that's hard luck, old fellow. Another whirl, if you like—"

"Oh, dang you!" said the robber with his first solemnity.

He jerked out the new check book and scribbled off the largest check he ever had written on an account.

"There's your twenty-four thousand, Jay. Go cash it! I'll go with you. Then—keep out of my sight!"

The latter waved the check in the air to dry the ink, and looked thoughtfully on his companion.

"It's more than any man wants to lose," he said. "Particularly, it's more than you care to lose today. I'll tell you what, Lynmouth—we ought to have a drink together and think this over!"

"It's done and ended, so where's the good of thinking?"

"Aye, but I have a thought, Larry. Will you have a drink with me?"

"No," said Lynmouth through his teeth. Then he realized that he was losing badly, and shame overcame him.

"I'll have one with you. I'm acting like a whipped puppy!"

"Not a bit! Not a bit!"

Jay Cress spread out his hands.

"Why, twenty-four thousand would touch any man to the quick. And I have an idea that will take away any need of cashing this check. A good idea. It's just come to me!"

"Crooked work? I'm through with that, too!" said the newly reformed bandit. "And I wish—"

He left the latter part of the sentence unfinished, and walked across the street, while Fortune followed like a good dog behind him. She stood outside of Bender's saloon, untethered. There was no danger that she would leave the door through which her master had disappeared.

Inside, they leaned at a corner of the bar and ordered drinks. Small beer for Larry Lynmouth.

"No," he said sourly. "I'm not drinking. I'm on the wagon. I'm not riding far, either. I'm going to try to keep clean, Cress. Starting at that, what sort of a proposition could you make to me?"

"Ah, you're going straight?" said Cress. "I always knew that you were the sort of a fellow who could go straight if you cared to. I always expected that you'd wind up on the right road, and I'm glad to hear you say this. For my part, I never wished you anything but the best of luck."

"Oh, drop that," said Lynmouth. "I'm sore. Let's hear what you have to say, and I'm off."

"Dry powder, dry powder, always ready to explode in a flash. But you're not as easy as you used to be, Larry. There's a woman behind this, or you'd lose with a smile."

"Yes," said Lynmouth. "There's a woman behind it. I'm

sorry that I grouch about it, but I intended to marry on
that money. Now you know—so don't mention it again."

"To marry on it! Well, I might have expected that,
too. To marry, settle down, and lead a straight, peace-
ful life."

He almost crooned forth the words, and a growing detestation sprang up in the throat of the robber.

"We won't talk about that, Cress," he snapped.

"Well, let me talk about myself, Larry. I've had the
same idea in my mind. A wife. That's the end of the trail
for any sensible man. I've made my pile—in one way or
another. Such a pile, old fellow, that I don't need your
share to stack on top. I've half a mind to tear the danged
thing up!"

He took out the check and made as if to rip it across.
Larry Lynmouth, with a grip of steel, caught and
crushed his wrist.

"Don't do that, Cress," said he. "I won't have charity.
I've talked like a kid after a thrashing. But I won't
have charity. Understand?"

He might almost have added that he guessed there
was little real charity or good feeling in his companion,
but he was frankly baffled by the attitude and the actions
of the gambler on this day.

A scoundrel Cress might be, but he actually spoke as
if he scorned to take the money he just had won—and
won without any apparent trick!

"Why, you're a man, old-timer," said Cress. "You
are a man, and a lot bigger than anybody I know, when it
comes to spirit. But I dare say that losing this money
spoils your marriage plan?"

"Postpones it for a while, at least."

"Aye, but not long. You'll soon have a pile together
again. You can't be kept back."

"I'd soon have it on the road," said Lynmouth bitterly.
"I'd soon have it if I were to step out and try my hand
again. But—I can't do that!"

"Well, why not, then?"

Lynmouth glanced aside at him.

"I've sworn to go straight!" he said quietly.

"Ah, you promised somebody?"

"Yes, I promised myself."

Cress whistled.

The bartender was drifting near, obsequiously, but a wave of the hand of Cress made him withdraw again. Other men were coming into the saloon. Some sat at the tables in the rear room. Others bunched at the far end of the bar, and Lynmouth guessed, with a certain pride and a certain scorn, that they had come in here to see him. They would not come close, however, to what was obviously a private conversation.

"It's a mess," said Jay Cress. "Here you are blocked, in a way. But then, you can make money again by going straight—a little more slowly, perhaps."

"Slowly?" groaned Larry Lynmouth through his teeth. "Man, don't I understand how money is made—honestly? Seventy-five a month, if I'm lucky. Live like a dog on forty. Save about four hundred a year. Ten years to gather up five or six thousand, if everything goes well—no sickness—"

"Well, ten years isn't a lifetime, but I—"

"Ten years?" cried Lynmouth. There was agony in his voice.

"Ah," said the gambler, "then I understand! You've found the right girl. Mad about her. She's mad about you, too. To postpone that marriage even one day is poison, eh?"

Lynmouth said nothing. He merely breathed heavily.

"I know exactly what you mean," went on the soft, easy voice of Jay Cress. "I'm not the sort of a fellow you expect to have a romance, Larry, am I?"

"I know nothing about that," said Lynmouth shortly.

"Well, I'm not. I know what I look like—a dried-up rat, sort of. But I've found the girl that I want to marry, old-timer. It isn't money that stands between her and me. It's you!"

5

REPUTATION!

INSTANTLY, Lynmouth turned fairly about.

"What the dickens do you mean by that?" he asked.

"Aye, how could my trail have crossed yours, Larry? Is that the idea?"

Lynmouth shrugged his shoulders.

"I don't know what you're driving at, Cress. Let's have it out in the open—or else let it drop."

"Why, I don't mind bringing it out in the open. I'd even name her to you—"

Lynmouth looked angrily up the bar. There was no one near.

"Well?" he said. "But I'm not asking for any names."

He thought of Kate Oliver, and prayed that he would not strike the fellow if he dared to mention her. With a fierce curiosity he listened.

"Name is Cherry Daniels. You know her, Larry."

"No. Never met her in my life."

"Think again. Down there in Jackson Ford. Little dark-eyed beauty. You danced with her once."

"I sort of half remember, now. What about her, Cress? If you're worrying about me, somebody's lied to you. I never spoke six words to her."

"Ah, there you are," said Cress. "Of course you didn't. But then, you didn't have to. You're Larry Lynmouth, and the girls are in love with you the minute that they put eyes on you!"

"Rot!" said Lynmouth, whom nothing pleased now. "Get to your point, if there is a point in all of this chatter."

"Aye, a point for me!"

"Let's have it, then."

"Why, Larry, it's simply that, after seeing you, she can talk about nothing else!"

Lynmouth sighed.

"What can I do about it, man? In the first place, she's only joking. No girl's as big a fool as that! I beg your pardon. I don't mean to insult your lady. But this sounds like the worst kind of rot."

"No insult, of course. I know that you're a gentleman, Larry. So does she. That's one of the troubles. She knows that you're six feet tall, and handsome, and have blue eyes, and walk like a stallion on a mountaintop, king of everything that you see.

"And ever since she saw you, she's been remembering. Poor girl! Not that she aspires to you, Larry. Mind you, she's not really rattle-brained. But there you are, up there in the sky, the great ideal. And no other man stands higher than the toes of your boots!"

He laughed rather sadly, and shook his head.

"A hard thing for me, Larry!" said he.

"Look here, Cress," said the robber. "You brought me in here to get something out of me. You wanted to get something out of me from the minute you dropped eyes on me. It isn't the money, it appears. Even twenty-four thousand dollars isn't much to you, it seems! Very well. Make it short and sweet. What can I do for you?"

"I'll tell you," said the gambler, looking him straight in the eyes. "You can make me ten years younger—your own age."

Lynmouth did not smile. He knew that even a Jay Cress in love was not actually a fool. Something was working in the back of the man's mind.

"I'm a wizard, then," said Lynmouth slowly. "I can make you ten years younger, if you say so. Though I've always thought that a gun was about the only way of altering a man's age. A pull on the trigger, and any one can be as old as Methuselah, and older, too. But go on, Jay."

"You can make me ten years younger. You can wipe the wrinkles out of my face. You can turn me from a homely mug into a handsome fellow."

"Easy," said Lynmouth, waiting. "Go on. What else can I do?"

"You can make me as great a hero as you are, Lyn-mouth!"

He stopped here.

Plainly, the man was in great earnest. Beads of perspiration glittered on his forehead, and filled the seams with moisture. He even panted a little, as though he had been running upstairs.

"You're coming to the point, I think," said Lynmouth. "Let's have it, then, and be short about it."

"Great guns, man," said the other, "how can I be short about it? How can I put into a nutshell the admiration that girl feels for you? How can I tell you, all in a moment, how she is always talking about you, or inferring you, even when she isn't using your name. Every time I go near her, I can feel the comparison darken her eyes. She knows what I am. A professional gambler. A no-good crook, in one sense of the word. To be sure, I can offer her a good home, good horses, a good carriage, good clothes, everything that she can really want. She knows that I love her enough to stay by the game. She knows that I'll even chuck gambling, for her sake. She's asked me. I've sworn it on the Bible—as soon as she'll say the word."

"But she won't say it?"

"Look here, Larry, she has in the house a pair of young brothers who are as wild as two streaks of lightning, and almost as fast with a gun. They're aching for a reputation. They burn up horses riding in posses. They've done the gun fighting already, both of them. Buck Daniels has got him a brace of horse thieves—two in one fight. Lew Daniels has dropped four different men, and the only thing he's sorry about is that none of them died. Cherry has been raised in that kind of an atmosphere, I tell you. Her father is forever talking about the grand old days, when death was always in the shadow of a man's heels. Her mother saw Indian fighting. She herself can shoot squirrels out of trees with a rifle. She can ride like a demon. You see the picture of her?"

"Yes, pretty well."

"And she doesn't imagine that anybody is a man unless he's a fighting man—a *gun* man."

"I can see that might be the case. I don't know what

you want to do with me, Cress. Are you asking me to go down there and shoot up the place to tame them down?"

"Nobody could tame them," said Jay Cress bitterly. "It's up to me to make a reputation for myself. And how am I to do it?"

"Go south of the river. Reputations can be—bought—there!"

He said it with quiet scorn, looking the other straight in the eye.

"I'm not a coward," answered Jay Cress. "I think you know that, if you know anything about me."

"No, I think that you have nerve enough," said the robber, nodding. "I'd never doubt that."

"But my fights have been out of some crookedness at a card table. Crookedness on my part, or crookedness on the part of the other fellow. Something quick. The flash of a card. Then guns jerked. Not even time for words. Well, I can fight, like that. I'm fast, and I shoot straight. In that kind of a brawl, I'm well enough. But to deliberately walk up to a rough character and ask for trouble —it simply isn't in my system!"

"I can understand that. Nobody likes to pick a fight."

"Nobody, Larry?"

"Nobody, I'd say."

"Well, I remember a time about five years ago when Boots Donelly was in a Phoenix saloon with his two guns as big as life, and a nineteen-year-old youngster walked in and made trouble with Boots. Donelly didn't want trouble on that day. He was tired of trouble. He'd spent too many years in prison. He'd killed too many men. But the kid wanted trouble, and he made Donelly open up. He taunted him, stirred him up, made him see red. And finally Boots pulled his gun. Aye, pulled his gun and had his head about shot off by that same nineteen-year-old boy, who wanted—what? You may remember that boy, Larry. His name was Larry Lynmouth!"

Lynmouth sighed. "I was a fool, and a cruel fool," said he. "I regret that day."

"Aye, you regret it. So does Donelly—whatever part of eternity he's in. He'd be cooler if he were still on earth. But what drove you at Donelly? What had he done to you? How could he expect that danger would come out

of you? He had no reason. Did you want reputation?
Great Scott, you had seven years of reputation behind
you, even then. It wasn't reputation that you wanted. It
was the fun of the thing. It was the chance. The fight.
Rubbing elbows deliberately with death. Smiling into the
eye of a gun. That's what you wanted. That's what you've
been dining on for twelve years. Confess that, Lynmouth!"

The youngster looked thoughtfully up toward the ceiling.

"Yes—may Heaven forgive me!" said he.

At this small exclamation, the gambler looked sharply
at him, amazed, but he swallowed his own amazement before it came to speech. He shook his head a little, like a
man rising from a plunge into cold water. It was plain
that he had not expected this note from young Larry Lynmouth.

"You're a changed man, Larry, aren't you?"

"I'm changed, I hope and pray."

"Almost religious? No, I won't ask that. But, to go
on, you're through with such gun plays, eh? You'd retire
from that field?"

"Yes, with all my heart!"

"Well, then, there's the point on which you can make
the bargain with me."

"What point, man? I don't understand."

"You will, in a minute. Listen to me, Larry. Guns and
gun fighting are nothing to you, now. You're through with
such things. Now, look here; the very thing that you
want no more is what I have to have."

"Then go out and get a reputation, man."

"I've told you before that I can't do such a thing."

"I don't follow this trail with you, Cress. Though I begin to think that you're in earnest about something."

"Never so earnest in all my life. Believe that!"

"Yes, I will."

"You still won't see what I want to point out."

"No, I'm trying to, but I don't, so far."

"Man, you need twenty-four thousand dollars to marry."

"That's true."

"And I need a reputation."

"So you say."

"Then let's exchange!"

Young Larry Lynmouth breathed out a puff of smoke, pretended to catch it in his hand, and threw it toward the other, with a faint smile.

"There's the reputation," said he.

"Listen to me! I take your check, here in my hand. That means marriage at once, and also happiness for you."

"Yes, Jay, it means all those things."

"In that case, you shall have the check. That is, I'll destroy it here under your eyes, if you'll give me what you say has no more value than smoke—your reputation!" He hastily added: "Not your new reputation as an honest man, a good fellow, a hard worker, a faithful husband, a fellow with a bank account—but your old reputation as a gun fighter and man-killer!"

"In the name of Heaven, Jay, will you tell me how I can give you that?"

"Yes, by right here and now taking water from me!"

6

"DON'T SHOOT!"

Now that the thing was out, it seemed patent that Cress had been driving straight in this direction for a long time, but even with the ultimate goal revealed, the robber was stunned. The enormity of the thing reverberated through his body, through his brain.

He to take water, to lie down, as it were, and admit that another man was better than he!

He had been thinking, all this while, that in spite of what he knew about Jay Cress, the fellow was, after all, not so bad. There seemed a certain unexpected heartiness about him, a certain direct simplicity that was a great pleasure to encounter. He had appeared almost unwilling to make the gambling ventures, seemed to insist on giving his victim another chance.

But now, in a sickening flash, poor Lynmouth knew that it had been no chance at all that Cress took. Whatever was crooked about the tossing of the coin—and he could not imagine what—he had been helpless in the hands of the trickster from the beginning. He could have gone on matching for a hundred times, until his debts had swelled into billions and thousands of billions, and yet always he would have lost and lost.

This, as by a side light, he saw.

He gripped the edge of the bar with both hands.

To give up the honorable reputation which he had built as a fearless man, to admit one smudge upon the bright shield of his honor? No, that was more than he could bear. They had called him cruel, a man slayer, a robber, a lover of cold danger, but never had they questioned the integrity of his courage.

He could tell himself that he was above being stirred by the admiration of the town as he rode through, and the fear and the awe which surrounded him, even when he had stepped into the two armed traps of the banks; but what he told himself was not the truth. He delighted in the sensation of power, just as he delighted in the speed and the grace of Fortune, carrying him.

He looked at Jay Cress.

The man was pale as a sheet, perspiring more profusely than ever. The drops were running down his face. He looked sick. Spiritually, no doubt, he was.

"Tell me," said Lynmouth, his voice sounding as though other lips than his were speaking, "tell me just what you want me to do."

"I've got it planned. I break out into a fury—apparently. I curse you— Mind you, it has to be something rank! And instead of answering, you back away. You blink at me. I challenge you to draw your gun. You make a motion. You seem to have your gun sticking in the holster. I pull out mine and cover you. You throw a hand before your face. You say: 'For Heaven's sake, don't shoot!' You see, Larry?"

"You cold toad! You poisonous sneak!" said Larry Lynmouth.

The other sighed. It was almost a groan.

"Think it over," he said rapidly. "Of course, I don't know. The girl you want——"

"Cress," said Larry Lynmouth, "if you breathe a word about her, mention her in any way, infer that she exists, I'll throttle your life out of your skinny neck!"

The gambler moistened his pale, cracked lips.

"Twenty-four thousand dollars is your price for thirty seconds of acting!" said he. "Mind you, after that, if any fool tries to challenge you on the strength of what I've done, you blast him like lightning!"

"Ah, yes, dang them!" said the boy. "And the minute they thought that my nerve was gone, they'd be at me like a pack of curs, right enough. I hadn't thought of that. That would be a satisfaction!"

"Yes, yes, Larry! Of course it would. You'd eat them alive. You'd stand higher than ever. As for this day—— it could be put down to a bad hand, or bad luck on the draw——"

He tried to smile. It was a leering smile so horrible that Lynmouth turned a sickened face away.

Jay Cress took the check which was in his hand and lighted a match.

"Mind you, Larry, you only have to say one word. You say 'Yes.' And, the minute you say it, I touch the match to the check. You hear me, Larry? That wipes out everything. You have your money again——home——happiness ——love——indeed, a quiet life to the end——children——honor ——respect——and you've saved me——given me my chance in life again——something more than blood in my veins—— another soul, for me! Say the one word, Larry——the match is half gone!"

Lynmouth tried not to see. Resolutely he turned his head toward the mirror, with the gleaming double row of bottles reflected neatly in it, the fiery glow of whisky; the brownish sheen of sherry; claret with a highlight on the bottle like a rich red eye staring back at him. He saw the mottoes and monograms of important firms plastered against the glass. And he was aware, at the farther end of the bar, of the increasing crowd which had come in here to see the great Larry Lynmouth, the undefeated champion, the hero.

A fly buzzed, drowsy as a bee, beside his ear. He trembled. It was as though he were in a delirium, and all this place was seen, for the first time, in the light of madness.

"Do you hear, Larry?" said the other, whispering beside him. He thought it was the fiend incarnate speaking! "There's still a spark of flame. Shall I touch it to the check?"

"Yes!" said Larry Lynmouth.

Then he trembled. He heard the other draw a breath like a thirsty man after drinking.

"Thank Heaven!" whispered the gambler faintly.

Then there was a flare of yellow fire. The check was gone. It was as though the weight of twenty-four thousand dollars were suddenly dropped into his pockets.

Life, therefore, was to go on as he had dreamed that it might. He was to have lovely Kate Oliver, a home, a chance to work honestly for an honest family—his own! Aye, there would be, as the gambler had said, only thirty seconds of horror.

He nerved himself. But he was weak. He trembled. He had to grasp the upper rail of the bar with both hands.

Suddenly a strange cry broke out beside him.

It was not a human voice. It was a wild shriek, yelling:

"Dang you, Lynmouth, you lie!"

He jerked himself around. He had been prepared for anything, he thought, but not for this.

He heard and vaguely saw the men at the other end of the bar dive out of the direct path of bullets.

But nearer at hand he was more distinctly aware of the face of the gambler. The man seemed to have gone mad. He was grinning, without mirth. His eyes were phosphorescent green, like a cat's.

"You lie! You lie!" shouted the gambler. "D'you hear? I'm not afraid of you and your guns! Dang you, go for your guns! Dang you, go for your gun now, and I'll blow you to blazes!"

"You little cur!" said Lynmouth, and whipped his hand for his Colt.

In that instant, as his fingers closed on the familiar handle, he remembered.

He gripped it. How infinite the hundredth part of a second seemed—how comfortably long a time to draw and let death enter the evil brain of the gambler. But then he remembered his promise, and the force of his word chained him like a dog.

He did not draw! And before him flashed the gun of the gambler. The directions came heavily into his brain. He must throw his arms before his face and say: "For Heaven's sake, don't shoot!"

Once before—why had he not thought of this sooner? —he had confronted a man in a little Nevada town, and there he had drawn from the other that very confession of weakness in exactly those words. But, obediently, he threw his arms before his face.

"For Heaven's sake, don't shoot, Cress!" he managed to say.

Then he started for the door. But, in spite of his masking arm, he had to see his way, and seeing it, he saw the faces of the spectators.

What was in them?

There was white horror mostly. But also there was savage delight in a cruel spectacle. There was enormous, incredulous joy, as if they had seen a bear throttled by a single dog, made helpless. In one face at least, he saw a sick shame at such action on the part of one who once had been a man.

But, in nearly all he thought he distinguished a green glare of keenest delight.

Then he came to the door. He missed it, half blinded, trembling as he was. He lurched heavily against the side of the building. It shuddered under the weight of the impact.

Behind him, there broke out a loud, crowing, raucous laughter. Behind him, too, followed on the sneering voice of the gambler, saying:

"You yellow cur, the next time I see you, I'll pistol you on sight! No, I won't use a gun on you, you contemptible bully, you cowardly murderer! You've shot 'em in the back, have you? Aye, and where else? But you've met a man—you've met a master, at last! I'll take a quirt and quirt you through the streets, the next time that I meet you—"

Then Lynmouth found the door and blundered out into the street.

The sunshine blazed before him, dazzling bright. A gust of wind blew off his hat. He did not pause for it. He mounted Fortune. The door of the saloon opened. He heard a slow, deliberate voice saying distinctly as the mare was turned up the street:

"This proves it. I thought there was one distinct exception, but I was dang wrong. There ain't a one of them that ain't a coward, at heart—not one of the murdering crew! I'd like to shoot him off his hoss right now!"

Then Fortune—how she seemed to hang in her stride! —was at last under way. She was galloping, but slowly, slowly. Slowly the familiar street staggered by him on either hand.

And the cold shudder clung in the small of his back. The dreadful fear of public scorn ate and consumed his soul. He could remember, in this wild moment of regret, how he had forced other men until their backs were against a wall, and how he had forced them to take water!

But his punishment was more than he could bear.

He had twenty-four thousand dollars saved to his pocket, to his marriage, to his future happiness. But, to him, they were like twenty-four thousand tortures. He burned, with a cold fire. He melted, he shrank, he shriveled. He felt as though he could not endure the weight of a single eye.

And, as he spurred hard out of town, he saw a small boy leaping up and down, and clapping his hands together, and he heard the crowing voice of the lad pealing after him:

"Hey, Eddie, Eddie! Look, look! There's Larry Lynmouth! And that's Fortune that he's riding. That's Fortune herself!"

7

NEVER AGAIN.

SOMETIMES racing at full speed, sometimes with downward head, at a walking pace no faster than the sound of slowly dripping water, Lynmouth went through the countryside, wandering here and there, but never able to escape from the horror of what had happened any more than he could escape from his own shadow.

At length, when the sun began to lose its heat and turn red-gold in the western sky, he came, by accident as it seemed, upon the sight of the house of the banker, William Oliver.

It was well out from the skirts of the town, where the hills began to roll, and the barrenness of that landscape was broken, here, by groves of cottonwoods, and by poplars which grew along the bottom lands, where there was almost a marshy surface a good part of the year. The house itself was like any other ranch house, except that its long, low lines had been added to, here and there, so that it sprawled upon the ground without much pattern; but just as the whims and the increasing fortunes of its owner suggested to him changes and enabled him to construct them.

It was altogether an odd place. The avenue which led up to its front, being of cottonwoods, was long and imposing; but it had been planted along the casual windings of a cow path of much earlier day. These trees, when the wind struck them, roared like a distant surf.

There was a good breeze blowing, when young Larry Lynmouth turned into the drive, and the sound of the trees closed like water over his head, so that he could not very well help lifting his eyes uneasily from time to time.

When he came up to the house, he saw old Si Tucker,

the Negro man of all work, washing down a rubber-tired
buggy in front of the wagon shed. Si straightened up, in
his glistening rubber boots, and stared at Lynmouth just as
though he never had seen him before.

"Is Miss Kate in, Si?" asked the boy.

"I reckon," said Si, in a mumble, and bent again to
his work. He was spinning the red-striped wheels, which
had been jacked up, and letting the sponge run along the
outer margin. It was a delicate bit of work, but not
enough to account for his preoccupation. There was another explanation for this indifference, and Lynmouth
shivered when he thought that the news might have
come this far, already.

He turned toward the front door of the house, frowning, when the screen opened and shut with a jingle, and
out came the banker himself.

He had put himself at ease, after his return home. He
had peeled off his stiff white collar that throttled him all
day long. He had unbuttoned the collar of the shirt itself,
revealing a large red blotch where the heel of the main
button had bruised his throat. And he was wearing loose
slippers, and a flimsy old gray alpaca coat which was as
cool and light as shirt sleeves.

Yet he looked to the robber even a little more imposing than he had seemed to be in the middle of the day,
surrounded by the varnish, the tidiness, the papers, in his
office, the many clerks and attendants upon his business
career and functions. For now, with the trimmings gone,
with the mark of the removed spectacles on the bridge of
his nose—sinking in almost to the bone—and with a certain lethargy making the lines of his face droop, one
could realize the burden which he had been carrying all
through the day, and of which he was now released.

He had a pipe with a long curved stem, such as once
was popular in Germany, and this he was filling with
mechanical care. He nodded and smiled a little at Lynmouth.

"Come up here and sit down, my boy," said he.

His voice sounded relaxed and weary.

Lynmouth hesitated on the uppermost step.

"I'd like to see Kate, if I may," said he.

"Kate's tired out," said her father, frowning down at the

bowl of the pipe as he lighted it. White smoke began to spurt from his lips, and presently obscured his face.

"Sit down, my lad," he repeated. "Sit down and stretch your legs. Fortune looks fit as a fiddle! You'd never suspect that she'd run herself almost to death a month ago. No sign of tucking up about her."

"No, she's well enough," agreed Lynmouth absently.

"That's the point about good breeding in horses," said the banker. "Men, too, for that matter. They fight through and recover under a strain. Whereas cold blood—well, it lets one down when least expected. Sorry that Kate is tired out and can't see you," he finished.

His tired eye wandered down the curving lines of the cottonwoods. And Lynmouth bit his lip. Something was being held back from him. He wondered if the banker really were foolish enough to imagine that he could keep him from the girl he loved, and who loved him, by such silly and slight expedients of conversation as this. A headache, forsooth, when he had not seen Kate for six months —six months of wild adventure and tribulation of all sorts.

"Yet Fortune is only a half-bred one," he said. "The other half is pure mustang, though she doesn't look it."

"Well, behind the mustang there were centuries of hot blood. In a manner of speaking, a clean-bred mustang is older blood than a thoroughbred, though not written about so much in books. Legs. That's all they lack. Length of legs to gallop with. But in the mountains, over the desert, I wonder if they won't lick a race horse almost every time?"

So said the banker. And Lynmouth saw that the herring was being drawn again over the trail that he wanted to follow.

He said quietly:

"Mr. Oliver, I really have to see Kate. I think if you'll tell her that I'm here, she'll be able to come for a moment."

Oliver sighed. "She knows that you're here, my lad," said he gently.

Still he looked down the lines of the cottonwoods, with pain in his face. But suddenly it appeared to Lynmouth that there was no fear in the expression of Oliver—not such fear as one would expect in the face of one who had in his mind the dread of losing his daughter.

The mismatching of Kate surely should have given him more trouble of mind and voice than this, unless he were a consummate actor.

"Kate knows that I'm here and she doesn't wish to come?" asked Lynmouth briskly.

"The headache—sick headache, my boy. You know how it floors a woman?"

Still he did not meet the eye of Lynmouth, and the latter leaned forward.

"Tell me, Mr. Oliver—" He paused at this.

"Well, Larry?"

"You've all heard about the fracas down in the saloon. Is that what's turned her mind?"

"Fracas?" The banker cleared his throat. "Well, Larry," said he, "naturally a good deal of talk was started around the town. I suppose that it couldn't be kept from the ears of Kate."

Lynmouth leaped at the truth.

"So you told her yourself?" he excitedly cried.

Oliver, drawing in a breath, nodded. "I told her myself," said he, "rather than have her pick up such a shock out of casual gossip."

"And what did you tell her?" persisted Larry Lynmouth.

"I don't think that you want me to repeat it, Larry. Listen to me, my lad. I think I understand. No man can be brave forever. There is bound to be a cracking point —I suppose."

"I'd like to know exactly what you told her," persisted Lynmouth, white and sick of face.

"I told her," said Oliver, "that Jay Cress, the gambler, slapped your face, dared you to draw a gun, and made you beg!"

His face set hard. Slowly he turned his head, and his eye sternly met that of the gunman.

It was impossible for Lynmouth to endure the weight of that gaze. He need not say that there had been no slapping of the face. No, there would be worse exaggerations than that, before long. They would say that he had fallen on his knees and begged for mercy, perhaps.

Well, it had been almost as bad as that. It had been so very bad, he decided, that nothing could make it much worse.

He looked up again. Oliver, as though in mercy, no longer looked at him. Instead, he regarded the sky, as it glimpsed rosily through the limbs of the cottonwoods.

"I'll have to tell you the truth," said Lynmouth hoarsely. "It's not much better than the part that I played down here in the saloon. But the truth is that Jay Cress bought me off. Hired me, I mean, to play the part of a cur!"

"Hired you?" murmured the banker.

"Yes, hired me. He wanted to get a reputation as a gunman. He hired me——"

His voice trailed away as he realized the horrible improbability of the thing. Oliver did not answer. He was shading his eyes with one hand, not to conceal mirth, but disgust.

No wonder. Who in all the world could be asked seriously to listen to and believe such a tale as this? Certainly no one of the hard-headed men of the West among whom Lynmouth had built up his repute. They knew guns, gunmen, and their ways too well.

He saw that he had lost. There was no sense in struggling against the impossible. He stood up, though to do so cost him more than any battle in his life.

"You'd better tell Kate that I'd like to have a last look at her," he said.

Oliver looked up in quick protest.

"There'd be no use——" he began.

"I won't beg," said Lynmouth slowly. "Not as I begged in the saloon. No, you needn't be afraid of that!"

"Well, it's your right to see her, if you insist. You're sure that you insist?"

Lynmouth laughed. He was amazed at the hard, clear ring of his voice.

"Yes. I insist."

Oliver disappeared through the door and presently there came a slender, white-clad form into the dimness of the hall. She paused behind the screen door, her hand upon it, yet without strength to push it open. Behind her was the vague shadow of her father.

"I wanted to ask you," said the boy, in this same new, hard voice of his, which he could not recognize, "if you have changed your mind? It used to be man slaying that you held against me. Have you changed your mind, and now that's what you want?"

He had to wait a long moment. Then she was able to merely say: "Larry, I—"

She could get no further. The music and the tremor of her voice shook him, and he could see her eyes staring at him, as at some horrible beast, not worthy of a name.

"That's all," said Lynmouth, as harshly as before. "I simply wanted to be sure. Good-by, Kate. What I've seen in your face makes me never want to look at you again."

8

THE WORLD IS A DESERT

BACK to Fortune went Lynmouth, and was just gathering the reins when Oliver came out to him. "Oh, good-by, Mr. Oliver," said the boy, and swung up into the saddle.

"A cruel speech that you've made to my girl," said the banker. "It will leave a scar on a heart like hers!"

"A heart like hers! A heart like hers!" cried Lynmouth, and the new, ringing laughter broke from his throat again. "A heart so filled with trust and faith! A good woman, good as gold. A woman to be proud of. Faithful for ten years. Never doubting a man she's once given her love to—"

"Can you look me in the eye and say that?" asked Oliver surprisingly.

"Look you in the eye?" said Lynmouth. "And why not, Oliver?"

He sent Fortune a pace closer, and stared straight down into the face of the banker, met his eyes, plunged his own gaze deep in it. Something blindly cruel rose up in him.

Oliver, with a faint gasp, stepped hastily back.

"I should have guessed," said he. "Of course, there's nothing for you to fear in an old and obviously un-armed man!"

"Is that why I don't fear you, Oliver?" said the boy. "No, I'll tell you the straight of it. I don't fear you because I know you, man. I know your daughter, too. It's over me in a flash. A banker's daughter. Of course she wanted to marry a headline, and not a man!"

Oliver started again.

"Is that your opinion of her? A very good thing that you've parted then, I should say. It's a step that you won't regret."

"Regret? I? No, no! I'll never regret it!"

He laughed again, deliberately, insultingly, keeping that cold, new glance of his fixed like a sword in the soul of Oliver. The he whirled Fortune quickly around and she scattered the gravel as she swept down the driveway.

Banker William Oliver turned back to the house, a little stunned, and very much embittered; and on the way he met his daughter, running wildly out of the house.

"Oh, please, stop him, daddy!" she cried.

Oliver stopped her, instead, and gathered her into his arms.

"Stop him! Shout to him!" said Kate feverishly. "I've got to speak to him again. I must! He's gone mad! Did you hear his laugh? Call him back!"

He held her firmly. There was not a shadow of a doubt in his mind or in his voice as he said:

"I'd rather recall my worst enemy. No, thank God that you're free from him! I thought that I knew bad men in my time, but a moment ago I saw a mask drop from a soul that is worse than the pit of darkness! Don't doubt me. Trust what I say!"

"Oh," she said, "if I can speak ten more words to him—otherwise, I never can get the thought of him out of my brain."

"I've always wanted your happiness first of all," said Oliver. "I've changed my mind, now. I'd rather a thousand times see you dead, than married to that fellow, for he's a snake, and not a man at all!"

But young Larry Lynmouth was already back in the town.

He turned his mare in at the stable behind the hotel.

"Give her the cleanest oats you can find in the bin," said he.

The groom shrugged his shoulders. The lack of one leg below the knee forced him to this sort of work. He could no longer back a horse, but on the ground he felt himself as good a man as the next. Now he turned.

"I'll give her what we've got," said he. "That's good enough for her."

"One minute," said Larry Lynmouth.

That musical, clear, cold voice, made the other pause. There was a peculiar ring in it, such as had made the blood of Tom Lambert turn, also. He carried, for the sake of old times, a good old revolver in a spring holster beneath the pit of his left arm; and every morning, when the larks were up and no other soul, he spent a solid hour of pistol practice in the hollow near the river, where the steep banks would muffle and throw back the waves of noise.

Lynmouth dropped a forefinger upon the breast of the stalwart cripple. And it seemed to Tom Lambert that a ray of icy coldness slid straight into his heart.

He stared up into the face of this newly disgraced man, and there he discovered a slight smile upon the lips of young Lynmouth, and looked into clearly shining eyes. Another ray of ice penetrated to the very soul of the groom. His hand fell numbly away from the revolver which he had been touching.

"Manners are beautiful things, Lambert," said young Larry Lynmouth. "They give grace even to old ruffians like you. When you answer a gentleman, you should raise your hat, Lambert. Do you hear?"

Old Tom Lambert dragged the hat from his head. His hair, all awry, slowly fell back in place.

"Yes," said he.

"Yes, sir?" said Lynmouth suggestively.

"Yes, sir," mumbled the groom.

"And so long as a gentleman is looking toward you, never turn your back on him. Is that clear?"

"Yes, sir," gasped Lambert.

"As for the mare, rub her down—carefully. Rub her down as though she were a diamond that needed polishing. Then pick out the purest and sweetest hay in the loft. After that, pick out the oats grain by grain, if necessary. You understand me, Lambert?"

"Yes, sir. I foller your drift, sir."

"Good night, Lambert."

"Good night, sir."

Even as the other left, Lambert still gaped after him.

"He would've killed me!" he gasped to himself. "He would've killed me like a dog—dang him!"

But he went with trembling earnestness to take care of the mare.

Lynmouth, in the meantime, went into the lobby of the hotel, walking slowly up the veranda steps. All voices were hushed, along the line of loungers whose chairs were tilted against the wall. All eyes regarded him, with lifting, sneering lips.

These were the men whose applause had gratified him, whose good word had meant so much to him! He read them, and he judged them with a glance, and with that new, cold certainty which never had come to him before. On this day he was reborn, and to the surety of dreadful knowledge.

Then, as he passed through the door, he heard some one say, not softly: "By Jiminy, he still can hold his head up! Can you come over that?"

And a tall man, a rough-looking fellow with a shag of hair above his eyes, leaning now against a wooden pillar of the veranda, muttered something in addition, and then laughed loudly.

Lynmouth stepped leisurely back onto the porch.

"Did I hear some one laughing? Or was it a dog that barked?" he asked.

He could see that line of loiterers stiffen with a jerk.

And yonder by the pillar, the tall man whirled about, equally suddenly.

"You laughed, I think?" said that new voice from the lips of Lynmouth, a sound of metallic clearness, yet musical.

"Yeah. I laughed!" bawled out the other. "I laughed, and what about it?"

"That's what I wish to know," said Lynmouth. "Because I love a good joke. Let me hear the story, my friend!"

He stood close to the other. It was not the full brightness of the day, but there was enough of the rosy twilight left to enable the stranger to see Lynmouth clearly, and what he saw made his jaws unlock and hang agape.

"No story, then?" said Lynmouth. "Was it only the barking of a dog, after all?"

He took a leisurely step forward, and the other retreated. He was unnerved. His very knees sagged.

"Dogs that bark ought to be silenced. With a whip, if necessary. Remember that!"

He turned again and walked back leisurely toward the door of the hotel. And how they gaped! Here he paused and reviewed them one by one, looking each man in the face, and each man turned his glance suddenly away.

Lynmouth went on into the hotel, and as he passed through the doorway, he heard another sound behind him, not of laughter, but a deep and sullen murmur, like the subdued snarling of many dogs.

He never had heard that noise before. Whatever deeds of derring-do he had performed before, it was at the expense of one or two, and always won the applause of the multitude. But now there was a change. He could distinctly hear some one saying:

"He knows very well that Cress ain't here!"

Aye, that had changed his entire life, and the attitude of the world of men toward him and his deeds!

He signed for a room and went upstairs behind the clerk to take it. It was a good room, and occupied a corner of the second floor.

"Anything you want—sir?" said the clerk.

He stood sullenly in the doorway, his head hanging. It was almost as though he already had heard of what had happened to Lambert.

"Nothing, at present."

The door closed, and Lynmouth was left alone.

So he stood at the window for a long time, looking out at the way the sunset smoked and burned in the west, and how the western windows of the houses blinked faintly with that light; and how the smoke columns rose in twisting lines above every house, like jointless arms reaching to the sky, without a hand to touch it.

So, it seemed to him, the lives of men were—reaching up, but unable to seize or even to touch the glory they might conceive. A world of folly and dreams, a world of dust and ashes, a world dissolving like smoke.

He knew that only the night before his very heart would have been touched by the immensity of the night closing over this little town; but now there was only ice where a heart should have been, and with the ache of frozen flesh he thought of Jay Cress, of Oliver the banker, and of Kate. But that pain did not disturb the clearness of his brain. All were worthless. They were, in a sense, like that line of fellows on the front veranda—a worthless lot. Dogs!

He looked back down the long avenue of his life.

Where had he known a man, or a woman, or a child, capable of real faith, real trust?

And therein, alone, lay divinity. Thereby alone could man make himself like the gods. He had found it nowhere. His eyes were open, and he saw the world as a desert.

9

ADVICE FROM THE SHERIFF

FROM this moralizing, Lynmouth turned to the prosaic task of washing. And in washing, it seemed to him that there was a slight stubble on his face, more than should be there for absolute cleanliness. And absolute cleanliness was what he now desired with a strange eagerness.

So he shaved, though he had shaved already, very early that morning, when, with such a bounding heart, he was preparing to ride in to collect the spoils of honesty and begin a happy life!

He told himself that he did not regret the change, for

the happiness which others found, and of which he might well have tasted also, was the happiness of a blind creature. Far better to have the eyes open, find what alone is pure and true, and failing that, die like an old wolf, driven out by the pack.

That word rang again in his brain. For every word, every smile, that likened men to dogs, seemed to him most true and just.

When he had finished shaving, he took a clean shirt from his pack, and brushed his clothes scrupulously, and rubbed up his boots. Even his spurs had to be polished a little, and his hat gone over.

At last, when he was speckless, he went lightly down to the dining room.

He paused in the doorway. All heads went up, there was a flash of eyes and faces turned toward him, and then all eyes and faces went down again, and he was only looking at the tops of heads.

How they hated him! How they feared him!

But he did not sneer. The same faint, cold smile was on his lips as he crossed to a small corner table and sat down alone.

The waiter bawled at him:

"Over here, mister. We ain't servin' any special parties when we're so short-handed—"

There was a quick jerking of glances toward the daring waiter, but Lynmouth merely turned his head with the same faint smile, and the fellow gaped and went backward a half step, exactly as though he had been struck on the jaw.

"I prefer to be alone," said Larry Lynmouth.

"Yes, sir!" said the waiter.

Had Lambert confessed his humiliating lesson in manners to every one, or was there simply an instinctive change toward him?

He was served by the fellow in a gloomy silence, far different from the almost breathless excitement with which gay, young, gallant, handsome, fearless, romantic Larry Lynmouth was greeted by every servant.

No, the whole attitude of the world had changed toward him.

He finished his dinner and lingered a moment on the veranda. Not a word was spoken by a single soul there, except in a subdued undertone. One might have thought that they were living over a mine of dry powder. Only when he went inside he could hear the voices grow up behind him, but even then it was not rollicking, foolish laughter but angrily, as though in dispute.

He could guess what they were disputing about—the sudden strength that had appeared in this apparently broken man, who had taken water from one and, therefore, in the ordinary course of events, ought to have been kicking stuff for every man's boot.

But he was far different. They could not understand it. And instead of giving him credit, they hated Lynmouth for the strength that remained in him.

Strength?

He raised his head, and his teeth flashed. He had been a weakling, a child, before. Let them try him now, to find how the child had grown into a man!

He had not been half an hour in his room, when there was a heavy knock on the door, and it was opened by a short, thick-shouldered, narrow-hipped man, with an old-fashioned pair of saber-shaped mustaches dripping down on either side of his face. A fearless, much-lined face looked out from beneath the battered brim of a sombrero. It was Sheriff "Chick" Anthony.

He came in without taking his hands out of his belt, inside of which he had slipped them. The white dust of long riding was layered in the folds of his blue flannel suit.

"Hullo, Lynmouth," said he.

"Hello, Sheriff Anthony. Won't you sit down?"

"No, I ain't gunna sit down." He pushed the hat farther back on his head. "I've come here to say—" he began.

"You overlook old rules, Anthony," said Lynmouth. "People used to be careful about such things, but manners have gone sadly to pot, and I've had to become a sort of missionary spirit in this rough world, sheriff. Therefore, if you don't mind, I'm going to ask you to remove your hat, sir."

"You're gunna what?" snarled the sheriff.

"Ask you to take off your hat, sheriff."

"I've heard about the new style you've took on since Jay Cress showed you up—" began the sheriff.

"Or else," said Lynmouth, "I have to ask you to leave the room."

"This dang nonsense—" began Anthony, when the other went on smoothly:

"Or else remove you, myself!"

The sheriff glared. He was as fearless a man as ever threw leg over cantle, but he did not believe in imperiling himself for the sake of trivial causes. He removed his hat.

"Now, do sit down," said Lynmouth. "You won't make me point out that you keep me standing, sir?"

"You're turned as sour as spoiled milk, Lynmouth," said the man of the law. "I wancha to ask yourself if you ain't got a screw loose?"

"Very likely," said Lynmouth. "I'm not aware of it; but anything's possible in this old rolling world, you know."

"You've always been too fancy and too highbrow for me," declared the sheriff, "but maybe you can buckle onto a couple of plain facts."

"Thank you. I'll try."

This politeness made the sheriff make a wry face, but he continued:

"You've made a couple of bum passes in this here town, today."

"You mean that I've crawled to Jay Cress?"

"Aw, I ain't sayin' nothin' about that," said the sheriff, his mustaches bristling to the side as he made a face of disgust, and then dropping again in their saber line, as before. "That ain't my business. But what's happened since is my business."

"And what's happened, then?"

"You've started lookin' for trouble."

"Ah?"

"You've been and rode old Lambert—"

"Lambert tried to snap at me like a spoiled old dog. I instructed him in a few of the essentials of good manners for one in his position. That is all."

He smiled at the sheriff and, still smiling, began to manufacture a cigarette, while Anthony almost forgot the last implied scoff and insult in the absorption with which he watched this act of delicate manufacture. The cigarette was molded in an instant, and the next moment was alight.

"I believe you don't smoke cigarettes?" Lynmouth explained to the sheriff. "And I have nothing else to offer you!"

"Yeah. You know a lot about me," growled Anthony.

"One tries to keep up with the eminent men—even in their foibles, Anthony. Man-catchers always have had a peculiar interest for me since I was a boy of twelve."

"I was gunna tell you something about yourself, young feller."

"I'm all ears, sheriff."

"After you rode Lambert, you come back here, and you tried to pick a fight out of a crowd."

"Not at all. I simply asked a man why he was laughing."

"You called him a dog!"

"Not at all. I said that a man who laughed at nothing was merely making a disturbing noise, like a dog. I asked him if he were a dog. But he seemed to have lost his tongue, and couldn't answer."

"You rode the whole bunch of 'em. You're lookin' for trouble, now. That's why you're hangin' around this town."

"Is it?"

"Aye, it is. If you want trouble, and to get yourself fixed up and respected again, why don't you take the trail of Jay Cress?"

"I couldn't catch him, Anthony," said Lynmouth, smiling again.

The sheriff stared at him.

"You've plumb turned to poison, Larry, ain't you!" he gasped.

"No. I've simply had my eyes opened a little. You're helping to open them now."

"I wanta say this," said the sheriff. "If you start revampin' your gun-play reputation in this town, and pull a gun on anybody, and so much as nick the edge of his ear, your life ain't gunna be worth half of a spoiled nickel, old son. You fasten to that! The way it stands, there's lynchin' talk in the air."

"Really?" said Lynmouth. He added, with that cold smile of his: "But with you in the town, it's very different. I'd be frightened otherwise; but knowing that you're here, Anthony, and understanding perfectly the fairness of your mind, your courage, your tremendous devotion to duty, I know that you'd as soon die a thousand deaths, yourself, as to see justice miscarry in the hands of a mob. I know that you'd protect me with your own life, Anthony!"

The sheriff stared again, as though he had heard something more than the mere words that were spoken, and as though he had seen something more, also.

"I dunno that I savvy you, no more," he said thoughtfully. "You kinda got me beat. But I'll tell you this, young son. You watch your step the rest of the while that you're in Crooked Horn, because if you don't you're gunna wake up with a broken neck, and no one sheriff on the face of God's green earth can save you from it. That's all!"

He turned abruptly toward the door.

"Are you going?" called Lynmouth gently. "Thank you for the warning, and good night, sheriff!"

The sheriff merely muttered something unintelligible.

Lynmouth stepped lightly to the door.

"Won't you let me go down with you, Anthony?"

"Oh, you be danged!" said Sheriff Anthony, jerking his hat firmly down upon his head.

He had the manner of one who has endured all that man can stand.

"Do mind the first steps, though," urged Lynmouth. "The runner on the stairs is so badly worn, and if you tripped at the head of the stairs, what a fall that would be, sheriff!"

Anthony looked up with a scowl, and then rapidly descended, while Lynmouth went back to his room, and opening the door, found that another man already had entered!

10

HARRY DAY COMES—AND GOES

THIS newcomer sat beside the window, so close to it that he could lean forward and look out through it, but at a sufficient distance so that no one possibly could see him from outside.

He was a little man. He looked like a precocious boy. That is to say, he had a boy's big round head, and little pinched neck, and rosy cheeks; and great glasses, and weak, blinking eyes behind them. He was dressed in gray flannel. He wore a gray silk tie, and a soft shirt with a wonderfully neat little collar. His feet were clad in the tiniest of shoes, which at a glance showed the care with which they had been fitted. In his hand he clasped a pair of chamois gloves of a light-yellow color, almost white from many cleanings and bleachings. Out of his breast pocket projected the corner of a handkerchief delicately striped with blue.

He waved his gloves to big Larry Lynmouth.

"Hello, old fellow," said he.

Lynmouth, closing the door behind him, instinctively turned the lock.

"Harry Day, of course," said he, and he swept the immaculate clothes of the other with a careful eye.

"How did you climb up that drainage pipe without getting rust on yourself?"

"One of my little mysteries," said Harry, and his boyish smile flashed.

"I'd like to know some other mysteries."

"Go ahead, Larry."

"How did you get here?"

"On a train."

"Cushion?"

"Blind baggage."

"What brought you?"

"Looking for the absent partner in my firm."

"What firm?"

"Harry and Larry, the disappearing artists."

"I told you that I was going straight."

"You're not the first actor to retire and come back again, Larry."

"No. So far, I intend to keep on going straight."

"You don't like it, though."

"What makes you think I don't like it?"

"By the grip of your jaws, and the flare of your nostrils. To an observant eye, Lynmouth, facial expressions are not a thing of a moment but a writing which fades in a second but is still legible with a microscope. Under the microscope you wouldn't look happy, old fellow."

"You were listening at the window while I talked to the sheriff?"

"Only heard the last few words. My arms were getting tired though."

Lynmouth smiled a little. He knew the wiry muscles with which that slender boy was strung.

"Come out with it," said he.

"Tell me, then. Do you want any help?"

"Help?"

"You understand, Lynmouth. I haven't been around the town long, but I've heard enough."

"You've heard," stated Lynmouth slowly, "how Jay Cress made me take water?"

Harry Day did not attempt to soften the balance of this statement.

"That's what I've heard," said he. "And that you're not the popular young hero, any more."

"How could you help me, Harry?"

"I could remove Cress, for instance."

"I don't want him murdered."

"Are you saving him for yourself?"

"Yes," said Lynmouth. "Heaven help the man who touches Cress before me!"

He set his teeth.

"That would mean that you'd have to hunt down the man who licked Cress? To reinstate yourself? But let me tell you, my lad, that if you've once buckled under before Cress, you'd always buckle under before him in the future!"

"Shall I?" said Lynmouth, with a sneer.

"Yes," answered Day. "I don't know the peculiar circumstances. And, judging from your face, there were peculiar circumstances. But if he once had the upper hand, he'll have it again when you next meet."

"You're wrong. I'll eat him," answered Lynmouth.

The little man shook his head. Now that he was serious, the boyishness seemed to leave his face. At a stroke, he was forty. Little crow's-feet were visible around the corners of his eyes. All at once, he was preternaturally old and wise.

"You'll never beat him again," said Harry Day. "Take my word for that and let me go blot him out."

"You're confident, Harry."

"I'm too small a target to be hit," replied the other nonchalantly. "Let me blot out Cress, and then come back to you. We have a lot of business ahead of us."

"I told you I was through with the game."

"You were through with it, of course. But that's past tense. I'm talking about the present."

"No, I'm through."

"What are you going to do, man? You've lost your reputation, lost your popularity, and lost the girl you were going to marry."

"You know that, do you?"

"Yes. And so does the town."

"Naturally, if you do. Then the Olivers have been talking."

"Apparently."

"That's worthy of noting," said Lynmouth, growing whiter.

"What I want to talk to you about," said the little man, "is not an ordinary common or garden variety of work. You've had enough of that—robbing for pleasure and excitement, rather than profit—robbing on a dare, so to speak. Picking out the banks which were the hardest, not the ones with the biggest store of honey in the hive."

"How big?" asked Lynmouth.

"Shall I tempt you?"

"I want to see if you can."

"It needs a jaunt to St. Louis. I've spotted a little old bank—good, solid, honest, old-fashioned place. And we'll always be able to clean up somewhere between a million and a quarter, and twice that sum."

"A nice big haul."

"Of course it is. And very simple, too. I have the straight avenue. No big sums to put out. No crowd to bribe. Nobody to make a big split with. You and me, we make the split between ourselves. I really think that there's a million each for us. Then retire, if you want to. You'll be able to live like a gentleman the rest of your days. Are you tempted?"

"Not a whit!"

"Honestly?"

"Not tempted a bit, Harry. I'm afraid that you'll never be able to budge me, if this won't work."—

Harry Day, thoughtfully considering, smoked a cigarette in silence. It was half gone when he said:

"I suppose I understand."

"What?"

"Why you're in this frame of mind."

"Tell me, then, because I myself hardly know."

"You were a robber, Lynmouth, not because you were too lazy to work, or because you loved crime, but because robbery was the exciting thing. The danger was on the other side of the law. So you went there, and you stayed there. Only a girl tempted you back into the fold. Now the fold is trying to kick you outdoors. That changes everything. It now becomes the romantically impossible task to attempt to stay in the fold. Am I wrong?"

"I don't know," answered the boy. "You may be right. That I can't tell. But the fact is that I'm interested in the job that's ahead of me."

"What's that job, then?"

"Hard to tell. First, to do something about the cunning sneak, Cress. Gun play? I hardly know. Why throw myself into the danger of the law by killing a little snipe like Cress? But whether I tackle Cress or not, I'm going to keep on this road. Yes, they'd like to run me out again. The whole town is sneering at me, and hating me because my spirit isn't entirely broken by Cress, as they expected it to be. I'll stay here and fight the thing out, whatever happens. Believe me, I won't quit!"

"You'll lose," said the other with much surety.

"Perhaps. It'll be a good fight, though."

"Not a good fight, either. When society wants to down a man, it always manages the job by first tying his hands behind his back, and then challenging him to a fight. Does it strike you, Lynmouth, that you don't dare to pull a gun on any man, no matter how right you may be and how wrong he may be?"

"Why not?"

"The honest citizens would lynch you. Didn't the sheriff tell you as much?"

"I'll have to take that chance, then. But I won't go back with you."

"That's definite?"

"Definite as steel."

Day sighed. "I thought I would have you with me," he regretted. "I met that old bungler, Steve Binney, and he wanted to throw in with me. I'll be down in company like that, before long, and it's a pity."

"Is Binney in town?"

"Yes, and looking hungry, too. He's kept his nerve, but he's lost his touch. They all do. Some of them get old, some get the shakes, some wind up in the cooler, a good many are nicked with bullets, and the rest die young with pneumonia—or some other athlete's disease. Some of them play the hypocrite and pretend to reform—if the place they land in is soft enough. But I've never before run into any one who really withdrew on the level, not for what he had, but for what he could get."

He shook his head mournfully, and then stood up.

"Are you going, Harry?"

"Yes, I'm going. Not by the door, thank you. I've operated in this little town before, and they may remember me too well. Hate to stir up a town's hospitality without asking for it beforehand. You're sure that there's nothing I can do for you?"

"Not a thing. Yes, there is one thing."

"Tell me, then."

"Go to Jackson Ford. Hunt up Jay Cress—I think that he'll be there. Don't lay a hand or a gun on him. But find out if he's expecting to marry a girl named Cherry Daniels. If he is, let me know about it."

"Is that all you want me to find out?"

"Yes. And give Jay one message from me."

"I shall, word for word."

"Tell him that I've given twenty-four thousand dollars to charity; that I believe he's a snake; and that I intend to treat him like one the next time I see him."

"The very sort of a message that I'd like to deliver to Jay Cress," said the little man. "So long, Lynmouth. I'll see you again, no doubt."

And he stepped through the window, as though into the dark door of his carriage!

11

A FEARLESS FRIAR

WHEN Lynmouth got up the next morning, it was already broad day—a very late hour for him to sleep. With a bucket of cold water he took a sponge bath, troubled the cook for a dish of hot water for shaving, and descended leisurely for breakfast at a time when the dining room was quite empty.

He ate sparingly, as was his habit. He had formed that habit through the many years when his eye had to be sure, and his hand lightning fast at any hour of need, and that need might come day or night. He had slept like a wildcat and walked like a wolf since he was a young boy. It was no wonder that he carried eyes, as it were, in the back of his head.

After breakfast he strolled out onto the veranda in front of the hotel, and received the same chilly dose of silence which had been offered to him the night before. He stayed there while he smoked a cigarette, and during that time he heard not so much as a whisper near by. Conversation was simply suspended.

He tried to overlook this treatment, but, in spite of himself, his anger was rising.

Then he went out to the stable, and from it he took Fortune, saddled her, and rode down into the river gorge.

He had thought, on the morning of the day before, that he had cast behind him the days of long and arduous labor with weapons; but he could see that he never had had a greater need of expert skill with guns than he had now. So he spent an hour and a half in the most laborious use of his Colts.

He fired from the back of the horse, at a walk, at a trot, at a canter, at a racing gallop. He dismounted, and shot from a stand, and from all sorts of positions, always making sure to slide the guns back into the spring holsters beneath his armpits after each bullet had been fired.

Mere shooting at a mark he disdained. To stand at ease, draw a careful bead, and then score a bull's-eye, was nothing to him. When need struck him, it was more likely to be from a whisper to the rear, or a stir on either side. It might be a gleam among the leaves of a shrub. It might be some intangible sense crossing his mind like a cloud shadow that would mean the vital presence of danger. There he worked almost like a gymnast.

He walked straight ahead. He ran. He halted from full speed, whirled and fired. He dropped to the ground, shooting as he fell. And always his brow was puckered with discontent. The calm content of the target shooter was not his, but the rock, the stick, the willow trunk which he selected as a target, was always, to his imagination, an armed man.

He was panting, and his guns were both hot when at last he stopped, cleaned the weapons, and restored them to their holsters, loaded. Nearly every day during the past several years he had gone through the same performance. It was an unpleasant medicine, but it was a preventive which had saved him from death fifty times. Other men, famous shots though they might be, who had built up their skill by honest hunting, and perhaps a few revolver rounds on a Sunday morning, might do very well and last a few years; but in the end they were either beaten outright by a more alert draw and a steadier hand, or else a gun stuck in a holster, or they fired wide, when taken by surprise. He, at least, would minimize these chances as much as possible.

If his life as an outlaw had been one of almost constant danger, it was nothing compared with the peril which he now endured, when every man was almost an openly professed enemy. He knew the meaning of that silence on the veranda. These men might be overawed and hesitate for a time, but eventually one of them was sure to pluck up heart and try the worth of the newly disgraced outlaw. Twenty times a day, the story of his shame was told and retold, he could guess. And eventually, by constant repetition, it was sure to inspire some gunman to make an attempt on him for the sake of glory.

So, sternly, bitterly, he determined to wait until that time came.

He went back to Crooked Horn, looked in at the hotel, and then crossed the street to the Merchants' Loan & Trust. As he entered, he heard the whisper rise and cease. The cashier looked through the barred window at him with a pale, forced smile, scrutinized his check for twenty-four thousand dollars, and disappeared for a moment. Then he came back and asked in what denominations his client would like the sum.

Lynmouth took it in hundreds. Two hundred and forty bills, in a thick, closely compressed wad. That treasure he stowed in a pocket, and then went out onto the street.

The brightness of the sun swarmed upon him, dazzling his eyes, baking him with heat, as he stood there trying to think. At almost the same time, the day before, he had encountered Jay Cress on this spot and lost the money. No matter for the way he had won it back. Now he was going to pay it out for good. But he could not tell to what charity. He saw the skinny spire of the church rising beyond the roof of the blacksmith shop. There might be a place to put the money, in order that it should be spent on charity, but he did not know much about churches and churchmen, and rather disliked them. Ministers seemed removed from the ordinary ways of common men. Professional goodness he strongly suspected.

At that very moment, while his thoughts were fixed

upon the subject of churches and churchmen, a Franciscan friar jolted down the street on a mule. The mule, to be sure seemed to have an execrably stiff gait, but the friar was such a very bad rider that his arms flopped and he grunted audibly at almost every step the animal took. The hat which he wore had fallen from his head, but, as though he were used to such trouble, the friar had secured it with a string that passed around his neck, so that it merely bobbed and danced between his shoulder blades. Another proof that he often went without the hat was that his tonsured head was as brown as a Mexican peon's face.

Young Lynmouth looked after him with a contemptuous sneer.

"No," he said to himself, "whatever I do, I'll never give my money to the church—not to any church! Hypocrites! They've been afraid of life and hard work, and jumped onto the safe side of the hedge to get fat and sit still. Confound them all! I'll find a hospital, or some such thing."

He was satisfied with this idea, and went slowly on until he came to the blacksmith shop, into which the Franciscan had turned. The blacksmith, attempting to pick up a forehoof, nearly was crushed under foot, for the old black mule—silver-sprinkled with age—jumped up into the air and tried to land on the poor man with all four feet.

The language of the smith became lurid.

"This ain't a mule. This is a danged old tiger," he declared. "You oughta muzzle her. She don't need shoes. She needs mufflers!"

"Now she'll stand like a lamb," said the friar, going to the head of the mule. "Alicia is very temperamental, and she has a particular dislike for blacksmiths. To her simple mind, you must remember, the glow of the forge fire, and the sulphurous clouds of smoke—"

"Must seem like Hades!" finished the blacksmith tersely. "Well, then she'd be at home! I never seen a mule that was simple. A wolf is a dog-gone quiet and foolish thing compared to a mule. A mule could pick out a good living where nothing but a buzzard would be happy."

"Alicia has a singular taste, to be sure," said the friar. "She has eaten two Bibles, a Book of Hours, a breviary, two gray robes, several hats, and at least one pair of shoes, in her life, and I'm afraid that she'll have more of the same diet before her end. In the matter of sins, brother, she is crowded with wickedness, but then she has her virtues, also."

"Yeah?" drawled the smith. "And what might they be, stranger?"

"She will walk on a trail among the clouds, where even the mountain goats might very well grow dizzy. She will swim like a fish through wild rivers. She will face a hurricane, even when there is hail like teeth in the wind. The sound of guns and the whizzing of bullets never unsteadies her. She has eaten sacred books, to be sure; but on the other hand, I have seen her, at least ten times, so thin that her stomach disappeared, because it was no longer needed, and her head looked like a pumpkin on the end of a Hallowe'en stick."

The blacksmith, now that the friar was at the head of Alicia, ventured to lift her hoofs again. She flattened her ears, but submitted, though her very nostrils curled with anger and with disdain. Of the shoes, two were gone entirely, and the other pair were in bad shape.

"Where you been riding her," said the blacksmith, "that you've had to be with the mountain goats and swimmin' floods?"

The little friar sat on a sawbuck, without dignity, and rubbed the bewhiskered muzzle of the mule.

"I must go," said he, "wherever I am needed. And who can tell where that will be? Sometimes here, sometimes there, and if one waited to turn the flank of mountain ranges, as you know, one would arrive very late!"

"These shoes," said the blacksmith, "they kinda look as though she'd been workin' in rocks right lately."

"Ah, yes! She's been among the rocks. Clear to Eagle Rest!"

He smiled with the pleasure of a child, as he mentioned the name. But the smith started back.

"Eagle Rest? Why, they've got smallpox up yonder!" he said.

"It is all over, now," said the friar. "There were four

sad deaths. How unfortunate that all people will not submit to vaccination, is it not?"

"You!" said the blacksmith. "You—move on! I ain't been vaccinated myself, never. The quicker you get out of here, the better."

The friar shook his head.

"You are perfectly safe," said he. "When I was among them, I put aside this robe; and when I left them, I purified myself, and gave the clothes a steaming in sulphur. Everything about me!"

He still shook his head, and smiled with conviction, though the blacksmith frowned in doubt and in dread.

"You need not doubt," said the friar. "I assure you that even Alicia I washed in a disinfectant three times, on three separate days. I am confident that you need have no fear."

"Well," said the blacksmith, "what fetched you up to Eagle Rest? Didn't you know that they had the plague there?"

The Franciscan opened his eyes in wonder.

"Of course, señor! And that was why I went there. Why else?"

The blacksmith pushed back his hat, scratched his head, and then bit off a whole corner from a black wedge of chewing tobacco. Staring at the man of God, he slowly masticated this lump.

Lynmouth stood silent as a shadow to listen.

"You went there because of the smallpox?" said the bewildered blacksmith.

"Nurses were hard to secure," explained the gray frair. "I had to hurry fast. In fact, when I got there, I found twenty souls practically lacking all care, and very sick; indeed—"

"You bein' vaccinated yourself?" broke in the smith harshly.

The friar sighed.

"Who am I to teach others, when I have neglected such a simple thing myself?" said he. "But at the first town where I have time to halt for a day, I intend to have it done."

The smith pointed a grim finger at him.

"Then you've been up there riskin' your life like a fool?" he demanded.

"Ah, my brother," said the Franciscan, "there is no risk. That which is willed, must be."

12

TWO KNOCKS AT ONE DOOR

THE blacksmith stopped chewing. With narrowed eyes he surveyed the Franciscan. And then the plug, stationary in his cheek, raised a white point on the skin.

"Well, you got me beat," said the blacksmith, and set about laboring on the shoeing of the mule.

Once the process had begun, and the old shoes had been torn off, and the fit of the new ones had been roughly estimated, there was a considerable time during which the smith was sure to be busy at his forge and anvil, and during which the friar would not be needed to look after the manners of his mule.

Here, from among the shadows near the door, Lynmouth raised his hand. The holy man came over to him at once.

He looked smaller, as he came closer. His head was as round as a ball and brown as walnut stain was his complexion. He had a waddling gait, like a duck; and his robe, which was of a rough gray fabric a good deal too big for him, he hitched up in front to give himself foot room for walking. When his features were still, they impressed Lynmouth with their preternatural gravity. When he smiled, however, all sense of fatigue disappeared. A merry kindliness drowned all other expression.

"Yes, señor?" said he, speaking in Spanish, which was apparently his easiest tongue.

Lynmouth answered him in the same language. He said, rather roughly:

"Brother, what is your name?"

"Juan is my name."

"And what's your job, on the whole?"

"To help where I can, wherever there is a need."

"What's your reward, then?"

"The honor of God's Son," said the friar.

"His honor, not yours?"

"Yes."

"What's the thing that would make you happiest?"

"To do a great good, in a great name," said the friar, patient under this string of terse questions.

Lynmouth held out the small package.

"Here are twenty-four thousand dollars," said he, "in hard cash. You can find the right places to spend it, I suppose?"

The friar stretched out his hand eagerly, but then checked the gesture.

"You mean this money for charity?" he asked.

"Yes," said Lynmouth.

"It is a very great sum," said the other. "You are a Catholic, my son?"

"I'm nothing," said Lynmouth. "I've only been inside a church a couple of times in my life. That business doesn't interest me. What I am interested in amounts to two things: to see that money well spent; and to know that my name will never be hitched to it. If you take it for charity promise that you'll never mention my name."

"And that name, señor?"

"Larry Lynmouth."

The friar opened his eyes widely.

"Señor, it will be a great honor and a great pleasure. But this is a fortune. You have some wishes, some desires in the matter of spending it?"

"Only," said Lynmouth, "that you don't found churches with it, but give it to people who are worth having it. Is that clear? There may be honest decent fellows who are down and out. Let them have a dip into the purse. I leave it to you."

The friar expressed no further wonder. If he felt it, he suppressed the emotion.

"You yourself," he said, "no doubt could find a use—"

"I don't know a man worth helping," said Lynmouth bitterly. "I know poor men and sick men. But they're poor because they're cowards or weaklings. They're sick because they haven't taken care of themselves. Barking curs, baying dogs, howling wolves—those are the people that I have known! I want no more of them. Never ask my advice, because I'd rather throw the money over a cliff than give it out to people I despise. Is it all clear?"

The friar held out his hand.

"Señor Lynmouth," said he, "I must thank you."

"For what?" asked Lynmouth sharply.

"For the sake of God," said the friar, "for He, also, is grateful."

But the sour cynicism which had mastered Lynmouth since his interview with the Olivers overcame him again. He turned on his heel, with a mere wave of the hand by way of farewell, and went back up the street to the hotel.

Once more he forced himself to stay for a short time on the veranda, in the silence of the loungers there. Then he strolled up to his room and threw himself on his bed.

He had a strange feeling that the gift of this money was the end of one part of his life. It was the clearing away of his last debt. From this point forward, he was at least his own master, with no necessary sense of guilt for his career of crime. Last of all, he had paid off the bribe money which he had received from Cress. That was the greatest load of all!

He began to breathe more easily.

With the past disposed of, there remained a few present problems. He must dispose of Jay Cress. He must dispose of Cress before the eyes of a mob.

Next, he must do something about Kate Oliver. What, he could not tell. But he only knew that he loved her still, and that with his love for her was mixed bitter contempt and a deep disgust, for she had failed him in the time of need, so far as he could see.

He was turning these matters in his mind. He was wondering how quickly public opinion, like a whipped dog, would come to heel again. How quickly would he once more be the idol of boys and the hero of young men, and the dazzling object of worship of the free-swinging Western girls?

There was a rap at the door. He turned a little, felt

the handle of a revolver beneath his arm, and called to the visitor to enter. It was the clerk of the hotel, bringing a note which, he said, had just been carried to the veranda of the hotel by a Mexican on a horse which dripped with sweat.

"If you're gunna find business in that note that'll make you wanta pull out, we'd like to know," said the hotel clerk, "because the way it stands, we sure gotta lot of users for this room!"

A very broad hint that Lynmouth's company was not wanted, but he paid no attention to the remark. There were other things for him to care about. He simply waved the clerk from the room, and then opened the letter.

It was written in large, sweeping characters, like the writing of a woman, and it was from Harry Day.

It read:

DEAR LARRY:

> I've been to Jackson Ford.
> I've seen Jay Cress.
> I've seen the Daniel boys.
> Above all, I've seen Cherry.

She leaves me a little dizzy. It's plain that she never has wasted much time in going to school, but what difference does that make? It isn't the clipped edges and the polish of words that makes them important. It's the spirit behind them, and she has plenty of spirit. Too much, you might say!

In short, she's a wonder. If I were half an inch over five feet, weighed ten pounds more, and looked a little less mature, I would fall in love. As it is, I can only keep hold of myself by an eyelash grip, and I keep saying over and over that I'm a fool, and a blanked fool. I put this in brief. I could write a book about that girl.

The situation down here is in part what you led me to expect.

I find old Mr. and Mrs. Daniels real ranchers. Hard hands and soft hearts, especially the old man.

The woman is not so easy. Women never are, when they've got three unmarried children.

The two boys are thoroughbreds. At least, they have plenty of hot blood, and they'll take a lot of cooling and tempering. However, they're neither red-short, nor cold-short, as the steel makers would say. It appears that you used to be the hero of the entire family. At present, however, the girl is heartbroken because you've apparently been beaten and showed the slightest degree of white feather. I've tried to explain that away. And she liked me so much for my excuses that I almost hated you.

But the boys have had a change of heart.

Buck is the quieter of the two. But Lew is raging to go up to Crooked Horn and establish a reputation for himself, and do the world a good turn by kill-ing the great bandit, Larry Lynmouth. Buck agrees, but he's quieter about it. The girl, in the meantime, won't look at Jay Cress. He's the hero of the boys, just now. The old folks make a good deal of him, too, because it's plain that he has plenty of money and would take good care of Cherry. But the girl hates him because he bested you. I would say, at the first flush, that she's in love. Either with you, or with her idea of you. Trust me when I tell you that one sight of her will make you forget the other one, old fellow.

I've seen Jay Cress. He asked me if you had sent me down. I smiled at him. He told me that if he ever sees you again, he intends to wipe you off the face of the earth. I gathered that this wasn't mere braggadocio. Having had the upper hand once, as I suspected, he was not at all afraid of mixing things with you again. I then gave him your message. He did not seem taken aback, but was infuriated. He called you a cur, and other things that would burn up the paper if I were to put them down even in this watered hotel ink.

The main point is that you'd better look out for Lew Daniels. He's a fighting chap, has killed his man—and more than once—and rides and shoots to suit a hero of romance. As a matter of fact, I think he already has started for Crooked Horn. Take care of yourself!

Let me know what more I can do. Believe that you haven't heard the last of me by a great deal. This is a mysterious business that you've stepped into, but I enjoy reading the romance, as it were!

Good-by, and good luck to you.

HARRY DAY

Lynmouth, having finished the letter, had barely crumpled it thoughtfully in his hand, when again there was a light tap at the door.

He remembered the warning in the letter, and rolling silently from the bed to the floor, he called out to his visitor to enter, at the same time stepping rapidly, and softly, to the side, so that he would not be located beforehand by the direction from which his voice had come.

But when the door opened with a jerk, he saw not a man, but the very prettiest girl he ever had laid his eyes upon.

13

CHERRY DANIELS

"HELLO, Larry," said she.

"Hello," said Lynmouth, with equal casualness, but looking a bit past her in order to see who had accompanied her.

"There ain't anybody with me," said the girl, "and you've forgot who I am."

"Not at all," he insisted.

She smiled a little.

"Anyway, I'm Cherry Daniels. I might've known that you'd forget me, and here you've done it. I'd better close the door, if you don't mind, because what I have to say ain't for the newspapers."

He pushed the door shut.

"Shall I lock it?" he asked.

"I guess nobody'll rush in on Larry Lynmouth," she remarked. "You don't need to lock it. And yet, I'd like to whisper. I've sailed up here from Jackson Ford because there's a pile of trouble. Shall I sit down? Thanks! I'm sort of winded. from running up the stairs and being scared of what I'd find at the head of 'em."

She dropped into a chair, pulled off her mannish hat, and fanned herself with it. She was almost as dark as an Indian, with black hair and eyes. Like an Indian girl's was the flash of her smile, and the wonderful supple grace of her body. But the glow in her cheeks, and something about the fine modeling of her forehead, told an eloquent story of white blood.

Lynmouth stood by the window, so that she would have to turn toward the light, for to touch her with his eyes was almost like touching a fine statue with a sculptor's hands.

"What's the trouble?" he asked her.

She paused for a moment, then she looked him straight in the face. like a man, and said quietly:

"Jay Cress came to Jackson Ford with a wild yarn about what he'd done. He wanted—but that doesn't really matter—"

"He wants to marry you. I know that."

"The little fellow wrote to you, did he?"

"What makes you think that?"

"I knew you'd sent him, though he didn't say so. But that doesn't matter. The point is that dad and mother, they think the sun rises and sets on Jay Cress. He's well-heeled, and all that. And my two brothers, Buck and Lew, they swear that Jay's the finest that ever came near the ranch. You understand how it is?"

"Yes, I understand."

"Well, you see how it is. I've got to be frank. They kept crowding me, and when I couldn't say 'Yes,' they—well, it's hard to put it, but I've got to tell you. They thought it was because I had oversized ideas about men from having met you."

She blushed, but her eyes were as steady as could be. Lynmouth nodded gravely.

"People get odd ideas," said he.

"And Lew," she went on rapidly, "swore that he'd wipe you out completely—to clear the road for Jay Cress, as he put it. I begged him not to be a fool. But he's too young not to want to get famous. And he's come charging up here from Jackson Ford. I cut across country, but I won't be ten minutes before him. And there you are!"

She stopped, panting and crimson with shame, but brave as could be.

"He'll be waiting for me with a gun, when I go downstairs. Is that it?"

"That's about the size of it."

"And you've come to hope that I wouldn't meet him?"

She shook her head. "I can't ask you that!" she declared.

Lynmouth hesitated. Somehow, this visit increased the bitterness in his heart.

"Tell me about Lew," he said kindly, forcing himself.

"Lew's a good sort," she said. "He's square. He's as good-natured as the day's long. But he's wild as a mustang. You've known plenty of his cut, but none just like Lew, I think. He's the best kind of a brother. He'd die for me. That's probably what he'll do today! And that's why I've come here to—"

She stopped suddenly.

"Go on," said Lynmouth.

"He may think, like the others, that you're not what you used to be. Excuse me for saying that!"

"They all agree that I'm a yellow dog, now," remarked Lynmouth coldly.

"I don't," said the girl. Her emotion made her stand up. "I know that you're the same as always, no matter what you did with Jay Cress."

"Do you really mean that?" he asked her.

"Of course I do."

"The whole world knows that I took water from Jay Cress!"

"The world's a fool!" cried the girl. "And they'll pay for finding out what I know already!"

There was fire in her face, and this utter confidence bewildered Lynmouth. He had seen her once, and that so casually and so long ago that he had even forgotten her face. To be sure, it could not have been what it was now. She must have been more child and less woman. Nevertheless, he had forgotten; but she, it appeared, had read him to the heart in that single meeting.

"You've a way of explaining the way I showed yellow to Cress?" he asked her.

"Why, I know that crooked things come out of crooked people, and straight things come out of straight people. And Jay Cress is crookeder than a dog's hind leg! That's how I explain it. I knew it before. I'm dead sure of it, now that I'm seeing you again."

"I haven't changed, then?" he asked her.

"Why, yes," she said, coming a little closer to him, and gazing steadily on his face. "You were iron, then. But you're sword steel now."

"I'll tell you what," said Lynmouth. "I thought that there was nobody who believed in me. You show me that I'm wrong. Well, put your cards on the table, and I'll do what you want."

She sighed out, "Thank Heaven!"

Her relief was so great that she gripped the edge of the little center table and steadied herself for a moment, her eyes closed. Then she said:

"Of course, I know what you can do!"

"Do you?" asked he.

"Yes, of course I do. I know, for instance, how Groney and Benson and Craig cornered you in Tombstone, and how you fixed them."

"Tell me," said he, "what you know about that?"

He was always curious to hear the tales of his exploits repeated, not to flatter his vanity, but because it amused him to see how rumor distorted the simplest things.

"You shot 'em up, all three. And the only thing you regretted was that Groney died."

"Groney meant nothing to me," he assured her.

"Of course he didn't! None of the others did, either. But I know. You didn't want to do real harm to fellows who'd had too much to drink!"

He started. He never had stated that to a soul in the world. It would not have been believed, had he sworn that he had purposely fired low against those three wild men, after they jammed him into a corner.

She went on: "You took a chance rather than shoot for the head, or the heart. You shot low, and it was only an accident that the bullet that hit Groney in the hip glanced up. Isn't that true?"

"Nobody would believe it," said Lynmouth, more and more amazed.

The girl laughed triumphantly.

"*I* know!" she said. "*I* could read your mind! Those three were hot with liquor, but all three of them were high-speed tool steel that cuts when it's red-hot. They were three fighting fiends, but you stood there and picked them off one by one shooting them through the legs. And what would keep you from doing the same thing with my brother Lew?"

"You want me to shoot him down?" he asked her.

"He's good stuff. He's real metal," said the girl, "but till he's tempered in his own blood, he's a dangerous fellow! I know that. I love Lew, but I know him. Besides, what else are you to do? When you meet him, don't I know that you could shoot him dead? Aye, and that would make them all respect you again!"

"Yes," said Lynmouth slowly, through his teeth. "That would make them respect me again."

"The curs!" exclaimed the girl. "But Lew isn't a cur. Will you believe that?"

"I'll believe," said Lynmouth slowly, very slowly, "every word that you tell me. You know, you're the one person in all the world that I would believe!"

She lost color. She stared at him, and he knew that she was shaking, by the tremor of the sunlight in her glistening hair.

"But when it comes to taking a chance with a cold-sober man—it's a different thing, Cherry. Those three fellows gave me two advantages. They were fairly full of redeye, and they were dead confident in their numbers. But with one steady, fast, straight-shooting man—"

"Ah, but you've done it before with dead-sober, cold-steady, fast men!" she exclaimed. "There was Pat Haskyns—"

He was amazed again. The girl seemed to know his history as well or better than he knew it himself.

"There's a better way," he said. "Do you think that your brother will be here soon?"

Providentially, uncannily, there was a knock at the door just then and when he called out a voice answered with a sort of snarling satisfaction:

"There's a young gent just come that's achin' to see you, Lynmouth!"

There was no doubt about the identity of that young man who was "aching to see him!"

He made a step toward the door, coldly angry. Then he stopped himself and remembered the girl.

"Tell him that I'll be right down," said he.

He turned on Cherry Daniels.

She moistened her lips and waited for his answer.

At last he said: "There's a better way than the one you suggest. I won't meet him at all. I'll slide my pack out this window and follow it down to the ground."

He stood at the window and looked at the drainage pipe from the eaves above. It looked a flimsy affair, but it had borne the weight of Day and must now bear his.

"D'you mean that you'll run out?" she asked him.

Her voice was husky and he turned back on her. Did she also doubt him?

"I wouldn't ask you—I wouldn't dare ask you to do it!" she cried. "Then everybody would say that you were no good!"

"Would you say it?" he asked her.

"I? Oh, Larry, I know what you are, and I know the misery that's fair eating you now. Go down and meet Lew—only for Heaven's sake, be as merciful as you can!"

"You go first," he told her gently. "You can get out the side door, no doubt, without any danger of being seen. They'll be on the veranda—everybody—to see the fight. Let me handle this my own way."

14

A NEW ADMIRER

HE WOULD never forget how she stood in the doorway, whiter than ever, with one of his hands caught in hers, and staring up into his face.

"Whatever you do, you won't throw yourself away?" she begged him.

"D'you think that I'm close to that?" he asked.

She nodded miserably.

"I can guess a lot," she said. "You're mighty blue, Larry, but I'm sure you'll pull through to the sunshine, pretty soon!"

He merely smiled down at her, and when she turned away, he quickly made his preparations for departure.

She was right. The world was filled with curs, except for this girl, and, perhaps, that brown-faced old friar, Brother Juan. As for the rest and their opinions, what should they matter to him? He would please the girl, he would save her brother, and let the others talk as they pleased. It made no difference to him.

So he told himself, though his heart ached wildly.

Rapidly he gathered his pack with the speed of one accustomed to quick moves. With its own rope he lowered it part way to the ground, then let it fall. Next, swinging out from the window sill, he took a good handhold upon the drain pipe and lowered himself rapidly.

Across that side of the house grew a number of trees and tall brush, so that he depended upon this to screen him from any eye that might be passing along the street. Yet he was not quite to the ground, but stretching himself for the drop, when he heard a clarion young voice behind him shouting loudly:

"Come and look! The skunk is gonna run for it! There ain't man enough left in him to face a mouse! Come and look at the great Lynmouth, will you?"

He heard a crashing of many running feet through the shrubbery, and, dropping lightly to the ground, he turned and faced the brother of Cherry Daniels.

There was no doubt about it. The youngster was almost as good-looking as his sister, with a big, capable pair of shoulders that promised well for hand-to-hand fighting of any sort. There was a dare-devil look about him that would have pleased Lynmouth on any other occasion, and he stood now with his hands on his hips, and beneath his finger tips dangled a pair of holsters, proving that he claimed the proud title of a two-gun man.

At the same moment, out of the brush broke a running group of eager punchers, the same lot who had been loitering on the veranda, reënforced by a clustering host of boys, eager-eyed little girls as hardy as wildcats, and all shouting and calling to one another as they came to witness the downfall of the great man.

And Lynmouth, breathing hard from the climb down, dusted his hands and looked around him. Then he stared young Lew Daniels fairly in the face. Bluff might do something.

He walked slowly, with long steps, toward the boy.

"You're Daniels, are you?" said he.

"That's my name, you yellow dog!" said Daniels. "Running out on me, were you?"

"I thought I'd spare your hide for you," said Lynmouth. "You want to finish yourself off, though, I see? Is that it?"

"All he's got is a four-flush," said a loud voice from the crowd. "Don't let him bluff you out of this pot, Lew!"

Lynmouth turned his head, and marked the big man whom he had disgraced on the veranda the day before.

A wide, delicious grin of expectation was on the face of that hero now. And all the rest wore the same expression. Indians around a torture post were amiable and gentle creatures, it seemed to Lynmouth, compared with this group which was before him.

The detestation which had grown up in him before now mastered him. It gripped his heart with a cold hand; it froze his very brain; it sharpened his wits to a cutting edge.

He looked back at Lew Daniels.

"Snake out if you want to," said Daniels. "I won't do more'n kick you a couple of steps on your way!"

And, as he uttered insults, it seemed to Lynmouth that the face of the girl floated like a ghost between him and young Daniels. No, he would not shoot to kill.

"You've asked for it, and you need it," said Lynmouth. "One of this barking rabble, here, can give a signal, unless you want to go for your gun first."

"Ah, still bluffing! Still bluffing!" howled the big man in the crowd.

"I'll tend to you afterward," said Lynmouth, "and if ever I see your ugly face again, my friend, I'll put a third eye between the other two. Your brains need more light! Are you ready, Daniels?"

That young man, suddenly sobered, but without a whit of fear, stood as if at a mark. He threw up his head, but did not move his hand for a gun.

"Let one of these undertakers raise a bandanna. We'll fire when he drops it," said Lynmouth calmly. "You, there," he continued to the groom, who was one of the lot that clustered near, "you pull that bandanna off your neck and use it for a flag."

"The yaller dog is quakin' in his boots," snarled the groom. "It's all pure bluff, Lew. Don't let him scare you a mite!"

And he tore the bandanna from about his neck and raised it high in the air.

"He don't scare me," Lew assured the crowd. "I'm ready when you are, Lynmouth!"

Actually, the boy was like a fighting dog, quivering on the mark. With all his heart, Lynmouth sympathized with that eagerness. He could remember the days of his first fights, with romance before him and the world all one golden opinion to be harvested. So he, Larry Lynmouth, had faced many a man. He knew that grim fire that was burning in the breast of this young hero. Aye, and perhaps there was a sufficient quantity of skill mixed with his courage to make him very dangerous!

Yet there had been a promise to the girl, and Lynmouth determined calmly, unalterably, that he would live up to it. If his reward was a bullet tearing through his heart, it would make no great difference. She would know why he had failed to fire a center target.

That which he picked out was a most difficult one—above all, for a snap gunshot. But he selected the weapon on the right hip. That would be his target. Two guns were very well to fill the eye of the world and impose upon the uninitiated; but he did not dream that young Daniels would be fool enough to attempt to snatch out both weapons when he faced such an enemy as this. No man in the world could move two hands as fast as one. No man in the world had sufficient brain and nerve power for such a feat.

"I'm ready," said Lynmouth, and that instant the bandanna was brought down through the air with a vicious swish.

Lynmouth's hand was instantly in motion. He did not have to think about what his hand was doing, as it flicked up inside his coat and snatched out the heavy Colt by the familiar, finger-worn handle. His hours of constant practice had made him a deft master of this technique. So his whole attention was given straight upon his target.

There was only a tenth part of a second, but to the leaping speed of his brain, that tenth part was split into ten separate fractions, in the first of which he saw the boy's eyes flash down toward his right-hand gun.

That look flicked up again instantly, but the indefinite glint of time was enough to tell Lynmouth that the game was in his hands. An expert young Lew might be, but he had much to learn of the mere essentials of a gun play.

His weapon was hardly starting from the holster on his right hip, when Lynmouth fired.

Holster and revolver disappeared with a great clang and a jerk that pulled Lew Daniels off balance. He reeled back half a step, clawing at his left-hand gun, cursing, his face contorted, but not with fear.

There was another hundredth part of a second for Lynmouth to regard this fact. If he delayed, the left-hand gun would be out, and who could tell what would happen then?

Straight for the left holster he fired his second shot; in spite of his thinking, the explosions seeming to those who stood there to follow right on the heels of one another. And fair and true the half-inch slug struck the mark. The second weapon went spinning.

But this time the body of the boy was turned, from the jerk of the first impact, and the sickening thump of a big-caliber bullet entering the living flesh of the thigh was audible.

"Dang you!" shouted Lew Daniels, furious and undaunted.

He snatched out a formidable-looking bowie knife and tried to rush at the other. But at the first step his leg collapsed beneath him. He fell heavily to the ground.

Lynmouth gave him no heed. He was down, and helpless for the moment. Unless the bone were broken, which seemed unlikely from the angle of firing, he would merely have his blood let—a thing which his sister had proclaimed a probable good for the boy.

There was other work for Lynmouth. And he stepped straight through the crowd, with his revolver poised.

"I want that black-faced, scowling dog who was barking here a moment ago," said Lynmouth. "Who's seen him?"

They melted away before him. Out of the distance, plunging through the brush, he heard the cry of a frightened man, like the yelp of a hunted dog, and he could guess that that was his quarry.

But he did not hasten forward.

Disgust mastered him once more. They were not even worthy of receiving a lesson at his hands. Only the boy who was lying there on the ground was worthy of attention.

By Heaven, they had not stirred a foot to succor the lad!

They stood about, gaping, watching the red form a pool. They dared not attempt to help him until the victor gave permission.

Lynmouth put away his gun with a snap of his hand.

"Are you going to stand about and let him bleed to death?" he demanded. "Pick him up and carry him into the hotel. Some of you get a doctor. Let's see, first, if he can move his leg."

He leaned above the fallen youngster, and gripped the

wounded leg at the knee. It moved freely. There was no sound of grating bone edges when he lifted the limb.

"Any pain when I move that leg, Daniels?" he asked.

The boy did not answer. Propped on one arm, the useless bowie knife gripped hard in one hand, he stared up at the face of his conqueror.

Then at last he broke out:

"You shot *both* my guns away, Lynmouth. By Jiminy, what a wonder you are!"

There was actually a smile of broad admiration lighting up his face!

And Lynmouth, looking down at him, knew that this was a true brother of Cherry Daniels, and that this letting of blood would do him much good indeed.

15

VICTORY FOR THE SHERIFF

THEN Lynmouth went back to his room. There he lay on the bed and tried to put things straight in his mind— no easy task!

There was Kate Oliver, for instance.

He felt that the lightness with which she had given him up amounted almost to treason, yet he also felt that there must be something more to the story than what he had seen. He could not tell, for example, how her mind had been worked upon. Always he had sensed in her a certain nobility and beauty of mind. This, now, he could not quite deny her, no matter what she had done to him in person. Besides, from the very first he had been conscious of unworthiness in respect to her.

But how contrast her with Cherry Daniels?

There was nothing airy, fairy, unstable, unearthly about Cherry. There was nothing to convince her of, for one thing, since she already was convinced. She understood him. In spite of himself, he knew that she could read his mind as Kate Oliver never would be able to do. To Kate, he would have to be a mysterious deity; to Cherry Daniels he would have to be himself. She knew and respected certain of his qualities so thoroughly that he could guess that she saw through to his weaknesses in other respects.

Far better, no doubt, that it should be so. Only young boys and young men wish to be worshiped; maturity wishes to be understood. Then she was made of stuff with which he was himself familiar, the jovial, buoyant, free-swinging Western spirit. He was touched to the heart by her willingness to confess to him what most girls would rather have cut out their tongues than mention—her fondness, her idealization of him. The very letter of Harry Day, brisk and worldly as it was, hardly had left less unsaid than the girl herself. She faced disagreeable or embarrassing facts for the sake of helping her brother.

He wished, vehemently, that ever such a woman had taken such an interest in him, as he began his wild life. Sister or ladylove, she could have molded him, he swore, like the softest wax.

He turned to the other things which had thronged in upon his mind—Oliver, the banker, a decent man, no doubt, and shrewdly practical; not unkindly, either, but unable to stretch his imagination to conceive certain vital truths about men and life. He had missed, for instance, the character of Lynmouth himself.

There was the president of the First National, bewildered by the touch of honesty in the ex-robber. Equally dumb, dull, and uncomprehending. These men, he felt, were not vitally enough touched with human sympathy, which can conceive sin in good men, and honesty in bad ones. Out of the same warp and woof all humanity, perhaps, was spun—except for the crowd of the street!

For, when he thought of the maudlin tears, hate, contempts, envies, and spites of the man of the street, his lips curled as he lay on the bed. They were not men at all, he told himself, but a herd.

And what was he, Larry Lynmouth?

He lifted his head and looked around him at the dingy room, the heel-worn matting upon the floor, the cracked ceiling, the cheap varnish on the wall partition, which had run into large, dull beads through the summer heats; and then there was the staggering wicker washstand, and the pitcher seamed with a great crack, ingrained with dirt.

After twelve years of taking danger by the throat, he could find himself in quarters like these, and with four thousand and a few hundred dollars in the bank! Other men worked harder, and for even smaller returns, to be sure; but they had not risked their lives five hundred times, as he had done! They had not lived with a gun leveled at their heads, so to speak!

Outside of the hotel, he began to hear a deepening murmur of voices, such as arises at a county fair.

He could guess what they were talking about. About himself—about his attempted flight—about his encounter with young Daniels. What did they make of it, he wondered? He was a coward to them, of course, for fleeing. But, if a coward, how could he have faced Daniels so coldly, so easily? That would puzzle their heads, and they would hate him the more because they were puzzled, for that was their way. He began to feel that five wise men would make a crowd, and every crowd is a multiform fool.

After this, he turned his mind toward his future in this town. He must stay here. That was plain. For having declared that he would fight the battle out on this spot, on this spot he must remain. But what could he gain? The respect of the mob, again?

Once more he sneered at the cracks on the ceiling, and with a sick mind he followed the branching lines.

Some one came to his door with a soft step; suddenly that door was cast open.

He got to his feet a little faster than a scared wolf; but that watch-spring reaction was still a trifle too slow. For, in the doorway, stood Sheriff Chick Anthony, with fate in his hands.

Fate in every country wears a different expression and incases itself in a different form. But in the Far West of those days it was embodied as a riot gun. The wide-belching spray of buckshot from the muzzle of a sawed-off shotgun could not miss at close range.

"Get up your hands," said the sheriff.

And the gunman got them up!

"What's the charge?" he asked quietly.

He was almost glad that some interruption had come, even if it had to be in the form of fate itself. For he felt that he could act on a problem much better than he could think about it.

"Yeah? What charge?" drawled the sheriff.

He came in, still presenting the shotgun, and he kicked the door shut behind him. Doing so, he could realize that the close of the door had pushed to a distance an ominous growl that came from many throats of angry men.

"What charge?" said Chick Anthony. "I'll have your guns, first, and then I'll tell you."

He laid the muzzle of the gun upon the lean stomach of Lynmouth. Then, keeping a finger upon the trigger, he reached inside the coat of the former outlaw and removed a single-action Colt from one armpit spring holster, then one from the other. He tossed these weapons upon the bed, without turning his head toward them to watch their fall. If he had, a twitch of the body might have removed Lynmouth from the line of danger, and then there were his fierce hands at the throat of the man of law. The sheriff could prejudge this probable action by the cold, steady eyes of the other.

When he had removed the major armament, he went further. He fumbled at the person of Lynmouth until he discovered the little two-barrel bulldog pistol which was his court of last resort in case of a surprise attack just such as this. He found, also, a knife with a blade long enough to split a heart, to say the least.

These weapons were tossed after the revolvers.

After a little further examination, the sheriff stepped back. He cuddled the stock of the heavy gun against his ribs, and said, as he still covered the mid-section of the other:

"Now hold out your hands."

Quietly, Larry Lynmouth obeyed. The sheriff reached into his coat pocket, and producing a pair of handcuffs, he kept his glance fixed upon the eyes of his prisoner while, like a blind man, he fumbled for the extended wrists. cautioning him, in the meantime:

"If you bat an eye, Lynmouth. I'll blow you to kingdom come! You hear me? To kingdom come, and be danged to you!"

Lynmouth merely smiled. This caution might be taken as a compliment, but he was beyond receiving or valuing compliments except from two people in the entire world. One was Cherry Daniels; the other was Brother Juan.

When, at last, the handcuffs were securely in place, the sheriff stepped back with a sigh of content. But still his eye was watchful and seemed a little puzzled, as though he wondered how, in spite of all his precautions, he could have managed to capture such a prisoner.

"Well," he said, "that's done."

"I suppose," sneered Lynmouth, "that your heart was beating rather fast when you stood in the hall outside that door?"

The sheriff assented with a wonderful frankness. The winner can afford such frankness.

"Yeah," said he, "I was scared stiff. When I pushed that door open, I thought that I'd have my face split wide with a .45-caliber slug. Somehow, it didn't hit me."

"I'm curious to know," said Lynmouth, "just what old charge you've raked up against me."

"Old charge?" said the sheriff.

"Yes, what old charge?"

"Why should it have to be an old one?"

"Tell me, then, what I've done since I had the pardons?"

Anthony scowled. "You couldn't guess, I suppose," he suggested.

"No, I couldn't."

"I'll tell you, then. It don't seem like nothin' to you. But in the first place, you've broke the peace. In the second place, you've attempted manslaughter. And if that ain't good enough to slog you into the pen for ten years, I'd like to know!"

"Manslaughter?"

"Whacha call it?" snapped the sheriff. "Jumpin' on a kid like Daniels!"

"Did I jump on him?"

"Whacha call it, then? Shootin' him down—that's tag, I suppose?"

Lynmouth said nothing for a moment. He could guess that argument was vain. But then he decided that he would try the effect of some slight logic.

"Tell me, man. Did I hunt for Daniels, or did he hunt for me?"

"What's that gotta do with it?"

"Did I try to get away without seeing him? Did I even climb out of my window and slide down to the ground?"

The sheriff merely scowled.

"Did he catch me there and call a crowd to watch him bully me?"

"A fine chance he'd have of bullyin' you—a kid like him!"

"He's as old as I am, about."

"Nobody's as old as you are," said the sheriff with conviction. "Nobody. A fair fight, I suppose—you'd call it? You agin' him?"

"I'd call it the fairest fight I ever was in, or that I ever heard of. At a signal."

"He had as much chance against you as agin' a lightning bolt!"

"Then why didn't the crowd stop him? I gave them plenty of time!"

"Listen," said the sheriff, amazed. "Are you tryin' to talk me into freein' your hands?"

"No," said the gunman. "I'm simply trying to see how much of a blind, ignorant, prejudiced fool you may be!"

"Well," said the sheriff, "I'll show you."

He threw the door open. Up through the hotel poured a loud, angry murmuring.

"I'm tryin' to save you from that!" said he.

16

IN JAIL!

IN THE sound of that many-throated murmur there was something infinitely convincing. Lynmouth, after harkening to it for a moment, nodded at the sheriff.

"They want me, Chick," said he.

"Yeah. And they want you right bad. You comin' along quiet with me, son?"

"Like a lamb," said the gunman, "only I'd like to know why you really want me, Chick. I've done nothing wrong today. Every man who saw that fight can tell you that I tried to get out of it. I would have played the yellow dog and run to get clear. Why do you want to climb on me?"

The sheriff considered for a moment. The idea engrossed him so that he made a cigarette and lighted it.

Through the smoke he said:

"I'll tell you, Larry. I'll tell you straight."

"Go on, then. That's exactly what I want."

"The fact is," said the sheriff, "that I've had trouble with pickpockets and sneak thieves, and I've jailed safe crackers, and thugs, and yeggs of all kinds, and highwaymen—and some of those things you've been yourself, they say, here and there in your life. But of the whole crowd there ain't a soul that I hate like I hate a gunman. I'll tell you why, too."

"What do you call a gunman?" asked Lynmouth dryly. "A man who will fight when he's cornered?"

"No," answered the sheriff instantly, "but a man who hunts for corners in which he'll have to fight."

"Hunts for them?" asked Lynmouth coldly.

"What have you done since you were a kid," asked the sheriff, "and found out that you had a faster hand and a straighter eye than other people?"

"Every man has two hands and two eyes," declared Lynmouth, with a frown.

"Two hands for a plow and two eyes for a furrow," answered Chick Anthony. "But not two hands or even half a hand, for a Colt revolver. You know that. Some are born for it. Most people never get anywhere near good shooting. And a man with natural talent and patience can't be touched by one fighter in ten thousand. You found that out almost as soon as you started, Lynmouth!"

The gun fighter listened attentively. He frowned at the ceiling, and then he nodded.

"That's fairly true," said he.

"Of course it is. Other fellows have no more chance against you than a sheep against a wolf. Chances? Why, you take no chances at all! You know yourself. You know what you can do. You've practiced every day of your life, nearly. Send a baby against a machine gun—I'd as soon as send myself, for instance, against you! I tell you what, Lynmouth, I work for the law because I believe that the law is what gives the weak man a right to live. You've worked against the law, because you thought that a man with a gun was better than a man with a hay hook, a pitchfork, or a rope. But you're wrong, and you and all your kind are wrong. And the best way out for you is to have your necks broke, and the quicker that happens to you the better it'll please me!"

"Then why don't you send the mob up here?" asked Lynmouth, sneering.

"Because, as I just said before, that ain't the law, and the law is my boss. The way of the law is gunna be the way of Crooked Horn, if I can manage it. Now march out of here and watch yourself, because if you give me a fair excuse, I'm gunna part you from yourself as far as buckshot will blow the heart of you!"

With a good deal of amazement, Lynmouth listened to this steady outburst from the man of the law. Then he nodded again.

"There's something in what you say, Anthony," said he. "You happen to be wrong about me now. But you're not wrong about what I've been in the past. Only add up one thing in my favor. Any puncher with any sort of a gun in his hand is a dangerous proposition; and the slickest hand in the world can have his revolver catch in the holster."

With this, he walked deliberately from the room, and went down the upper hall and so along the side stairs to the ground floor. No one was at the side of the building, so that they stepped out into the open street, unobserved.

"Now run for your life, and head for the jail!" said Anthony.

A yell went up from the front of the hotel, at that moment, and with a glance over his shoulder, Lynmouth saw that the alarm had been given.

In spite of his tied hands, he went like a race horse for the steps of the jail, bounded up them; and although the sheriff was loaded down with the weight of the shotgun he was hardly two steps behind. His ready key he fitted into the lock; it turned; and the door swung open to give them safety.

Lynmouth, as he passed through, looked back to the rush of the crowd, coming in one frantic stampede that threw the dust as high as a run of horses. They yelled with rage and disappointment. Two or three fired into the air, and one low enough to send a bullet thudding into the front of the jail.

The door shut. They were safe.

"A brave lot, they are!" said Lynmouth, listening to the roar of the human wave as it broke around the building.

They were whooping. They were screaming.

"They're brave enough—they're good enough," growled the sheriff. "They're only a crowd. And that's different. But they're workin' men that've kept their wives and their kids. What've you kept, Lynmouth?"

For some reason, the tongue of Lynmouth was stopped by this remark.

Then heavy blows fell on the jail door.

"Anthony, Anthony!" yelled a loud voice, which Lynmouth recognized as that of the big man whom he had twice humiliated.

"Well?" asked Anthony, inside the wall.

"Is that you, sheriff?"

"This is me. Whacha want? Who are you?"

"No matter who I am. I'm the voice of Crooked Horn, and I'm tellin' you that if you like a whole skin, you'd better unlock that door and let us in there at Larry Lynmouth. Because we're gunna have his hide!"

The sheriff hesitated not a moment.

"If I open that door," said he, "I'll unlock his irons at the same time and put a loaded Colt in each of his hands. How fast'll you come through that doorway, then?"

"You keep on this way, Anthony!" screeched the other. "You just keep on this way, and there ain't a gent in town that would vote for you for dog catcher!"

"If a dog catcher come here," answered Chick Anthony readily, "the first neck he'd look at for a license plate would be yours, whoever you are! Back off that porch and shut up!"

"I ain't gunna back off. I ain't gunna shut up!" roared the other. "We want his hide, and we're gunna have it, and Heaven help you if you stand in our way!"

"Go back home, all of you," said the sheriff. "I ain't gunna waste no words with you. If it pleases you to caterwaul around the jail, here, go ahead and do it. But don't try to talk to me! There ain't gunna be no lynchin' in Crooked Horn. You hear me say it, and it'll turn out that way!"

He turned his back to the door, after carefully sliding the last bolt.

A heavy weight fell against the door from the outside. The door shook; a reverberating hammer stroke echoed through the building.

"But they won't beat it off of those hinges and bolts," said Anthony, "unless they get a battering-ram."

"And then what?" asked Lynmouth.

"Then we'll see what we'll do. Maybe you and me agin' the whole lot of them!"

"That's not logic," said Lynmouth. "If I'm no good, I'm not worth running a risk for."

"You?" cried the sheriff. "D'you think that I'd raise a hand for twenty of you? No, sir, never in my life; but on account of the law, I'd fight ten thousand Injuns for the sake of a mangy cat! Come back here and we'll find a cell for you!"

There was plenty of room. There were only two other occupants of the jail, at the moment, and both of these were tramps who had been picked up a day or so before by the deputy.

Anthony, as the roaring of the crowd continued, introduced the new prisoner to the others, pausing at the doors of their cells.

"Alabama," said he, "here's Larry Lynmouth, that you've heard about. Larry, this here is Alabama, by his account of it. He's a bindlestiff, a blowed-in-the-glass one."

Alabama lifted his reddish, swollen face, which looked as though it were irritated to rawness by the stubble of beard that grew upon it.

"Dog-gone right honored and pleased to see you, Lynmouth," he said. "This here is an honor. I been with them that've killed their one man or their two or their three, but I never shook hands before with no butcher out of a slaughterhouse!"

He grinned as he spoke. It was hard to tell whether he was ironic or earnest.

"And here's Bud Shine."

He indicated a young mulatto.

"Bud, he's a tramp royal, by his account. Set-downs are the only meals that he'll eat. Regular meal hours is what he keeps, or none at all. Lookit the way he's all fixed up. Like an end man at a minstrel show—nobody no smarter than Bud Shine."

The mulatto stood up leisurely. He was a handsome rascal, and his smile flashed as he listened to the words of Chick Anthony.

"How are you, Mr. Lynmouth?" he said. "I've seen you before, sir. I saw you when you were on the way to jail in Denver, one day. Sorry to see you locked up in a little place like this, sir, but perhaps you'll find the walls thinner, down here?"

"Eddicated, too," said the sheriff with admiration. "Yeah, he's eddicated for fair. He could read as big a book as there is in the world, most likely; but I dunno that print would ever do him much good. So long, Bud."

He went to a corner cell, to which he introduced his prisoner.

"Cot's bolted to the floor," he commented. "These here bars are tool-proof steel. Might be that you could hang yourself with the bedclothes, but outside of that, I dunno what harm you could do! Gunna be comfortable enough in here?"

"I'll be comfortable enough," said Lynmouth, looking slowly around him. "Thanks about the tool-proof steel. I wouldn't want to wear my arms out on that!"

"Welcome," said Chick Anthony. "Anything special to eat?"

"I'll eat anything you have."

"All right, then, my lad. So long for a while."

He closed and locked the door, and went slowly down the aisle, While Larry Lynmouth looked thoughtfully after him; for he had seen in the sheriff a thing quite new to his mind and his life. It was a new and a great idea, that men could be honest merely for honesty's sake!

17

ON TRIAL

It was a noisy day.

Until late that night the crowd milled about the jail, shouting, singing, yelling like Indians who have won an important battle. And sometimes they shouted in a chorus, "We want Lynmouth! We want Lynmouth! We want Lynmouth!"

They wanted him in order to break his neck, he was well aware; but he listened to them in a detached manner. It was as though he were divided from himself.

In the middle of the afternoon, William Oliver came to see him, and reached through the bars to shake hands, while the sheriff's jailer stood by, at watch.

"I've come to find out what I can do for you, my boy," said Oliver.

"I don't know," said the prisoner. "I'd like to find out, first, what they charge me with."

There was a slight contraction of pain, or disgust, on the banker's face.

"They charge you with felonious assault with intent to kill," said he. "They accuse you of having attempted the life of that boy—Daniels is his name! I've come to find out if you're provided with a lawyer fit for the work of defending you, and to learn in what else I can be of help to you."

Lynmouth regarded him carefully.

"Oliver," said he, "tell me if Kate sent you?"

The banker started a little. He gripped at the bars.

"What made you ask that?" he demanded. "No, Kate didn't ask me to come here—that is to say—"

"That is to say, she doesn't care," said Lynmouth, nodding. "I asked because I was curious. I'm not curious any longer."

"You have a lawyer, Larry?"

"I'll have one when this comes to trial, I suppose. I don't need help. Thanks. But I never have used charity."

Oliver delayed uneasily at the bars of the cell. He found it hard to raise his eyes to those of the young prisoner.

At last he said: "I'm sorry, my lad. I'm very sorry. That's all that I seem able to say!"

He went off, and the door was closed, as Larry Lynmouth felt, upon all of one section of his life. His very soul shrank at this dismissal of the past.

He had a pair of visitors of another sort later on in the afternoon. Young Tom Daniels, called "Buck" by some people, arrived with his sister. Their attitude differed greatly from that of the banker.

Tom was very like his brother and sister in looks, but his manner was grave and retired. He shook hands through the bars under the careful supervision of the jailer, to make sure that nothing was flat on his palm.

"I'm Tom Daniels," he said. "I've come up here to see what's what. I've seen Cherry, here, and I know what she said to you before Lew dropped in. And I've seen Lew, and know what happened at the fight. This here town is plumb crazy, Lynmouth. I dunno what's got into its head. But I do know that I never heard of a more sporting chance than you give to Lew. He says it was the slickest shooting that he ever saw; and sure it's the best that I ever heard of. You could've planted both of those slugs dead easy between his eyes. Well, Lynmouth, I'll tell you what. The Danielses are a funny bunch. They never forget a bad turn, and they never forget a good one. We sure ain't going to forget you, Lynmouth, if you'll believe what I say!"

The prisoner looked steadily at his visitor.

"Yes," he said at last. "I believe you. I'd believe nearly anything good about a family that has a Cherry Daniels in it!"

Cherry gasped. She turned crimson with emotion.

"Thanks, Larry," said she. "That sounds straight from the shoulder. But we want to know what we can do to make you comfortable here, until we get this suit squashed. We're going to see the sheriff and the judge right away; you'll be out of this before night!"

"Not before night, I hope," smiled Lynmouth. "I don't want to leave the jail while the town can see to eat me."

They left him, all smiles, all good-fellowship, and Lynmouth stepped to the bars to watch them go.

But no one came to set him free that afternoon or that evening. The next day came around, and still there was no word from any of the Daniels family. Lynmouth found this very hard to understand. Perhaps, in the meantime, they had heard something greatly to his disadvantage; yet he could have sworn that they were people who could live up to their promises.

On the very next day was the trial.

It was as strange a trial as ever was held in the West, in those days when strange trials were a matter of everyday occurrence. The judge never had been through a law school. Election somehow had given him office without qualifications. He was simply an honest, hard-headed rancher who had drifted into an unusual occupation by pressure of public request. He was as honest as the day. He was as brave as a lion. And he hated gun fighters and criminals of all kinds, and when he saw Lynmouth in the courtroom, a red haze danced before his eyes. Personally, he had known three of Lynmouth's victims of the past. He had not esteemed any of the three. But he could detest the ruffian who had shot them down.

Lynmouth's lawyer was a pale youth just out of school, his eyes not yet recovered from the strain of midnight study. Therefore, they were masked behind glasses. His

one interest seemed to be to escape sharing in the lynch-
ing of his client, which, he was sure, would be the termi-
nation of the trial.

Under such auspices, after the assistant district attorney
had bludgeoned Lynmouth in his opening speech, after
the jury was chosen, the trial finally began.

The young lawyer, Twill, who represented Lynmouth,
could not help noticing a singular lack in these proceedings. He pointed out that the complainant was not present.

"How can he be present," demanded the district attorney, "when he's lyin' at death's door, owing to the bullet of this ruffian, here?"

Mr. Twill, overwhelmed by this outburst, nevertheless
managed to answer that at least there should be some dep-
osition from Lew Daniels.

"It ain't needed!" said the attorney. "I leave it to
the judge if it's needed when the whole town knows the
way this here butcher shot down young Daniels, as fine
and upstandin' a young feller as ever rode a hoss into
Crooked Horn!"

This stirring speech brought rounds of applause from
the audience, which packed the courtroom.

They snarled toward Lynmouth like a pack of hounds,
and he sat back, calmly at watch. Oliver, the banker, was
in that crowd. He did not join in the snarling, to be
sure, but he was there, giving weight to the proceedings,
as it were, by his respected presence.

Still there was no sign of the Daniels family, and the
wonder grew constantly in the mind of the prisoner.

His testimony on his own behalf was a straightforward
story of all that had happened.

Then the assistant district attorney cross-examined.

He began by saying: "How many men have you killed,
Lynmouth?"

Young Mr. Twill rose to object. He was crushed by
the judge. For Judge Bore pronounced this mysterious
ruling:

"I dunno what's wrong with that there question," he
said. "We all know that Lynmouth has killed a considerable parcel, and it's only right that we should have his
word how many. There's a pile of knowledge that young

gents don't get out of books!" he concluded, with a withering scowl at Mr. Twill.

This ended that young man for the day. He turned a pale green, and felt at his throat, as though he were afraid that a rope already might be closing around it.

He interposed no more objections, and the course of justice flowed triumphantly on its way. The trial was amazingly brief. The judge, in his address to the jury, naïvely regretted that this charge was not one under which they could sentence the criminal to hanging by the neck till he was dead.

"Vigilantes beat the law all hollow in a lot of ways," declared Judge Bore. "But I sure gotta say that we'll soak him as hard as we can. Go and bring in your verdict, and I'll see what we can do."

The jury retired, and returned in five minutes!

Lynmouth was, of course, guilty.

At this, the judge made a speech. The one reason he had accepted office—outside of his desire to clean up the cattle thieves—was that he liked making speeches, and he made one now that lasted a half hour. He reviewed the entire career of the accused man. At his door he laid all that wildest rumor ever had attributed to Larry Lynmouth. In conclusion, he sentenced him to ten years of hard labor in the penitentiary, and wished, he honestly admitted, that he could have made it twenty, or life!

This speech was received by a tumult of applause that lasted for a long time. Hands were laid on the judge. He was carried shoulder high into the street, where he had to repeat his speech with certain flourishes and additions for the benefit of those who had not been able to crowd into the courtroom.

This tumult served to permit the sheriff to get his prisoner safely back to the jail. The vocal thunder of Judge Bore covered the retreat, and when the more alert members of the crowd looked around for the victim, the doors of the jail already were closing behind him!

They made another rush upon the building. They stormed and swept and ranted about it. But the sheriff, inside, was smoking a cigarette and communing with his prisoner.

"Nothin' never happened no better for you than this

here sentence," he declared to Lynmouth. "Now, you take it the way that you are—twenty-four, and headed downhill so fast that your head oughta be spinnin'. Ten years to take a rest and think things over and find out that the law is stronger than you are—why, you'll only be thirty-four when you get out again, and that's exactly the right age for a gent to settle down and start his real life! You gotta chance to make yourself into a useful citizen, an honest man."

"Chick," said the prisoner, "this is a fairly large jail."

"Yeah? What about it?"

"Go and talk in another corner of it, will you?"

The sheriff arose with a snort, and from the "blowed-in-the-glass" tramp adjoining there was a loud burst of laughter.

"Good advice," said the sheriff, "never made the grass grow, and I reckon that a crook never can be straightened except with a hammer!"

At this, he withdrew, and Larry Lynmouth settled down to a gloomy vigil with his own dark thoughts. The Danielses no doubt were like all the rest of the people in Crooked Horn. In other words, when a pinch came, they could change their minds!

Then he stretched himself on his cot, and by sheer effort of the will, forced himself to go to sleep.

18

A GOLDEN BOOK

THAT evening, when the interior of the jail was half dark and half rosy with the sunset light, there was another visitor for Lynmouth. The jailer brought him with a grin, and said:

"Here's an easy way to heaven, Lynmouth."

It was Brother Juan, the Franciscan.

"Hello!" said Lynmouth ironically. "I need some good advice, brother, and I suppose I'll get it now!"

"Do you need advice?" asked the Franciscan.

"I need it," nodded Lynmouth.

"This is a very strange thing, then," replied the other.

"Why strange?"

"Because I've never before found a man who needed advice."

The jailer laughed. "Juan, he's a rare one," he commented. "There ain't another like him, if you hunt clean to New Orleans."

"Hold on," said Lynmouth. "What do people need, if it isn't advice?"

"They need hope," answered the friar.

"Hope, eh? A cheap thing, I should say," replied Lynmouth.

"Yes," said the friar. "It is the one thing in the world which has no value, and yet I suppose it is the cure of all evils."

"What can it cure?" asked Lynmouth. "Heart trouble, for instance?"

"Well," replied the friar, "all men must die, but hope can let us die happily."

"And a broken leg, Brother Juan?"

"The trouble of a long sickness in bed is the slowness with which the time passes, and hope can make the days fly, my friend."

"Well," answered Lynmouth, "give me the kind of hope that will make ten years in jail pass like a day."

"That I cannot do," said the friar.

"Why not?"

"Hope cannot enter a hard heart," said the friar.

"Is my heart hard?"

"As flint," said the other.

"How do you know that?"

"By your eyes, Señor Lynmouth. They are too bright. They shut me out from your mind."

"I'll open them wider, Brother Juan, if you can put this hope, that you speak of, into them. But when you come right down to the facts, isn't it true that hope is like blinders—and only horses should wear them?"

"Well, perhaps there's something in that," answered the friar gently. "Hope keeps good men sitting still with their hands folded, when they ought to be up and about their

work. You, señor, if you were free, would jump from here
to the mountains at a single leap."

"No," answered Lynmouth, "I don't think that I
would go very far from Crooked Horn."

"Are you in love with this town, señor?"

"I'm interested in it," said Lynmouth. "I'm interested in
the people here. I want to find out if everyone in the
world is like this crowd."

"I can answer for that," said the friar.

"Can you?"

"Yes, I can tell you, safely, that all men are alike."

"No matter where they have been born or bred, or
the way they've been raised?"

"Yes, because they go through the same experiences."

"One man in a palace, and another in a shack, say?"
sneered Lynmouth.

"We are all born; we all live with hope for tomorrow
and groans for today; we all love, hate, suffer from envy
and spite, and at last we come under the shadow of death,
sooner or later. So kings and beggars are just the same,
under the skin."

"You've known a good many beggars," said Lynmouth.
"But suppose you tell me how many kings you've talked
to?"

"Three," said the friar gently and calmly.

Lynmouth gaped a little.

"You mean spiritual kings, such as starvation, greed,
crime, and those things, Brother Juan?"

"No, I mean what you mean. Kings on thrones."

"You've talked to three of them?"

"Yes. To three of them."

"And you found them exactly like other men?"

"A little difference, but the difference was no deeper
than the skin, as I was saying before."

"Listen to him!" broke in the jailer with a gasp. "He
says that he's talked to real kings, and three of 'em!"

Brother Juan turned and looked gravely at the man of
the law.

"I am not lying, my friend," said he.

"Why, Juan, I didn't mean that," declared the jailer. "Of
course, you're not lying. Only—it sounded kind of funny—
the look of you and the dust in the wrinkles of your

robe, or whatever you call it—and then to think of a king."

"The first king I talked to," said the friar in his gentle, cheerful voice, "was much dustier than this."

"Maybe there was a door open into his throne room," grinned the jailer.

"His throne was a camel's back, and his scepter was a scimitar," replied the friar. "He nearly took my head off with it. I still have the scar."

"Well," said the jailer, "if you got anything more to say to Lynmouth, better hurry it along. It's supper time for me, and for the three of them."

"You read Spanish as well as speak it, señor?" said Brother Juan to the prisoner.

"Yes."

"Then I have here a little book in which you may learn patience and hope."

He offered it to the jailer.

"Aw, give it to him," said the latter. "I guess there ain't a set of keys to the jail between the pages."

"There is something which may be as useful," said the friar.

"And's what's that?"

"A way to the road of good life."

He passed it between the bars, and the prisoner took it with his manacled hands.

He thanked Brother Juan, and the friar left at once. But he paused an instant to speak to the young tramp royal— he who disdained cold "handouts" and insisted on "sitdown" meals. Then the Franciscan departed from the jail, while the chief prisoner examined the book. It was on very bad paper, with thick, cardboard covers, and the small print, crowded close together, repeated in Spanish the Golden Book of the great emperor.

These meditations Lynmouth conned over for a few moments, until supper came. It was simple, but there was plenty of it. He ate with a good appetite.

Afterward, the lights were turned out, except for a single lantern which hung in the farther end of the jail room, and filled the apartment with a flickering and uncertain illumination. The tramps tried to open a conversation with their more celebrated comrade, but presently gave up the useless attempt, and both began to snore heartily.

There was not nearly enough light for reading, but with the book open in his hands, which were manacled before him, Lynmouth meditated, strange to say, on nothing except the little, common-looking, gentle-voiced friar who had talked to kings, and nearly lost his life at the hands of one of them. There was nothing at all remarkable about Brother Juan, except that now and then he would fix one with a glance as straight as the edge of a sword. Yet Lynmouth knew that this was one honest man in the world, and a strong man, as well.

This thought made the covers of the little book bend under his increasing grip. That is to say, one cover bent. The other remained rigid. This stiffness surprised him, for the board seemed of the cheapest and most pulpy sort. He examined that side of the binding again, and almost at once he was aware that the cardboard was flexible enough, except in the center, where it seemed that a rib extended.

This made the prisoner sit up.

Feeling the surface dexterously, he could detect a slight rise. Instantly, he parted that board to the middle, and there fell out a thin blade of steel with a sharp saw edge.

This, then, was the hope which the wily friar had passed to him through the bars of his cell!

An excellent hope it was. He knew at once that the little saw was of the finest sort. He raised it. Even in this dull light he could see the glitter of the diamond points! At that sight, the shadows of ten years of prison life were swept from his mind. He set to work.

To free his hands was the first difficulty. He turned his left hand as far as he could in the grip of the manacle, caught the saw between his fingers, and began to work back and forth the short chain which united the cuffs. The matchless edge of that saw bit into the good steel almost as though it were wood. It sank into a groove. It ate straight through a link, and for the first time since his arrest, Lynmouth could separate his hands.

This made him feel free already.

However, he must get rid of the dangling, jingling chains. And so he spent a patient half hour cutting through the main body of each manacle. Twice the saw squeaked, small and shrill as a mouse, but it did not disturb the two sleepers.

He went to the door.

The lock passed through two strong bars. If these were tool-proof steel, even with this jewel of a saw he probably could not work through them before the morning; but he had an idea that the sheriff had rather overstated the security of the prison for the sake of discouraging all attempts at escape.

The first touch of the saw told the story. It bit into that unworthy stuff with the greatest freedom!

Even so, he had two patient hours of work before him. It was nearly midnight before the bars were severed around the lock, and the door of its own weight sagged gently outward.

He stepped cautiously out into the aisle.

A groan from the nearest cell froze him to his place. But it was only a murmur in the midst of sleep, and the snoring recommenced. From his position, Lynmouth could see the dark faces of the three windows which gave a meager supply of air to the cell room. And there was also the door of the jailer's room, roughly sketched in the lamplight which slid through the crack from the other side.

From the windows he surmised that he could make an easy exit; but within the jailer's room were his pocket cash, his guns—those old and proved companions—together with his hat and his roll, which had been brought from the hotel.

Straight toward the jailer's apartment, therefore, he took his way.

19

LYNMOUTH FINDS HIS WINGS

In spite of the light, Lynmouth more than half hoped that the man might be asleep; but when he came closer to the door, he heard the guard clear his throat gently, and even made out the crisp rustling of the page of a magazine being turned.

This complicated his attempt.

The door might be locked. Even if he could open it, however, he would have an armed man in a lighted room to deal with, and the keen eye and the surly brow of the guard seemed to indicate the nature of a fighting man.

Lynmouth hesitated. After all, the windows would be easy and safe, and as for his personal property, that could be replaced easily, later. New guns actually might be better than the old ones, if he had a chance to grow accustomed to them before the hounds of the law ran out on his traces and cornered him.

A pair of riders galloped down the street, calling loudly to one another, laughing, rollicking. He even heard the creaking of the stirrup leathers, and the snort of one of the horses.

This, for some reason, determined him. He had a reputation to recover, and to leave without all his belongings would hardly be a creditable action, whereas, to go at the jailer with empty hands, would be something worth talk.

Straightway he tried the handle of the door, turning it softly, slowly—so slowly that even a careful eye fixed upon it from the other side would hardly have been able to tell that the knob was in motion. When the handle began to take up the spring of the catch, he was still more delicate in his operation. At last, he felt the door free beneath his hand, and knew that it was not locked.

This he accepted as a promise of success.

He allowed the door to open a fraction of an inch. Then, when he could peer in, he saw the guard sitting exactly opposite the door, with a riot gun across his lap!

This seemed luck too bad to be true. At the least, he could have expected that the fellow would be seated to the side. And a riot gun, of all weapons!

It appeared that the man did not feel altogether safe with Lynmouth in the jail, not even though manacles and bars were between him and his prisoner. Yet he had taken to the reading of a magazine, and the story which held his attention made him bite his lips with excitement.

A door slammed somewhere near the jail.

To the high-strung nerves of Lynmouth, it was like the striking of a thunderbolt.

The head of the jailer jerked up. He frowned, and looked straight at the door, which was now a full half inch ajar.

Lynmouth could almost have sworn that the gleaming eye of the man had seen him in the inner darkness.

"Dog-gone my hide!" said the guard. "That door latch is gettin' wore out."

He laid aside the magazine and got up—but he carried his shotgun with him!

Yet Lynmouth did not hesitate. He braced himself with his right foot against the wall, and his left hand on the doorknob. He dared not breathe until the swarthy face was close to his. Then he snatched the door wide open!

At the first touch of great danger, the coward shrieks, but the brave man strikes, and this fellow was brave. His face convulsed with the shock, but he uttered not a sound, merely swinging the muzzle of the gun toward the face of the prisoner.

But he was much too slow, for Lynmouth's hard fist already was in the air, and his blow landed fair and true, with every ounce of his weight behind it. On the tip of the chin that stroke went home. It made the jailer tuck down his head against his breast and stagger back. The shotgun fell—into the hands of Larry Lynmouth.

He was afraid for a moment that he would have to use his advantage. The jailer did not yell, even now. But reeling as he was, hardly more than half conscious, though on his feet, he staggered back to resume the fight.

He brought up against the gaping muzzle of the gun, and this restored him to his wits. Down at the double gleam of the steel he looked; then up, with clearing eyes, at the other. Finally, he groaned:

"You've done it!" said he.

"You can put your hands up for me," said Lynmouth, "and get back into the corner, right there, away from the window."

Keeping the gun tucked under his arm, in the very fashion in which the sheriff had carried that same weapon, he enforced his command, while he reached behind him with his free left and and shut the door.

The guard, like a man in desperation, looked from one side to the other; but he could not quite make up his mind to rush against such a weapon in such hands.

"How'n the name of Heaven did you do it, Lynmouth?" he asked. "It don't look possible!"

The robber thought of the saw and the book which were now in his coat pocket, and he could have smiled.

"Iron won't hold an honest man," said Lynmouth.

"Oh, honest be danged!" said the jailer. "Tell me the truth. Because we'll find out the minute you're gone."

"I did it with my teeth," said Lynmouth. "You see, they have diamond edges?"

He smiled to illustrate his point. Then he secured his man. It was done easily and expeditiously by using a pair of manacles which hung on the wall. With these, he fastened the hands of the jailer behind his back, and after that he went about his search.

Most things were in plain view. The roll was in a corner; his hat hung from a peg on the wall; and in the very top drawer of the desk he found his two guns and their spring holsters.

He fitted these on with the most eager haste.

"Aye," said the guard, who seemed to have lost most of his hostility, now that he saw his position was hopeless. "Aye, there you go. I should've known that we couldn't keep a fire like you inside of this dinky jail. And now there you are with your wings on!"

He nodded at the guns, which the robber was now fitting into the spring holsters.

"You'll be flyin' far before mornin', Lynmouth," he suggested. "You'll stop for the mare, I reckon?"

"Is she still at the hotel stable?" asked he.

The other shurgged his shoulders. Then he added, with a change of expression:

"Why shouldn't you have her back? She's yours. She'd look wrong under any other man. No, Lynmouth, she ain't in the hotel stable."

"Who has her?"

"Why, who'd you think?"

"The sheriff, maybe?"

"That's it. She's bucked him off three times today, and that's why he ain't here tonight. That's why," he added with inexpressionable regret shining in his face, "this ain't happened to him."

"Where does he keep her?" asked Lynmouth.

"In the stable behind his house. In the box stall. He has sense enough to give her the best."

"What right has he to her?"

"I dunno. He'll keep her till she has to be auctioned off, and then I reckon that nobody'll be fool enough to bid against him. He's as happy about her as a kid about a new toy. Why, he says that she's fast enough and clever enough to make any fool win in a race. He says that now he has her, he'll be like an eagle, sailing high and then dropping at the crooks in his country like they was fish hawks, and no more."

Lynmouth chuckled softly.

"He'll have to get another set of wings to follow Fortune, when I'm on her back again. Tell me another thing, will you?"

"Why not?" asked the man, with a shrug of his shoulders. "After this evenin's work, there ain't gunna be any room for me in this town of Crooked Horn. I'm a Jonah here, and so why shouldn't I tell you anything I know?"

"Then tell me if you know where the Daniels people are. Have they gone back to Jackson Fork?"

"Them? Why, Lew Daniels won't be able to ride for a month. No, they're here."

"Where are they?"

"You say it kind of mean," replied the jailer.

"I don't mean them any harm. I'm just curious."

"There ain't five men in town that know, and I'm one of them," said the other. "Fact is, they wouldn't come through with the right kind of testimony. So the sheriff got rid of 'em."

"What does that mean? Got rid of 'em?"

"Why, it means just that. You take a gent like Chick Anthony, he don't care a whack about the forms of the law. He cares about the real thing, and when he has a man that he's sure is guilty, he wants to see him convicted. If the Daniels crowd was around loose and not willing to testify agin' you, why, the case was lost, and you'd go free. So he just arranged to have some of the boys take the Daniels lot and herd them into a house on the edge of the town, and keep them there, whether they wanted to or not."

"A strange kind of a sheriff," said Lynmouth bitterly.

"Well," declared the guard honestly, "he might be wrong, but not often, and mostly he's workin' his head off to do what he thinks is right. That's the way with him, you see!"

"I understand what you mean, at least. His sort of honesty is hard on the nerves of the men who don't agree with him, though."

"That may be, but old Chick Anthony is all right about most things. He may be wrong about you."

"Now tell me, what house are the Danielses in?"

"Tom King's house. D'you know it?"

"The one by the old mill?"

"Yes, that's it."

"How many men has he for a guard on the place?"

"Hello!" said the guard. "You thinkin' of raidin' the house?"

"I didn't say that."

"Well," said the other. "I've talked enough, and maybe a good deal too much. I won't say no more. You wouldn't be fool enough to walk into a hornet's nest like that, would you? Why, there's—"

He checked himself and even bit his lip, so afraid was he that he might have talked too much.

"I have to gag you," said Lynmouth, taking a clean

bandanna out of the drawer of the open desk. "I'll manage it so that you won't choke, though."

"Sure," said the guard. "You gotta gag me. And when they find me, they'll wish that I had choked."

He submitted with perfect patience while the bandanna was deftly wadded and inserted between his teeth, and corded around his head.

"If you start trying to yell," explained Lynmouth calmly, "you'll be apt to work that gag onto the back of your tongue, and then you may choke. So long, my friend!"

And he slipped through the window, dropped his roll before him, and jumped to the ground

20

OUTSIDE THE MILL

THE mill of Tom King was a relic of the days when freighting was so expensive that it paid to turn a water wheel in the river—when it was running high enough to do the work. But with the decline of freights, and the decline of population, this need no longer existed; and, therefore, the mill had fallen to pieces. It merely made for Lynmouth, a spectacular silhouette against the stars as he worked his way carefully through the underbrush toward the house.

The house itself had a broken back and sagging knees, and was frequented by Tom King only on the rare occasions when he came in from his trapping in the higher mountains. The cleared land about it, where once grew a large part of the grain that passed through his mill, now was given over to a second-growth forest as high as the head of a man on horseback. The shrubbery grew thick in between, and Lynmouth had to stalk like an Indian to get through the growth without making overmuch noise.

He came up from the side of the barn, where he heard horses stamping inside and munching hay. At the door, lighted by a lantern which was partly hooded by a sombrero dropped over its top, were a pair of armed men. They sat on boxes tilted back against the wall, their rifles beside them, and one of them was yawning hugely.

"This here is a fool game," said he who had yawned. "Keepin' a man out of his honest sleep for—"

"How can an ol' crook like you have an honest sleep?" demanded the other. "Have a heart, and talk straight, will you? Chick Anthony knows what he's about."

"Well, ain't Lynmouth in jail, sleepin' in chains, and dreamin' about crossed bars and a shaved head?"

"He's been in jail before," said the other. "But he ain't never wore stripes."

"He'll never get loose from old Chick Anthony," said the sleepy man. "And here we are watchin' hosses—" He groaned as he said it. "I could sleep for a week!" he vowed.

"Lookit that owl skidding along low over the ground."

The mournful voice of the night bird sounded close and loud.

"Gives me a shudder to hear it sing!"

"She's a fine-lookin' girl, that Cherry Daniels," said one.

"Yeah. You ain't sayin' anything new. She's the girl that Bud Carey and Lefty Grey had the fight about."

"I never heard nothing about that."

"Why, you ain't? Everybody knows about that."

"I never heard nothin' about it."

"Why, they went out to a dance at Jackson Ford, and Lefty Grey, he took her, and Bud Carey was pretty jealous. He passes a coupla remarks, and Lefty asks him outside to settle the fight. But the girl, she seen by the look of them that they meant trouble. So she got out into the anteroom of the schoolhouse, where all the hats and the guns was piled, and she pulled the charges of those two Colts, and when those two poor suckers got out under the stars, they blowed chunks of fire into the air but they never hit nothin'. And them that had gone to watch, they begun to laugh, to see twelve shots fired at six steps, and all of them clean misses. Then Bud, he pulls a knife, and he starts for Lefty; and, all at once, there's the girl standin' in between them, with her back turned to Bud.

" 'Lefty,' says she, 'I guess this here is our dance.'

"Well, there wasn't any dance music playing, just then; but she captures Lefty and takes him back into the schoolhouse; and, sure enough, there wasn't any fight, and poor old Bud, he sneaked away home, feelin' mighty small, I guess."

"She's got her nerve with her," said the other watcher.

"Yeah. They ain't nothin' but nerve in her. I seen her ride Bill Maker's roan hoss."

"Did she sit him out?"

"Yeah. For a coupla minutes."

"Then he piled her?"

"Sure. Right on the bean was where she hit. She woke up ten minutes later. 'I must've lost a stirrup,' said she; 'I'll ride him now, and make him know what's what!' "

"Did they let her?"

"Naw. It would've been suicide. The first time, the roan bucks. The second time, he eats you alive. But she's game!"

"Yeah. It's a dead game family. Think of that Lew Daniels, the way he stood up to Lynmouth."

"Yeah, and think of Lynmouth shootin' his guns away!"

"A coupla lucky shots, that was meant to kill!"

"Everybody can have one lick of luck with a gun, but nobody can have two. No, they sure was aimed bullets, old son."

"Leave me be! You been reading so many books that you'll be writin' one, pretty quick!"

He slumped back against the wall of the barn and pulled his sombrero over his eyes, while the other tilted his head and began to whistle very softly to himself.

Lynmouth went on to the house, all of whose life seemed to be concentrated in a single room, which flared with strong lights.

The window was low. He could easily look in and see that it was the big old kitchen which was so used. This was the camping ground of the three prisoners and their guards.

On a couch in the corner, Lew Daniels lay, his eyes on

the ceiling, one hand behind his head, smoking, and blowing the smoke upward toward the ceiling. Near him was Cherry, sitting on a high stool, with her heels hooked on a rung of it. She was bent over a magazine from which she was reading a story aloud to her wounded brother.

As for Tom Daniels—otherwise called Buck—he sat at the round kitchen or dining-room table with four other men, all of whom were playing poker. His own hands were tied together, but he had sufficient freedom to pick up the cards and handle them. A good pile of money in front of him indicated that he was a winner. Nevertheless, he yawned as he played.

"It's about time to quit," he declared, as Lynmouth first looked through the window.

"What's the matter?" asked one of the four. "You got all of my money, Daniels!"

"I'll match you for the lot," said Daniels carelessly. "Double or nothing."

"I lost it at poker, not at matching," complained the other.

"Well, I've finished playing," said Daniels. "That's all!"

"Go on, Tom," called his sister. "Don't be a sorehead, but play the game out."

"Yeah. He's learned his poker manners south of the river," said the offended loser.

He was one of those narrow-shouldered, lank-bodied fellows who have the strength of a hawk's talons in their bony hands.

"When I have my hands free," said Tom Daniels fiercely, "I'll show you how far north you learned what *you* know!"

"Ease up and shut up, Tom," insisted the girl. "You forget that you're a guest in this here house."

Tom Daniels laughed.

"I'm a guest, all right," said he. "And they're going to slog poor Lynmouth into prison, while we sit around here."

"What can we do?" said the girl.

Tom ground his teeth. He got up abruptly from the table and walked away, leaving his stake behind him.

At this, the lean fellow, who had complained, rose abruptly also, and headed him off.

"Just keep away from the guns, old son," he said malevolently.

Lynmouth craned his neck. He could see them, then. A stack of rifles and cartridge belts gathered against the wall near the sink. There were plenty of weapons still making the guards uncomfortable, and forcing them to sit awry in their places, but the heavy part of their armory was stacked in the one spot where it could be under the eyes of all concerned.

"You're looking for a lot of trouble, Bell!" said Daniels angrily.

"Look at here, son," replied the tall puncher. "Trouble is what I've been raised on, trouble is what I'm gunna die of, but it will have to be a lot more of trouble than you can deal out!"

Tom Daniels, in a frenzy, wrenched the power of his strong young arms against the ropes.

"If I had free hands," said he, "I'd soon show you, Bell!"

"Shut up and be still, Bell, and you, Daniels. We've all had enough of your lip," said the older companion, who seemed to be in charge of the party.

"I've known 'em before," said the sardonic Bell. "These here kind that are mighty brave when they got their hands tied. 'Hold me, boys, for fear that I might get at him!' That kind of a hero. That's exactly what the kid is like!"

It looked as though Tom Daniels would fling himself at his tormentor, even helpless as he now was, but the voice of his sister cut in sharply: "Be quiet, and back up, Tom."

"Yeah, she does his thinkin' for him, when it comes to a pinch," declared the tall man.

"When he's free again," replied the girl coldly, "he'll lick you to within an inch of your life, Bell, and you already guess it. You're talking to keep yourself warm. Oh, I can see it in your face!"

He snarled at her, but silently, for no ready words would come under this stinging rebuke.

"Shut up, Tom, and you, too, Cherry," commanded the wounded lad. "It don't do no good to argue with this crowd of mavericks. Keep still. When Larry has gone to prison they'll have to turn us loose, and then there'll be another kind of a yarn going around here. We'll get that case appealed double quick!"

"No matter what you say," said the oldest of the party, with perfect conviction, "you won't get any judge to listen to you. Lynmouth is in the pen, and no matter how he was railroaded, that's the place for him. When he was a man, that was one thing. But since he took water and showed up yellow as a Chinaman, that's a different matter. Nobody can think of nothing now except that he's killed twenty men an' is likely to kill a few more."

It was a perfectly neat and explicit statement of the sheriff's case, and the sheriff's policy. Anything to get this malefactor into jail, where Anthony was certain that he belonged.

When once the doors of a penitentiary had closed behind the robber, then the sheriff was childishly certain that the law would not be foolish enough to set the bad man free again, no matter what small irregularities of procedure there might have been in his commitment.

All was perfectly clear to Lynmouth, now. He waited no longer, for he had other things to do on this night, but now pushed open the kitchen door and walked in, with a gun in either hand.

21

ALARM

IT WAS an amazing thing that no one so much as glanced up at him. The game of cards continued. The girl went on reading her book, and Tom Daniels, with his bound hands, stood looking on at the progress of the poker. Yet a door had been opened, and the screen slammed!

They were so secure that the only remark was:

"Say, Chuck, if that's you, stick some more wood in the stove, will you?"

This from a busy player, considering a bet.

He got no answer, and this silence caused him at last to turn his head.

What he saw there by the door made his mouth open and his hands go up above his shoulders instinctively. The others jerked their heads around at this, and every one of them, in silence, imitated the first observer. The girl started up beside the bed of wounded Lew Daniels. And Tom was the only soul who uttered a sound, which was a sort of wheezing gasp of astonishment and of pleasure.

The first to speak was the man in charge of the party. He merely said, in a tone of the greatest disgust:

"I might've knowed. This jail wouldn't hold him! Whacha want here, Lynmouth?"

Larry Lynmouth smiled.

"I wanted news," said he, "and I have it now. Cherry, have you a knife to give Tom free hands?"

She had out a small penknife instantly. Lynmouth, amazed that she made no outcry or exclamation, almost turned himself and his guns from the four guards, a movement which would have made four revolvers whip out at him. As it was, from the corner of his eye he saw her obey his directions, sawing through the rope that tied Tom's wrists together. She did not speak, but her eyes and her face were flaming excitement; her lips were pinched together, but a smile tugged at the corners of her mouth. She looked as though she were in the midst of a thrilling game, not in a house where guns might begin to thunder and men die at any moment.

"Fan those fellows for their guns," directed Lynmouth to Tom Daniels.

The latter obediently removed the weapons of the four, stacking them by the stove, where he picked up and put on his own gun belt and Colt.

"Can you handle a gun, Cherry?" asked Lynmouth.

"Pretty fair," said she.

"Give Lew a Colt and take that long .38 on the .44 frame. If these fellows try to rush you, let them have it —and you don't have to shoot for the wings, either. Whatever they get is coming to them. Come on, Tom. We'll get the horses."

They got the horses with greatest ease.

From whatever direction the two guards at the stable expected danger, they never dreamed that it would calmly saunter out from the house where their four companions were known to be sitting.

Chuck and his companions were presently "stuck up" by the guns of Lynmouth, while Tom Daniels went into the stable and got out the horses belonging to himself, his brother, and to Cherry. Saddled and bridled, and with the packs behind the saddles, these animals were soon equipped. An extra pair of reins served to tie the pair of "vigilantes" back to back. Then they returned to the house, where they found Cherry sitting across a chair, with her gun leveled across the back of it.

"Lew," said Lynmouth, "these people will do you no harm, here. You can stay while Cherry and Tom go get a stretcher and come back for you. We'll soon have you comfortable at the hotel."

"Wherever you have me," said Lew, "I've got no right to bother you, old-timer. Account of me you've had this trouble, Larry, and as long as I live, or Tom, or Cherry, we've swore that nothing we can do will be enough to make it up to you!"

"Mind you, Daniels," said the middle-aged chief of the party, "mind you, now, that you're helping at the escape of a condemned man. You're liable to the law, for that!"

"To the law?" said Lynmouth. "There is a shred of law, here and there in Crooked Horn. But there's a great deal more law in the capital. And when this case is appealed, you'll find that Chick Anthony is out of a job, the judge will be kicked off the bench, and the lot of you are liable for kidnaping—which means about five years minimum sentence. There's an idea that will warm you up a little!"

It did not warm them up. It appeared to chill them to the marrow of their bones. One of them stirred violently in his chair and exclaimed:

"I told you so! I told you there wasn't no law for grabbin' Tom and Cherry, this way. We'll have a chance to think it over behind the bars, the fools that we've made of ourselves!"

He had no comfort from his companions. And Lew

Daniels was laughing softly on his couch and sneering at his guards.

"You tried to railroad Lynmouth," he declared to them, "but you've only railroaded yourself! Go ahead, Larry. I'll be all right, here. Go ahead and take your time. I don't deserve that you should turn a hand for me—but that's the kind you are. I only hanker after one thing."

"And what's that?" asked Larry Lynmouth.

"To shake hands with you," said the boy.

So Lynmouth crossed the room and gripped the hot hand of the wounded man. The eyes of Lew Daniels burned up at him. He said rapidly:

"I came here to make a reputation off of you, Larry. I was a fool. I was a cur. But you've give me a chance to try to be a man again, and I'm gunna take it. I'm gunna try to be—I'm gunna try to be—like *you*, Larry, because you're a hundred per cent!"

This speech had come out in confusion and stammering haste, but it made Larry Lynmouth feel like a very old and sinful man. He shook his head and smiled at the other.

"You're better as you are, Lew," said he. "Guns don't make a man. If you live by guns, you live in hot water. I've found that out. So long, and good luck to you."

The gun in the hand of Lew was hardly needed to keep the four watchers from interrupting the retreat of the others. There was no heart at all in those guards. They wanted only one thing, and that was to get as far as possible from their prisoner, and to be disassociated as much as might be from the evil aftereffects of their work "for the sheriff" and in the cause of "Western" justice. Gloomily they stared at one another and at Lew Daniels, while they heard the sound of mounting outside the house.

There, Lynmouth, Cherry, and Tom Daniels rode away through the woods and across the edge of the town. They halted in the middle of a narrow lane, shrouded with trees on either side, so that they were safe from being discovered.

"Take Cherry to the hotel, Tom," directed Lynmouth. "I'll say good-by to you here."

"If you leave him, Tom," exclaimed the girl hotly,

"you're no brother to me. If you leave him, you're a quitter!"

"Me?" exclaimed Tom Daniels. "I wouldn't leave him for a million dollars!"

"Not leave me?" said Lynmouth. "Why, Tom, you're a crazy man! With Cherry alone here in Crooked Horn—"

"I'm as safe as if I were in a grave!" said Cherry earnestly.

"And with Lew wounded—"

"They'll give us no more trouble," answered Cherry. "They were a sick-lookin' lot after you talked to them, Larry."

"But I don't want you to come on with me," said Lynmouth. "I'm an outlawed man, Tom—and—"

"And Lew is a living man," answered Tom solemnly. "The Daniels blood ain't so thin as all that, Larry. It's pretty close to red. And there never was a Daniels from the beginning of time that ever forgot a friend. Leave you, Larry? You couldn't pry me loose!"

"D'you see, Tom?" explained the robber earnestly. "The fact is that if you go along with me, they'll hunt you exactly as they'll hunt me. And this time they intend to hunt me as they never hunted before! They want my head, and they'll have it if they can. I can't have you along!"

"I'll foller you, then," said Tom Daniels patiently and obstinately. "I'll foller you along as fast and as far as I can, so long as you ain't got Fortune under you to run away from me. I won't be much good. But I can guard your back, anyway. I can sit up through the night watches. And I'll fight till I drop when the pinches come."

He said these things simply, as one who had thought them out with care, and saw nothing extraordinary in the proposal which he made.

"Of course he'll fight till he drops," said the girl almost fiercely, "or else he's not a Daniels! And, of course, he'll stay with you until Lew is fit to ride—which won't be very long. And if Tom and Lew both go down, my father'll come to you, Larry. And if he goes down, I'll go myself and boil coffee for you, anyway, and keep on watch."

"Aye," said Tom, before Lynmouth could answer a

word. "You took a chance with Lew. You've put yourself in prison. You've outlawed yourself and taken to a dog's life, because he drove you into a corner like the fool that he was. And there ain't a drop of Daniels blood that don't belong to you!"

He meant what he said. It was staggeringly clear that they both meant their speeches. And again Lynmouth was amazed.

To have a companion on the long outward trek would be something pleasant beyond words. He felt that he could not accept the self-sacrifice of this open-hearted youngster. And yet he did not see how he could avoid the company which was pressed upon him.

His mind flashed back to other meditation which had been his, recently, during which he had vowed that there was neither truth, decency, honesty, nor loyal manhood in the whole world.

Here he could change his judgment. Here was a whole family as ready to die for a friend as a good dog for its master.

Before he could speak again, a bell began to ring rapidly. Apparently the rope was jerked so fast and without regular rhythm, that now and then the beats were checked, and then again they rattled out in confusion. It was, in a way, like the frantic chatter of a breathless person, gasping out words, choking for breath, gasping again.

"The alarm bell!" said Cherry Daniels. "They've found out that you're no longer in the jail, and they'll raise the town, Larry! Ride fast. They have good horses in Crooked Horn, and they'll burn them up like grass for the sake of catching you if they can!"

"If they catch me before morning, they'll have to catch Fortune, too. I'm going to the sheriff's house!"

He waved to Cherry, and called a brisk good-by, then put his borrowed horse—it was the one which Lew Daniels had ridden into Crooked Horn—to a good gallop, and whirled through the lane toward the house of Sheriff Chick Anthony.

Behind him pounded up the hoofs of Tom's horse. And side by side they came into sight of the house of the sheriff just as a match light sputtered dimly in a window, and then the stronger glow of a lamp or lantern followed.

Almost immediately afterward, the light was snatched away. It swung across another window. A door slammed. And then the sheriff himself was seen running for the barn, his grotesquely bounding shadow running across the ground beside him.

22
THE SHERIFF SAYS "SHOOT!"

THE house of Chick Anthony stood at a little distance from the other dwellings of Crooked Horn. He had built where he could have some elbow room, and therefore he was surrounded by some open fields, with borders of slender, graceful poplars, and willows straggling along a brook that ran near his house, bankful in winter, and spotted with slimy pools at this season of the year.

"Stay here," said Lynmouth to his companion. "I'll go forward and have a look at things."

"I'll go with you," said the boy.

Lynmouth turned quickly in some impatience.

"You young fool," said he. "Don't you realize that what's going to happen may be penitentiary—or even hanging?"

The "young fool" shook his head.

"I'd do as well at the end of a rope as you would, Larry," said he.

Lynmouth argued no longer. He swore softly to himself, and then rode on until he was close to the fence which shut the house away from the road. There he dismounted, behind a clump of poplars which stood close enough together to make a green wall.

Young Daniels did the same, and at the same time they heard a door of the house slowly open upon its creaking hinges.

"Chick! Chick!" called the penetrating voice of a woman.

"Aye?" called a distant wail, stifled by the walls of the barn.

"Don't you dare to leave till you've put on a flannel shirt!" screamed Mrs. Anthony. "A night like this, you'd catch your death. I never seen such a man!"

A distant mumble answered this appeal.

Lynmouth, in the meantime, was over the fence and gliding down the bank of the creek toward the barn, for the trees at least made a background against which a moving body could not be clearly seen, though the stars were wonderfully bright.

He stopped once, to grip the shoulder of his companion and say almost desperately:

"Do you hear, man? I want you to go back there with the horses—and guard the retreat!"

"I'm here with you," answered young Daniels doggedly. "I'll retreat fast enough when I've gotta."

There was no time to argue. Again, Lynmouth cursed beneath his breath the stubborn courage of this lad. He hurried on and reached the barn door just as there came a trampling of shod hoofs on the wooden flooring, and the sheriff rode out into the starlit night.

He was on a horse slenderly but strongly made, wiry, high-stepping, with a lordly fling to its head. And Lynmouth with a leap of his heart, recognized Fortune.

"Waiting, sheriff!" said he.

Anthony jerked about in the saddle, and stared at the winking starlight upon the steady barrel of the revolver.

Then, after a vital second, he said:

"You've got me dead to rights, Lynmouth! I thought—"

The rest of his speech was broken off by the fresh clangor of the alarm bell, which began again with an even more stuttering and desperately jumbling haste than before.

What had been found now? Or had the report of the freeing of the illegally held prisoners reached the ears of the townsmen? Did they care to call out for help for such an occasion as that? Perhaps. Law was an idea rather than a strict form in Crooked Horn.

"Just step off that mare, and step on this side, Chick," said Lynmouth.

"Chick! Chick!" yelped the voice of his wife, from the house.

"Aye!" he called back.

"You forgot your old pipe. Don't you forget to stop for it. And I gotta new package of tobacco for you to take along."

"Aye!" answered Chick in a cheerful tone.

He stepped down from the stirrups, in the meantime, upon the side of the mare nearest to Lynmouth.

Fortune, the instant she was liberated, came with a rush for her master, but he waved her aside with his left hand. The right kept the gun steady upon the sheriff.

"I might have guessed," said Anthony with wonderful calm, "that you'd be out of that dang jail, no matter what I thought of it. Right out in spite of the tool-proof steel and everything?"

"Yes," said Lynmouth, without smiling, "in spite of tool-proof steel and your tool-proof contemptible meanness, Anthony!"

"Aye, aye!" said the sheriff. "That's the tone, is it?"

"That's the tone," answered the other fiercely. "What sort of a tone did you expect, Anthony?"

"I expected a good sporting tone, Lynmouth. It's not the first time that you've been in a jail, and it's not the first time that you've got clear."

"It's the first time," said Lynmouth, "that I've been run into a jail by crookedness."

"Then you're lucky. But what's the crookedness?"

"You don't know that, Anthony?"

"Not exactly."

"You don't know that you herded the Daniels family out of the way so that they couldn't testify in my favor at the trial?"

"Hello!" said the sheriff as calmly as before. "You know a good deal, it sounds like."

"I know this, Anthony," said the other. "I know that you're going to pay me now for it."

"I've got seven dollars and fifty-five cents in my pocket, by my last count," replied the sheriff, with his amazing coolness. "Is that worth while to you, Larry? It won't be out of my own wallet. I can charge it up to expenses."

"Back up three steps, Anthony," said the other. "I'm going to have this out with you here and now."

"Oh," answered Anthony. "It's to be a duel, is it?"

"Yes, a duel."

"With your friend here to shoot me in the back when I try to pull my gun?"

"You infernal—" began Tom Daniels.

"Hello! It seems to me I've heard that voice before," said the sheriff. "Who's this that you've picked up, Lynmouth?"

"Get back—get out of sight!" said Lynmouth fiercely to the boy.

"I won't get back, and I won't get out of sight!" declared the youngster. "It's my fight more than it is yours. I was the one that they bulldozed into that house by the mill. I'm gunna—"

"Shut up!" cried Lynmouth. "You will—"

"Well, it's young Tom Daniels," said the sheriff. "You've picked out a good one to make the other end of your couple, Lynmouth."

"You'd never accuse a Daniels of shooting a man in the back?" demanded Lynmouth.

"No, I reckon that I wouldn't. They fight from in front, and they fight fair, by all that I know of 'em!"

"Then back up to your distance and grab your gun, Anthony."

"Not me."

"You won't do it?"

"Not a step!"

"You won't fight?"

"Not a move!"

"I'll let the world know about this. No, I couldn't do it! You've seen young Tom Daniels with me, Anthony, and you'll have to die for that!"

"All right, then," said the sheriff. "Draw and shoot."

He thrust his hands into his trousers pockets. He even whistled very softly to himself as he faced the younger pair.

"Are you a yellow dog, after all?" said Lynmouth fiercely.

"I'm a reasonable, sensible man," said the sheriff. "I've

got a wife and a kid that depend on me, and a county that looks to me to keep it in order. D'you think that I'll chuck myself away for the sake of pleasing you?"

"I offer you a fair chance, man! D'you think that I'll go back on my word?"

"No, no, Lynmouth. I don't think that. And I think that you'd kill me sure enough if I pulled a gun. That's why I'm not going to."

"If you don't draw," answered Lynmouth, his voice quivering with his anger. "I'll shoot you down in cold blood!"

"Maybe you will," answered Anthony. "But I'll take a chance that you won't. But if I pulled the gun, there'd be no chance at all. I'm only a common or garden shot, Larry. I'm no hothouse expert, like you, my lad!"

"Why don't I do it?" said Lynmouth to himself.

The unexpected answer came to him from the sheriff's own lips.

"Because you ain't down to the level of murder, yet. Not down to the level of cold-blooded murder, I mean. You'll be there soon, though. You're on the way. I've seen these here Galahads and Launcelots before. But they wear off the knight-errant stuff before long, and get plain bad. You'll be there in another few months."

"Shall I?" said Lynmouth through his teeth.

"Aye," said the sheriff. "You're like all the rest. Yegg, thug, safe-cracker, stickup artist, gunman. Murder will come along next. But you ain't there yet, I take it!"

Lynmouth straightened, with a deep sigh.

"I want to, and I ought to," said he, "but I can't. You've railroaded me into jail. You've kept me there by crookedness. You've had a crooked trial. You've held out my witnesses who could have saved me. But still I can't give you what you ought to have."

"No, Larry," said the sheriff. "There is half an ounce of decency left in your system."

"And when I've started, you'll be on my trail again with your posse, of course."

"Why not?"

"Why not? You've got the sporting sense of a ferret, Anthony."

"D'you think that hunting down crooks is a sport to

me?" said the sheriff. "No. It's a business. A hard, dirty, dangerous business. But it has to be done, and I'll do it. Ask a street-cleaner if he has a sporting sense, but don't ask me."

His very frankness seemed to stagger and silence Lynmouth. He actually recoiled a step or two.

"You think that you're right, Anthony," said he. "That's the wonder of it!"

"I know that I'm right. And one day you'll know it, too, unless Jay Cress hunts you down before you've lived long enough to get an understanding of things, including yourself."

"Hey, Chick! D'you hear me?" shrilled the wife from the house.

"Aye," said the sheriff. "I'm comin' for that pipe and tobacco now!"

And he turned upon his heel and started for the house.

23

JAY CRESS HAS A PLAN

ON THE very next morning after these occurrences, Jay Cress arrived in the town of Crooked Horn, and he did not come alone.

There had been two things left for him to do. That is to say, he could run away as fast and as far and as silently as possible to escape from the wrath of the outraged and discarded hero, Larry Lynmouth; or else he could turn about and face the danger like a man. He decided that he would turn and face it, because he loved Cherry Daniels better even than a crooked set of dice, and he could not help telling himself, over and over again, that when once he had wiped Larry Lynmouth out of his path, she would certainly revert to him, Jay Cress.

However, he also knew that he had no chance of wiping out the great enemy with his own unaided power. He had to assemble a host, as it were, to fight this battle for him. And so it was a host that he gathered, and at the head of which he rode into Crooked Horn. It was not a host great in numbers, but it was mighty in fighting prowess.

First of all, when he entered Crooked Horn, he went to the bank of the Merchants' Loan & Trust. That might seem a strange place for him to call, but then he had a strange purpose in his mind.

He asked to see the president, and was asked to wait for a few moments. Every one treated him with the greatest respect. Since his overthrow, in the public eye, of the great Lynmouth, he had been surrounded with enough adulation to satisfy even a king. And if he had not won the love of Cherry Daniels, the great immediate reward at which he had aimed, he was at least looked up to with almost aching necks by all other people.

Twenty men who had despised him as a gambler now became cordial. They were men of importance. They counted heavily in the community. For there were many things in the favor of Jay Cress. To be sure, he always had been a gambler, but, on the other hand, he had a quiet, almost a withdrawn manner. He talked little. He had a low, quiet voice. He rarely obtruded his opinions upon other people. He had a soft chuckle which seemed to appreciate every man's humor. Equipped with these qualities, he was exactly the type of man who sweeps public opinion before him in the West, where men and women liked to be surprised by those who are around them. Something up the sleeve, a hidden strength, an unobtrusive touch of courage, wit, greatness of soul—those things are valued, and men are valued for them.

It was in this manner that all the world of the West was astonished by the feat of Jay Cress in subduing the famous Lynmouth. And, as much as it was astonished, it was still more pleased. The quiet, dried-up, withered little desert rat, so to speak, had downed the brilliant, young, handsome, heroic figure of Lynmouth. It would have seemed extravagantly impossible to other sections of the world but the West believes in quiet, silent, unobtrusive men. It has seen them at work before.

The stock of Lynmouth was wiped out; everything that

he had was transferred to the credit of the gambler, and something more was added. Still the credit of the gambler soared, because he never boasted. He never spoke of guns. He never exhibited feats of marksmanship. He never referred in any way to the disgraceful scene in the saloon, in which he had crushed Larry Lynmouth.

His reasons for that reticence were strong ones, because he knew that he who speaks about trouble will eventually find it.

Nothing could restore the credit of Lynmouth now, it seemed. A flaw had been found in the strong chain, and, therefore, no one would trust it to support any weight. To be sure, since the affair with Jay Cress he had crushed his heel in the face of Crooked Horn's manhood, in a way of speaking. And he had downed brilliant young Lew Daniels in battle. And he had broken from the jail. And now the Daniels family talked freely about the abominable treatment they had received, and declared that judge, sheriff, and jury ought to be jailed for misusing the law. But all these things were taken with a grain of salt. Men simply raised their shoulders and their eyebrows a little. They had faith in the judge. Bore was a known man and a good man. So was the sheriff. If they had seen fit to arrange things in a slightly unorthodox fashion, it did not really mean that they had broken the law. They simply were serving it in an original way.

Without any further thought, the crowd declared that Jay Cress was a hero, Lynmouth a ruffian "bad one," and the sheriff a thoroughly good officer of the law.

This was the situation when Jay Cress, as has been said, came into Crooked Horn. He went to the bank. He was told to wait for a moment, and while he sat in the outer room, he saw Kate Oliver come from her father's office. He stood up and tried to melt into the shadows in the corner of the waiting room. For the whole world knew that Kate Oliver had loved the great Lynmouth— and the whole world knew why that engagement had been broken. Such news cannot be kept under a hat, it seems.

Now, when Cress looked at Kate and saw her pale, lovely face, and the darkness of her eyes, their expression somewhere between the blank suffering of a child, and the sorrow of a woman—and when he knew that she saw him, but was blinded to the meaning of his face by her great misery, even the soul of the gambler, which was as small and as cold as the soul of a snake, was touched with amazement and warmed to a certain admiration. And he said to himself that there were greater things in this human world than ever had been touched even by his imagination.

Then he went in to speak to President Oliver of the Merchants' Loan & Trust Co.

He found Oliver with a far-away look of pain in his eyes. And the gambler was sufficiently subtle to understand what was in the mind of the other. Therefore, he named it with his first word.

"Lynmouth—" said he.

He watched the shot take effect. Oliver swayed his shoulders back in his chair and changed color. He was so nervous that he was almost tremulous. This man had changed, recently, almost as much as the reputation of Larry Lynmouth.

"Lynmouth," went on the gambler, "has started up his operations near Crooked Horn again."

"What makes you sure of that?" asked the banker.

"There've been three stages held up in the last ten days. They've been stuck up by some one with the nerve of a lion. Well, everything points to Lynmouth. Two men have been seen. That would be Lynmouth and young Tom Daniels. Besides, there have been other robberies in the countryside. Houses entered. Phil Naylor's house was broken into. Nearly eight thousand dollars' worth of stuff taken away, money and some old family jewels. Of course, you know all about these things, Mr. Oliver."

"The two stage robbers," said the banker, "are brutes. So are the men who have been raiding across country. However, Lynmouth's crimes never were brutal."

"No, Lynmouth has changed," said the gambler gently.

Oliver colored as though the words had been almost a personal insult.

"Perhaps he has," he admitted jerkily. "At least, I know it is true that every one in Crooked Horn declares that Lynmouth is the master robber."

"Well, then," said the gambler, "I thought that I would throw in with Crooked Horn."

"In what way, Cress?"

"You see, my life's in danger from Lynmouth."

Oliver tried to smile, but he could not flatter in this case. Something sickened him.

"I imagine that you can take care of yourself, Mr. Cress."

The gambler did not smile, either. He merely made a hasty gesture, as though casting away any sense of self-assurance or pride in accomplishment.

He merely said: "I have reason to think that Lynmouth wants me dead, and I know that he has a way of getting what he wants. I'm afraid, to put it frankly."

The banker nodded. He liked this plainness of speech, this simplicity, this confession of fear in one whom the world called a staggeringly great hero.

"And we're afraid, in Crooked Horn," he replied with equal frankness.

"You're afraid," said the gambler, "that Lynmouth may slip into town and open some bank vaults, among other things."

"We are, exactly," said Oliver. "And the other stores which have cash drawers, and the jewelry shop, and every place which has a vaulable and portable stock—every one is afraid of what he may do."

"He's apt to try everything," said Jay Cress. "He's as cunning as a fox, and he's as fast as a hawk. He can do almost anything. And so I thought that we could throw in together. I don't want to be driven out of the country by Lynmouth's band—"

"Do you think that he has a band, actually?"

"Well, I should say so," said Cress. "If there were only two, I would not—"

He checked himself, though it was plain that he had been about to say that if there were only two, he would not be in the slightest degree concerned. Then, as though seeing where his words were leading, and in haste to avoid the least semblance of boasting, he went on rapidly:

"Of course, we have the sheriff, and a good sheriff he is. You don't find many better men than Chick Anthony. He'd never be found wanting when it came to a pinch. Of course, we all know that. But still it seemed to me that I'd feel safer, and perhaps that I could make Crooked Horn safer, if I had a few good fighting men gathered together as a sort of extra police."

"A very sound idea," said Oliver gravely.

"Then," said the gambler, "I got together four men."

"Who are they?"

"Jud Ogden is one."

"The Chihuahua horse thief?"

"Yes. Harrison Riley is another."

"That's the fellow who killed Ben Chipper?"

"Yes. Peg Leg Sam Dean is the third."

"That's the fellow with the wooden leg—the gunman and yegg?"

"Yes. And the last is Happy Joe."

"He's the one they tried in Denver for the Clauson murders?"

"Yes."

"I never could imagine a sourer lot of murderers and ruffians than those four, Cress!"

"But they are so brave that any pair of them would face Lynmouth; and they shoot so straight that any pair of them might kill him."

"Kill—" exclaimed the banker. Then he nodded, and passed a handkerchief across his face. "And what do you want us to do?" he asked.

"Pay the four men."

"And you?"

"No. Don't pay me. I'll pay myself and lead the four. I mean to say, we'll plan together."

"Cress," said the banker, "I like your idea. There's only one exception that I'd take to it."

24

FOUR LITTLE LAMBS

CURIOUSLY, Jay Cress waited. He was relishing this interview for many reasons. Not so many days before, he could hardly have got into this room to see Oliver without first picking the lock, or climbing through the window.

Now he was "Mr." Cress.

He enjoyed that difference with all his heart, and he also loved the slight shadow of awe with which the eye of the banker was veiled, from time to time, when he looked at his visitor. Yet the gambler did not boast, did not strike attitudes. All was quiet, simple, and almost gentle in his manner.

So he waited for Oliver to expound his idea.

"As a matter of fact," said Oliver, "there are reasons why I'd like to see Lynmouth out of the way. There are other reasons which would make his death a tragedy in my house."

He paused. It was difficult for him to speak. Finally, he went on:

"It appears that the proceedings against Lynmouth in the recent trial were highly irregular. If that case is appealed, he may be entirely cleared."

"It's rather a hard thing," said Jay Cress, "for an outlaw to appeal his case. If he had remained in prison— that would have been a different matter."

"I understand," said Oliver. "Personally, I have no doubt that unlucky young man would be better off behind prison bars. However, I must tell you that I won't be a party to any murder plot, Mr. Cress."

The gambler nodded. He kept his grave, steady eye upon the face of the banker. This was an honest man, and honest men, to Jay Cress, were like an undiscovered country. They dawned on his eye, but they never could be thoroughly known. He dreaded that he might make a false step at any instant.

"Does this seem like a murder plot to you?" he asked.

"No. Not on the face of it. It's simply a plan of defense. But with four such men as Peg Leg Sam Dean, Happy Joe, Riley, and Ogden, I should say that no one could be better equipped for murder. I would like to know if you think you can keep them thoroughly in hand?"

Cress did not answer offhand. He looked at the ceiling as though considering the question carefully, accurately, honestly. As a matter of fact, the one thought, the one desire, in his mind was to murder Larry Lynmouth; or, at least, to surround himself with such a strong cordon that the bullets of Larry Lynmouth never could break through to his life. He wanted that cordon approved of by public opinion. He particularly wanted to have the indorsement of such an honorable citizen as the banker, Oliver. Furthermore, it would be pleasant to have his four ruffians paid for by the town! In this manner, he became a sort of extra-legal agent, a self-sacrificing hero, laying himself in dreadful danger for the sake of Crooked Horn.

These were the thoughts which passed through his mind behind the mask of his cunning eyes. But then he looked down to Oliver and nodded.

"I hope I can handle them safely," said he.

"You hope so, and I hope so," said Oliver. "However, four such characters are four bottles of nitroglycerin, liable to explode unless properly cared for—liable to wreck Crooked Horn, if they burst loose. I'll tell you what I'll do, however. I'll talk to the First National people. I'll talk to some of the other business men. I think that they'll agree to your proposition. How much pay do the four want?"

"They ask for ten dollars a day, and hotel keep."

"That's very high pay," said the banker.

"I don't think so," said Jay Cress in the same thoughtful manner. "The fact is that I don't believe they'll be needed for very long."

"What makes you think that?"

"I believe that Lynmouth is desperate."

"And that he'll act quickly?"

"Well, he has a certain reputation which he would like to regain. Either he'll—"

Cress hesitated.

"You can speak your mind freely to me, I hope," said Oliver.

"I think, then," said Cress in the same cautious, judicious manner, "that he'll try to establish his reputation as a 'bad man' again either by committing some robbery in Crooked Horn on a great scale, or else he'll—he'll—well, in short, he'll murder me. Mr. Oliver." He frowned a little, and shook his head. "I don't like to say that, Mr. Oliver," said he.

"Do you think that he'll face you again?" asked the banker.

"I didn't say that he would do that," answered the gambler. "I said that I thought he would murder me!"

"Impossible!" exclaimed Mr. Oliver. "Why, his entire life has been honorable so far as his battles with—"

He checked himself suddenly.

"Perhaps you're right," said he. "Goodness knows what that poor young man may do now! As you say, he's desperate. His old life is thrown away. The light has been let in on him! Do you know, Cress, that sometimes I wish to Heaven you never had outfaced him there in the saloon, and let us see the miserable truth about him?"

Cress lowered his eyes and raised a hand to his face.

Smiling exultation was what he wanted to hide, but his attitude was that of a man who has the unpleasant past brought up before him against his will.

"I'm sorry you spoke of that, Mr. Oliver," said he. "The fact is that I try never to think of it. It wasn't—it wasn't what I expected," he went on in a lower voice, speaking rapidly, as though to himself. "I lost my temper. I was sure that he would fight back when—"

He made a brief gesture. He looked at Oliver with an assumed horror and regret in his face.

"I never spent ten worse seconds in my life!" said the gambler.

The face of Oliver was wet with the mere thought of that distressing exhibition of cowardice. He mopped the moisture away. He opened the window, and leaned out, breathing deeply; while the nostrils of Cress expanded suddenly, and a single flash of triumph appeared in his eyes.

"Tell me one thing," said the banker, his back still turned, his voice shaken.

"Whatever I can," said Cress.

"What do you think could have made him so afraid of you that he would stand that public humiliation—a man who never had shown the white feather before in a life filled with fighting?"

Cress allowed himself to brood for a moment over this question before he replied; though, as a matter of fact, it was an answer which he had prepared long before.

"I've wondered about that," he said. "But once we were riding together through an Arizona forest. And as we went along, I saw a squirrel on a branch of a tree. I took a snapshot, and by mere luck I hit the squirrel. Pure luck. But I'm afraid that the thing stuck in the mind of Lynmouth."

"It did, of course," said Oliver, "and, therefore, when he faced you in the saloon he—"

Suddenly the gambler raised both hands.

"Excuse me," he said in a stifled voice.

"Yes—yes—yes!" said Oliver. "Of course you don't want to hear any more about it, and I ought to ask your pardon. I do, in fact. About the other part of the affair— well, I'll talk to the others, as promised. I think that I can have an answer from them in the course of a couple of hours. Will that suit you?"

"Yes."

"That would be forty dollars a day in wages, and say another twelve for keep—or, make it fifty dollars altogether?"

"The hotel will put them up in good shape for two dollars and a half a head, board and room. They don't ask for the best. They simply want plenty!"

"And no drunkenness—no shooting up of the town, Cress?"

Jay Cress made a little gesture with both hands.

"Of course, I can only do my best with them," said he.

"I think that best will be good enough," said Oliver. "I must ask Gregory, the lawyer, if this affair is strictly honorable and legal."

"Yes, yes," answered Cress in much haste. "We have to be sure about that, of course."

"Then that's all for the time being. Where are your men now?"

"At the hotel."

"I'll drop around and see you all when I've rounded up some public opinion and support."

So Jay Cress left the bank, having come to the verge of accomplishing his move to checkmate the great Larry Lynmouth. With an elastic step, lightened by joy, he went back to the hotel, and there he met his legion.

They sat together at one end of the veranda in front of the hotel. The other loungers were gathered as far away as possible. There was a no-man's land in between the two groups, and at the sight of his four heros, Jay Cress did not wonder.

For they looked a great deal more like four animals rather then like four men.

Of them, one might have called "Happy Joe" a baboon. He was the most horrible-looking of them all. He had the high, globular forehead of a philosopher—or a half-wit. And the lower part of his face was as repulsive as that of a monkey, and, like a monkey's, it was covered with a short growth of red hair, which he never shaved, but kept clipped close to the skin.

"Peg Leg" Sam Dean, a great, gross, old, mangy bear, was always marked and incrusted with shiny spots of grease, which fell on his clothes from his gluttonous and unmannerly habits of feeding. A bear he was in the face, too, with his receding forehead and his great, gross, pig-fat jowls.

Harrison Riley was obviously a cat. Even his thin mustaches helped the illusion. And so did the three thin wrinkles in the center of his forehead, and, above all, his smile, which appeared good humor at first, but was presently seen to be intolerable, incredible ferocity, and coldness of soul. He was well dressed. He had the vocabulary and the manner of a gentleman, but if one wondered at the company he kept, the very first inquiry would be answered with the information that he was the blackest heart among them all.

Finally, Jud Ogden was a little, red-eyed, sharp-faced

ferret, consumed by an insatiable appetite for evil, habitually sitting with his head thrust forward, picking his fingers rapidly, nervously, and leering into the empty air in which he saw his visions of detestable crime.

Up to these men the gambler marched. The very air seemed to darken around them.

They looked up at him. The mouth of the bear, falling open a little, leered at him.

"Well, what is it?" they asked him.

"You're going to have your easy time and your fat pay," he told them. "But a quiet life it will have to be. You agree?"

The four looked at one another and smiled. Their amusement was of an unearthly kind.

"We'll be four little lambs!" said Harrison Riley.

25

THE STATE OF THE MOON

ON THAT very morning, through the gray and the chilly pink of the mountain dawn, Lynmouth came down from the Lansham Mountains. He had beside him young Tom Daniels, and Tom was far from well. There was a bright flush in his cheeks, alternating with moments of pallor. Sometimes he shook violently; sometimes, his head sagged with unutterable drowsiness.

They had marched nearly all the night across the range, for the sheriff of the next county had brought out a hundred well-mounted men, and has split them into five parties with which he combed the highlands so industriously that Larry Lynmouth, even with Fortune under him, decided that it would be better to turn back to his older hunting grounds. For that purpose he had crossed the Lanshams and come back toward Crooked Horn.

Moreover, he was seriously bent on discovering the

identity of the pair of robbers who, mounted on horses which resembled Fortune and Tom Daniels's bay gelding, had been holding up stages and single journeyers in the neighborhood of the little town. All these purposes were a good deal altered now, however. Tom Daniels was sick.

When Lynmouth asked him how he did, he usually chuckled and waved his hand.

"Sick for a good sleep, Larry," he would say. "Don't need nothin' more than that to get me right again."

So Lynmouth asked him no more questions. He simply cast about in his mind to find a proper retreat for the youngster to rest and recuperate. He had a fever, and a high one. He would need careful attention, and the best of good care. And Lynmouth knew that, for his part, he never could aid Daniels in this way. The hunt for him was too close.

From the very first, he had regretted Tom's joining him with a peculiar fervor. Company on the long trail was a pleasant thing, and Tom was an excellent hunter, a good cook, a cheerful fellow at all times. The trouble was that Lynmouth never could get out of his mind the fact that Daniels was practically outlawed for his sake.

He carefully had kept the lad's hands free from any suggestion of real crime. But the time had come when real guilt was not required. It had merely to be known that Daniels was with the notorious Larry Lynmouth in order to have half the terrible crimes in the calendar imputed to him. Since they departed from Crooked Horn, they had every species of highway robbery laid at their door. Plainly a pair of criminals were masking their true identity by pretending to be that of Lynmouth and his traveling companion. Besides, several brutal murders had taken place in the mountains and these were likewise laid to the door of Lynmouth and young Daniels.

So great was the feeling that had arisen, that men did not consider it strange that a hundred men had actually been enrolled and split into five posses for the sake of hunting two wanderers. And it was taken as a personal triumph for the sheriff when the fugitives were harried across the range.

That march through the snows above timber line had

been the undoing of poor Tom Daniels. The wind blew through him and chilled him properly. And then the fever followed.

A miserable anxiety possessed Lynmouth. If the boy died, he would feel that he was the murderer. If he had to be taken to a habitation, his capture by the police would follow almost as a matter of course, and then his sentence to prison. There would be little sympathy shown to the professed comrade and champion of the outcast, Larry Lynmouth!

Sometimes it seemed to Lynmouth that he had been a madman when he permitted the youngster to join him that day in Crooked Horn. He should have turned him back to the town, or, once mounted upon Fortune, he should have ridden away from him and left him hopelessly outdistanced.

He knew, however, that there was no use lamenting over spilled milk. He had to get a shelter, and a good nurse for Tom Daniels, and he wracked his head, trying to think of one. Outside of the Daniels family, did he know of a single human being whose faith he could put trust in? No, not one!

Unless it were the little brown-faced friar, Brother Juan!

Now, as if there were a mysterious force in that mere thought, they heard the clicking of hoofs in the distance and turned into the brush to let the traveler go by.

"Riding a mule," said Tom sleepily.

And Lynmouth nodded.

For the short, quick, precise step of a mule is easily distinguished by those who once have taken the rhythm into their hearing.

Then, around the next turn of the trail, dizzily outlined against the thin blue of the morning sky, they saw the squat, huddled form of Brother Juan himself, in the saddle on the back of Alicia.

His hands regarded not the reins. They were clasped at his breast, leaving the wise old Alicia to pick out her way as she pleased, while Brother Juan looked toward the east with such adoration in his face, and with such a smile of joy upon his lips that Larry Lynmouth was touched to the soul.

He knew, before, that the friar was a good, practical,

charitable, and godly worker in the name of his religion; but suddenly a door was opened by which he was permitted to see that some portion of the beauty of the soul of St. Francis himself had descended to the poor brother.

Lynmouth did not hesitate. He rode straight out onto the trail.

Alicia stopped with a grunt—for she was coming downhill at a sharp angle—and bracing herself on her crooked legs, she cocked her long ears at the interrupters.

"Hello, Brother Juan!" called Lynmouth.

The friar raised up both his hands in salutation. Then he came forward and shook hands with both of them heartily, cordially.

Lynmouth went straight to the point.

"My friend, here, is sick, brother. What can I do with him? Do you know of a single honest man in the mountains who would take care of him without showing him to the police—or without talking about him so much that the neighbors would do the same trick for him?"

Juan did not have to stop to think.

"I can take you to the very man inside of half an hour," said he. "You've heard of old Jarvis and his wife?"

"I wouldn't trust a woman—they gossip!" declared Lynmouth.

Brother Juan allowed his eye to pause upon the face of Larry Lynmouth for a moment.

"If we cannot trust women, can we trust men?" he asked. "Come, come, my friend! We are all made up of parts good and parts bad, and lately you've touched the bad parts of a good many minds. I don't wonder that you're sour, but old Jarvis and his wife will help to cure you of that!"

"Who are they?"

"You will see!" said the friar, and, turning Alicia about in spite of her groans of protest at having to retrace her way, he led off up the trail.

In another moment, they turned off the main trail on a little byway, which was almost too dimly marked among the rocks and the shrubbery of the mountainside to be visible. Along this they went for a short distance, when they encountered a tall old man with a pack strapped behind his shoulders, and an old-fashioned, long barreled rifle slung in his hand.

He looked on the verge of eighty. He was so old that his handsome, clean-shaven face had the pinched lines of a boy. His eyes were wonderfully blue and bright, and he stood under his burden as erect as a tree.

"I come back to you again, señor," said the friar. "I have brought two friends of mine."

"Take 'em right up to the house, Juan," said the other. "Mary has got enough kindness left in her to be decent to strangers."

"You'll come with us, Link?"

"I'll never go near the tarnation house again!" said Jarvis.

He turned and shook his fist at the direction and the thought of it. "I'm a free man, Juan, and I'm gunna stay free."

"What's happened, Link?"

"That woman has clean run to tongue," declared the old trapper. "I never seen nothin' like her. She was always free with her words, but now she ain't nothin' but a noise. Like a mockin' bird that has been raised up next to a screakin' sawmill. All the noise she makes is bad."

"You've had an argument, brother," said the friar.

"How can you have nothin' else but arguments?" demanded the ancient with heat. "How can you have nothin' else with a woman that won't agree to no sense?"

"Well," said Brother Juan, "we must have much patience."

"I've had it. I've had fifty-five year of patience with her, but I've used up the last grain of patience that I've got! I'm a free man, now, and I'm certainly gunna stay free to the end of my time!"

He stamped his foot to give point and emphasis to his remark, and jolted the stock of his rifle heavily against the ground.

"It was a bad argument, brother?" asked the friar with wonderful gentleness, while Lynmouth looked on to see in what manner, if possible, the man of religion would bring peace to this dispute.

"It's the most foolishest thing that I ever heard a growed-up woman say," said the trapper. "Now, then, I leave it to you, brother. When the moon is a-lyin' on its back, with its horns stickin' up, ain't that got the meanin' of rainy weather?"

"I've heard so," said the friar.

"Of course you have, and so has every one that ain't closed his ears to sense and right thinkin'. Now, you lookit. She says that it's when the moon is lyin' on its face, with its horns turned down, that it's always rainy weather."

"It seems to me," said the friar, "that I've seen the moon in both phases during the last month or so, and yet there hasn't been a drop of rain that I know of."

This seemed to stump old Link Jarvis for the moment, and he scratched his head, turning his eyes from side to side.

"Chances and occasions, they alter things," he said. "But when I told her that when the moon showed by turning over upside down that it was empty, and couldn't hold nothing, she wouldn't make no sense at all. She tried to argue that when the bowl was turned up, it would shed no rain, but was only gatherin' the moisture. I traced right back to last winter and told her the way that the moon was fixed every time. But it didn't make no reason to her. A woman, she can't think. What you call a woman's mind it's just plumb made up of meanness and pig-headedness. Lyin' on its back, anybody knows that that's the sign of rain!"

Brother Juan argued no longer. He merely said: "This will be a severe punishment to her, Link."

"Aye, and she's got it comin' to her," answered Link fiercely. "Her always talkin' about her rheumatism around the house, and wishin' that all she had to do was to take a nice saunter along under the open sky and take a few coyotes out of traps—let her try and do it now! I've left everything. I ain't takin' anything away from her except my freedom. And now let's see what happens to her!"

26

AN ARGUMENT ENDED

THE old man looked over his shoulder with a grim satisfaction, as he said this, and the friar answered:

"Link, of course you want your freedom, but here's a poor sick boy who needs to be taken care of."

"Let the old woman go and take care of him," he answered. "She can do everything so dog-gone well!"

"He's a very sick boy," said the friar.

"I'm all right," answered Daniels sleepily. "I can take care of myself and——"

The trapper, as he heard this drowsy tone, gave one quick glance at the boy, and then toward Larry Lynmouth. His eyes seemed to clear suddenly, and the meaning of these two wanderers entered his brain in a flash.

He pointed to the boy.

"That's Tom Daniels," he said.

"Yes," agreed Lynmouth.

Then he waited, almost smiling, to listen to the bitter denunciation which was sure to break from the lips of this acid old man.

Instead, to his amazement, Link Jarvis gently patted Tom's horse on the neck.

"We'll go right on up to the shack, son," said he. "We'll have you into a bed in no time. That's what you need."

Now, the voice in which he uttered this was so extraordinarily soft and deep and gentle that Lynmouth hardly recognized it as the same tongue which he had heard before.

Tom Daniels, his eyes glazed with fever, stared blankly back at the old man.

"All right," said he. "I reckon you know best!"

And straight up the trail they went, winding leisurely on the mountainside, until they came in view of a little shanty which had a tall rock at its back, and around it a pleasant clustering of poplars. A small stream went glimmering and flashing down the slope, and on a stone beside this running water sat a white-haired woman, her face bowed into her hands.

"Look!" said the friar softly to old Link Jarvis. "There is Mary, crying for you, Link."

At this, the trapper halted, frozen in mid-step, and struck his fist against his forehead.

"I'm a bully and a coward and a dog!" he said between his teeth, and he began to run forward. Though his walking step was light and elastic enough, one could see the stiffness of age in his running. He came at once to his wife and leaned over her.

"Mary," said he, "here I am, back again!"

She lifted her head with a cry. Lynmouth could see that her face was wet, glistening with her tears. But she snapped out:

"Oh, I knew that you'd be back quick enough, when you thought of sleepin' out on the hard ground, you and your rainy moon!"

Her husband recoiled with an angry exclamation.

"I'm back here with a sick gent for to be taken care of, and the minute that he's well, I'm off ag'in. I wouldn't stay here and live with you no more. I wouldn't and I won't!"

"Nobody wants you to," said Mary Jarvis in equal anger.

Then, as her glance fell upon Tom Daniels, she exclaimed:

"The poor boy's in a fever. Help him off of his horse, Link, and see if you got something besides thumbs on your hands. I'll hurry in and get a bed ready for him."

She went hobbling up the hillside as fast as she could, panting with haste, with gentleness, with pity, and casting a glance or two at the sick lad as she went.

They got Tom Daniels off his horse and into the house. The sun darkened with a sudden sweep of clouds across its face; a chilly wind whistled around the shack. But soon Tom was stretched in a narrow bed, groaning with uttermost relief, while a fire began to roar and crackle and shake the flimsy stovepipe.

Lynmouth was cutting wood with rather an unpracticed hand. Old Link busied himself about the stove and the heating of water for tea. And his wife cared for the boy. There was no thermometer. Upon his forehead she laid her wise old hand, wrinkled with time and hard with labor. Still it was sensitive enough to gauge the strength of the fever to a nicety. She listened, also, to his breathing, spending a long time at this, and canting her ear with the utmost concentration.

Then she was ready to announce her opinion.

There was a high fever, she said. But the lungs were not yet affected by the disease. If all went well, in a week or ten days the boy would be ready for the saddle again. If all went wrong, he might be in his grave in the same time. But she hoped that there would be no complications. And straight-way she began to take from a cupboard certain small paper packets of dried leaves and little roots.

She made up a brew of these with the boiling water, and gave it hot to the patient.

It would reduce the fever rapidly, she hoped. But rest and quiet would have to be the main agents in his cure.

"As much rest as he can get, poor boy," she murmured, "with Link a-yippin' and a-yappin' all around this place!"

"Me yippin' and yappin'!" exclaimed Link. "Why, there ain't been a time for fifty-five year that I've been able to hear myself think!"

"You and your moons!" said the wife in scorn.

"Me and my moons!" he repeated angrily, but lowering his voice on account of the patient. "And where's the moon now, I ask you?"

"In the sky, I reckon," she answered curtly.

"Aye, it's in the sky. Thank goodness that there's something you'll admit. And where's it lyin'?"

"Why, it's a-lyin' on its back, holding up its arms to collect all the rain, and keep nary a drop from fallin'. I told you that before! Common sense, it don't make no impression on a brain like yours, Link Jarvis!"

"Don't it?" he said, a sort of terrible triumph and exaltation in his face.

Then he raised his hand, with one finger pointed.

At last she had to look at him. She could not help herself, so commanding and victorious was his attitude. And behold! Lightly on the roof, swishing in the grass, tapping with a muffled beat upon the dust of the path, the rain began to descent. The odor of laid dust, and of the drinking ground, and the wet smell of pollen, came slowly drifting into the cabin.

"Don't bother me with your nonsense," said Mrs. Jarvis, more angrily. "The way you stand and look there, you'd think that you knew something."

"And what d'you know more?" he asked her.

"Why, I'll tell you. Exceptions always prove the rule. That's what I know!"

Her husband writhed with wrath.

"I might've knowed," said he, "that nothin' would stop her from talkin'. She'll carry on and have her own way out of pure cussedness. Night and day, she's gunna think nothin' but what she wants to think, even when God Almighty sends down his rain to show her that she's wrong!"

"Who's carryin' on and talkin' and ravin' and disturbin' the sick now?" asked Mrs. Jarvis sharply. "Reach me that tablespoon, and be quiet. And clear out of here, all of you. I gotta have peace in here. Link, you go and cut me a strip of bacon out of the smoke house. I'm gunna fry him up some bacon, crisp and thin, and see if he'll be able to eat it, pretty soon. Lookit him asleep already, and smiling, poor lad, poor lad! God send him strength right quick and make him well. Get along, you Link Jarvis and your moons!"

Her husband obeyed at once, and from the little shed behind the house came back with the desired strip of bacon, which he soon had frying on the fire, before he was banished from the house again with a wave of Mary's hand.

He joined the friar and the outlaw before the shack. The rain already had ceased, but the smile which he wore seemed to indicate that he was about to rejoice in his victory. However, he said not a word about it.

"Such a woman like Mary is," said the husband; "she could heal the dyin'. Would you wanta know why, Brother Juan?"

"Tell us why," said the friar in his gentle voice.

"By the goodness of her," answered the trapper. "The

goodness of a good woman, Juan, is somethin' that would melt away mountains, and make the rain stop fallin'. Fifty-five year of happiness she's give to me!"

Then, as he saw the faint smiles upon the faces of his companions, he was forced to qualify the remark a little by adding:

"Exceptin' now and then, when her tongue gets to runnin'. But a woman's like a river, and her talk has gotta keep running along downhill, tearin' away ground and rocks, wearin' away the men that've gotta be around to listen to her."

He paused and sighed.

"She was settin' right there yonder on the stone," he muttered, "cryin' after me. Don't you never forget that, Link Jarvis!"

Lynmouth, greatly moved, called the old trapper to one side.

"You're going to be put to a lot of trouble, Jarvis," said he. "I want you to take this money and use it any way you see fit for Tom and yourselves!"

He held out a hundred dollars in small bills.

Jarvis looked down at this treasure with a rising flush in his face. He cleared his throat, but at last he was able to say:

"I been a poor man mostly all my days, though I seen the time that I had two hundred and forty-eight dollars all at once in my hand, and all my own, exceptin' for twenty-two dollars that I owed that thief of a blacksmith, Chalmers. I been a poor man all my life, exceptin' for that day, Mr. Lynmouth; but I never seen the time that I would need to take money from them that come to me sick and hungry. And Heaven forgive an old man that swears that time will never come that he'll take pay for doin' a man's decent duty by them that are down!"

He seemed to feel that there was too much heat in this remark, and he went on more gently:

"The day that they're houndin' you, Lynmouth, you'll be needin' all of your money for yourself. I couldn't use it, anyway."

"It's honest money, Jarvis," said the robber.

"Why, that I don't doubt," said the trapper, "as much as any money is honest, and as much as any of it ain't dirty with the blood that's been shed for it. But I couldn't take your money for doin' what's right that I should do. Give it to Juan, yonder, that turns every penny into bread and meat for them that need it!"

Lynmouth, without a word, turned to the friar, and the latter took the little sheaf in his brown hand. He did not thank the giver. Instead, he said to the trapper:

"May Heaven bless you and give you happy days for this, Link."

"Heaven has blessed me already," answered the strange old man. "My blessing is yonder with that sick boy."

27
THE STAGE STARTS

IT WAS not long after these events that the Paradise stage left Crooked Horn on a trip which never was forgotten in that part of the world, either by those who were in the stage or by the townsfolk of Crooked Horn, who saw the stage start out under such cheerful auspices that morning.

Because of what followed, every detail of the start was remembered, down to the fact that old Dick Logan, the driver, had left his favorite leader behind, and was trying a new five-year-old bay, all fire and danger, in the place of the veteran. It was instinct on the part of Dick, said those who always are wise after an event. No one could have surmised danger.

In the first place, Dick Logan was as capable a driver as ever handled six wild horses around a hairpin turn. In the second place, in the high seat beside him was Chet Ritchie, who was wonderfully handy with rifle or revolver, and who had, besides, a sawed-off shotgun braced against the seat near by. It was said of Ritchie that he preferred to load his shotgun at a junk pile rather than with buckshot. He had served as guard on that line for three years. He had shot five men in performing his duty, and three of them had died—all victims of the murderous loads which he placed in his riot gun. There was not, in fact, a more respected man in Crooked Horn than Chet Ritchie. To see him whirling in on top of the stage, with his bandanna fluttering behind his neck, and his mustaches blowing, was proof beforehand that nothing could have gone wrong during the preceding journey.

Dick Logan, too, in spite of his sixty-five years, and his wonderfully bent back, was a known fighting man.

The stage was not overloaded.

It carried Lou Thomas, the teacher of the Paradise school, who was returning to her post. There was William Oliver, the banker, and his daughter Kate. They were going up to Paradise because he had some business to transact there, and because, furthermore, he wanted to distract her mind with a little shooting. Deer were reported thick around Paradise at that season of the year. With them went Oliver's new guest, Desmond Reardon. He was a lean, clean fellow of twenty-five, newly out from the East, with a fine clear eye, and an ability to sit even Western saddles that had won for him the early respect of every one. People whispered that Oliver hoped for a match between his girl and young Reardon. Perhaps not entirely because Reardon was reputed vastly wealthy, but rather because he was such a decent sort. He knew how to hold his tongue and listen to other people yarning. For that, above all else, he was valued. Both Reardon and Oliver were fighting men and good shots.

The last member of the company was a stranger who had dropped into Crooked Horn the day before.

Nothing was known of him except that he had said that he understood the air of Paradise was exceptionally bracing and pure; furthermore, that he had a deadly white skin, that his voice was low and husky, so that he rarely spoke, and then with evident pain; and finally, he had kept his neighbors in the hotel awake by coughing most of the night through.

These details were enough.

It was patent that this man was a consumptive, hunting for health in the good clean Western air of the mountains. It seemed equally obvious that he had come too late, for his broad shoulders were relaxed, his head was sunk between them, his very eyesight seemed to be failing, for he wore great dark glasses that sat across the bridge of his nose almost like a robber's mask.

This was the cargo of the stage, aside from some light luggage. This was the cargo, except for a single box belonging to Mr. Oliver, which had been loaded into the back of the coach. It was amazingly ponderous. In fact, it weighed two hundred and fifty pounds, all gold coin, and worth about twenty-five thousand dollars.

If the presence of that treasure had been known to the others, perhaps pretty Lou Thomas, at least, would not have been so eager to take the trip, because it is a well-known fact that gold, at least west of the Mississippi, draws danger more surely than honey draws bees.

There was nothing of importance or interest at the start, except the familiar sight of Logan on the driver's seat, swinging his restless leaders a little as they pranced on the bit, cursing them affectionately, and promising them all the work they could want before that day was ended.

Then, just before the embarkation, the stranger, with a linen duster's collar turned up around his neck and the lower part of his face, came to Mr. Oliver, told him that he understood he was a prominent citizen, and wished to know if he considered this trip perfectly safe?

As he finished his question, he took a handkerchief with his gloved hand and covered his mouth during a brief, harsh fit of coughing. The banker gave back a little with that look of fear, disgust, and pity with which healthy men are so apt to face an invalid who suffers from the white plague.

"This road is as safe as any in the West," he assured the sick man.

"But I've heard that Lynmouth and Daniels are haunting this very road," said the other, in his panting voice. "Are they—"

Coughing stopped him again. He pressed a hand against his breast and waited in an attitude of anxiety for the reply.

"Lynmouth and Daniels," said the banker, "have robbed twice on this road, and for that very reason they're not likely to try it again. Besides, the pair of them—Lynmouth, certainly—never would have the courage to face two such men as sit on that driver's seat."

"It's all right, then," said the other hurriedly, still wheezing so that his voice was almost indistinguishable. "And there's nothing in the stage likely to draw trouble, sir? I mean, I've heard that when valuables are in the boot—"

Oliver looked at him sharply.

He did not like to lie. On the other hand, he could not be such a fool as to betray the presence of that valuable shipment of specie.

He said finally: "I don't think you have anything to fear, Mr.—"

"Ford is my name, Mr. Oliver."

"I don't think that you have anything to fear, Mr. Ford."

Mr. Ford climbed into the coach accordingly.

He seemed so weak that he faltered on the long step, and the strong grasp of Chet Ritchie under his arm was needed to steady him and get him up to his place.

That grasp revealed certain things to Ritchie, and he talked of them to his friend and old companion in labor and in danger—Dick Logan—after the stage had started, and whirled down the street of the town at a furious gallop. (The entrance and the exit of a stage always must be at fullest speed. It is a point of ceremony, a point of etiquette.)

"Dick," said Chet Ritchie, "I'm gunna tell you about that lunger, back there."

"What about him?" asked Dick Logan. "I could tell you what about him. I'd like to have him ten miles instead of ten feet behind me!"

"He's one of these here athletes," answered the guard of the stage. "You know what happens. They get strong too quick and too young. And then they go bust."

"I dunno how that could be, but I've heard it," said the driver, taking a sharp turn at a rate that brought a squeal from Lou Thomas behind them.

"I'll tell you how it could be. They gets their lungs big for football and rowing. Then they get out of college and set themselves down in an office and push a pen, and them big lungs aint used, and into the unused corners all the germs they love to settle, and pretty soon they got consumption."

"Yaah. That sounds reasonable. What makes you think he's an athlete? He acts more like a sack of potatoes."

"I had a hold on his arm close up to the shoulder. India rubber, Dick. Like takin' hold of the forearm of a mule. You could feel the pull of the tendons, and the slide of the muscle. I bet it ain't been more than a couple of years back that that boy was plowin' down a football field leavin' the other team behind him like a growed-up bull goin' through a flock of yearlin's."

The driver looked behind him.

"No matter what he's been, he's about finished now," he said. "Look at him hangin' onto the side of the seat and wabblin' with every jerk like his head was goin' to fall off of his shoulders."

"Aye," said Chet Ritchie. "Pore feller! Paradise up yonder in the hills is only gunna be a short step to the journey he'll be makin' before long!"

They shook their heads over this, and then settled down into a resolute and grim silence.

For the stage had stretched away out of Crooked Horn, and now went over the level where the dust flew thick up into their faces, and horses, drivers, and passengers were instantly covered with a thick, sliding, ever-renewed layer of dust.

Bandannas were bent over mouths. Eyebrows turned white. The whole party swayed and suffered through the increasing heat.

However, the foothills began soon, and after that the motion of the big vehicle was something like that of a small boat, laboring up the near side of a wave, and then lurching down the farther slope. The brakes were good; the wheelers were skillful in taking some of the weight on their breeching straps; and old Logan knew to an ounce how much burden of speed he could give to the wheels as they flew down slope after slope, and negotiated the dizzy corners.

Sometimes every one stewed in windless heat; sometimes their breath was taken as the stage shot downward. The horses were covered with a mud of sweat and wet dust. They were streaked with foam. They tossed their heads in the impatience of laboring—helplessly suffering creatures.

But the way toward Paradise was more than half covered, and the people in the stage began to talk a little.

Lou Thomas took the lead. She always did! And her very first remark was like a blow in the face of Kate Oliver. Said Lou:

"What's the news about Larry Lynmouth, Kate?"

Kate did not answer instantly. Her father looked sharply, attentively at her, but there was too much dust on her face to permit her color to be noted.

Lou gracefully explained, in the slight interval:

"They say that you were kind of fond of Larry for a while, Kate. I mean, before that awful bust he went when Jay Cress called him and made him take water."

"I hear that he's just come over the mountains," said Kate indifferently. "I don't know anything in particular about him."

Her father sighed with relief. He was almost glad that the teacher had been so hideously tactless as to bring up this tender subject, for the voice of his daughter was steady as could be.

"Yeah," said Lou Thomas. "They say they gave him a run, but you can't tell. He's slippery, I'll tell a man! He's all grease. First he's here, and then he's there. Run him through the mountains a hundred miles away, and only the day before, he and Daniels were out on the Chipping Road, holding up poor old Doc Grey! You heard tell about that?"

Lou Thomas left her grammar for her schoolroom. She never carried the extra burden abroad.

"I heard something about that," said Kate, still perfectly calm.

"The way they beat up old doc, that was what got me!" declared Lou.

"Beat him?" asked the other with a sudden sharpness.

"Yeah. Slammed him. Doc only had twelve dollars and a half with him, and they expected that he'd have the whole payroll of the boys on the ranch. They was so disappointed that they took out the change in beatin' up poor doc. Something awful! They flattened out his nose, and they knocked out his teeth. Lynn Ferris saw doc. Said he looked like a borax team had walked straight across his face."

Lou Thomas took a breath; she gasped with indignation.

"A hound like that, hangin' is too good for him," she said aloud.

"Ah, well," said young Desmond Reardon, "it's a big new country!"

He always wished to show that he was reserving judgment upon the faults and the sins of the Wild West. He looked at Kate Oliver. She was all the West that he really cared about.

She lifted her head, now. He looked at her profile and the faint, proud smile that touched her lips.

"For my part," said she, "I think that Larry Lynmouth is incapable of cruelty."

28

THE STAGE STOPS

THIS she said in a fairly loud and very clear voice. And as they were at that moment topping a rise, the wheels were not rattling so much as usual, the harness was not creaking, and every soul in the stage heard the words clearly. They reacted in different ways.

Banker Oliver started as though a pin had been stuck into a tender part of him. Young Desmond Reardon frowned, and then bit his lips because he had shown displeasure. He did not know much about the affair between the girl and the desperado. He had only heard a hint of it, and the fact that she had been able to love such a wild fellow had not altogether displeased Reardon. It gave spice, piquancy, and mystery to her gentle nature, in his eyes.

Lou Thomas opened her mouth a little too wide for speech, and rounded her eyes, so that she made three silent O's.

On the driver's seat, Chet nudged Dick, and both of them nodded in silent understanding.

As for the stranger, Mr. Ford, he turned his head quickly away, and stared across the valley, as though he saw something very wonderful upon the farther side.

"Oh, but lookit, Kate," said Lou Thomas. "You don't mean to say that you don't believe what everybody knows about—"

"No," said the girl, "I don't believe anything."

"You mean that Larry didn't stick up the Danville bus the other day, him and Daniels, and kill old Pete Larsen?"

"I don't believe he did," said Kate Oliver.

She looked fairly and squarely at the other girl.

"But—Kate!" exclaimed the teacher breathlessly.

"He never murdered old men in the days before—though he did commit plenty of crimes, I suppose."

"Before what? Before Jay Cress made a Chinaman of him?" said Lou Thomas. "But everybody knows that he's gone to pieces since then. Why, I've seen the day when I'd rather've danced with Larry Lynmouth than anybody—almost!"

She grew dreamy for a fifth part of a second, as she considered a certain exception in her mind. He was not, at that moment, more than four feet away from her. She had been trying for an hour to take the eye of young Desmond Reardon.

"But now," said Lou Thomas, "I'd rather be hitched onto a wild Indian! A lot rather!"

Kate Oliver did not reply. She simply turned her head away and looked out across the valley, in the same direction toward which the invalid on the back seat was staring.

He, with a gloved hand pressed across his mouth, worked feverishly at a short, dark mustache which fringed his upper lip and, together with the large dark glasses, quite completed the covering of his face.

"The scoundrel!" said Lou Thomas, determined to press the point. "The way that he's run off with poor young Tom Daniels that used to be as nice a boy as I ever saw. But, oh, Kate—great heavens!"

She stopped with a gasp.

"Yes?" said the other girl quietly.

"Maybe—maybe I was wrong. I mean—I should've remembered—I didn't think you'd care a whit since—I mean—" She had stumbled into deeper and deeper confusion.

"It's all right," said the banker's daughter.

She was so perfectly in command of herself that she could even smile at the teacher.

But her father and Desmond Reardon were studying her face with an almost frantic intensity.

All that they could see was a calm and deep resolution, and a spiritual strength such as neither of them had expected to find in her. It made Reardon feel that he had thrown away a month of time. It made William Oliver wish that Larry Lynmouth never had been born, and that he might die soon.

Here Lou Thomas whose head moved on her graceful neck as restlessly as that of a bird, turned and looked back.

She saw the white, dust-misted road winding along the gentle slope behind them. She also saw the face of the invalid and a peculiarity about it which made her hold her breath. Suddenly she leaned forward and touched the knee of Oliver.

"Mr. Oliver! Mr. Oliver!" she whispered. "We've got a stage robber or something with us. He's not a consumptive at all!"

"What are you talking about?" said Oliver, who almost hated this girl because she had forced into view the true mind of his daughter. He might have at least been grateful for the revelation.

"The man on the back seat—the dark glasses—the mustache—he's just rubbed half of his mustache away!"

Oliver, without a word, reached a hand inside his coat. He was brave as any man, and ready for battle if there was need.

"Stand up," he whispered back, "and tell the drivers. We'll stop the coach at once. Stand up. You're nearer to—"

She did not stand up, however, for just at that moment the stage swept about a corner and dropped down a dangerously steep slope at a rate that made every one hang on.

This pitch flattened out somewhat at the bottom, only to swerve around a sharp bend, with a five-hundred-foot drop of naked cliff on the right, and a tangle of brush on the left. At the very moment when the stage was staggering with speed on the point of the turn, with the leaders half out of sight, a rifle clanged, the new bay leaped straight in the air, and that stage was on the verge of being flung off the road and into eternity.

Chance saved them from immediate destruction.

Old Dick Logan had taken that curve a good deal faster than he had intended, and the result was that he had swung wide, and too wide.

The fall of the bay leader piled up the horses behind him; the stage skidded violently out, but on the verge of the precipice its rear wheel struck a rock that pitched it high up. The lumbering stage staggered for an instant in mid-air, as though hesitant as to whether it should topple over the cliff's edge or back against the safe slope. Then it suddenly inclined with a lurch toward safety.

There were some active people on that stage.

Dick Logan, to his eternal credit, thought only of slamming on the brake and driving it home to the last notch with his foot, while at the same time, with wonderful skill and presence of mind, he jerked the span in the swing and the wheelers to the left, and the inside of the curve.

They fell and piled up. But they would otherwise have spilled over the ledge and inevitably have drawn the whole stage and all its passengers to death with the pull of their four tons of writhing weight.

William Oliver was not young, but he managed to get to his feet and jump. So did Desmond Reardon, like a tiger cat, and Lou Thomas, screeching wildly.

Chet Ritchie, true to his duty, snatched up the shotgun and fired it; but as the seat swayed, the shot went wild, and did no harm to the riflemen whose weapons peeked from the dusty screen of leaves straight ahead. Both he and the driver, however, on account of their high positions, were flung, not under the stage, but clear of it into the bushes which received those who jumped. They were stunned and scratched, like the rest, but not a bone was broken.

Only Kate Oliver did not stir, but sat petrified, or as though her mind had been too far away, too deeply involved, to be snatched back in an instant to the concerns of this world, no matter how physically perilous. She merely freshened her grip on the edge of the seat and closed her eyes.

Then hands with a grip like a giant's grasped her beneath the arms. She was torn from her place and pitched high into the air. And a near-by stout shrub received her with wonderful gentleness.

That was the act of the invalid about whose shoulder muscles Ritchie had waxed so eloquent.

He had time to do that as the stage heeled and staggered.

As it lurched in toward the bank, he himself leaped, but not toward the safe brush. Instead, he sprang out into the center of the road and landed like a cat on his feet.

He landed running, as it seemed, and headed straight past the tangle of struggling horses.

In the meantime, two men had come quickly out from the brush.

Their work had not been perfectly done. Instead of pitching the stage over the rim of the cliff, they had merely stopped and overturned it. However, that stunned and scattered group at the verge of the road was incapable of making the slightest resistance to the two good rifles which the robbers carried.

They came forward rapidly, confidently, eagerly. The taste of the loot was already theirs, in anticipation, when danger ran at them around the piled horses.

It came in the form of a man with dark glasses thrust up high on his forehead, and with half of a black mustache, and a gun in his hand which spat confusion upon them.

The smaller of the two was the first to see the peril. He whirled, with a yelp like a wolf, in time to take a bullet through his right shoulder. The weight of the slug knocked him flat.

The taller of the pair swerved also, and even had time

to get in a shot, but it flew hopelessly wild, taken by utter surprise as the marksman was. Then the strength of his legs turned numb beneath him, and he fell upon his face, shot straight through both legs between knee and hip.

29

HORSES AND MEN

SEEING the two drop, Mr. Ford did not waste so much as a glance at them. The horses were in danger of trampling one another to death, and, therefore, he ran in at them, and with wonderful agility—for a consumptive, at least—he avoided their plunges and their striking hoofs, and cut the traces of the most entangled.

The bay leader lay dead. The other five lurched to their feet, and some of them ran to a little distance, but Ford took no more heed of them, hurrying on into the brush.

There he found a mare which might have passed off tolerably well as a sister of the beautiful Fortune on which Larry Lynmouth rode, together with a second mount which was reasonably like Tom Daniel's gelding.

The gelding he left alone. The mare he mounted and rode off, going at a foot pace down the hillside for a little distance. Then, when he was out of hearing, he put the mare to a good round gallop, and went down the hollow of the valley as fast as the footing allowed the animal to run.

He left confusion behind him.

The two masked bandits were helpless in the roadway. The bigger man, who had been shot through the legs, uttered not a sound of complaint, but the smaller groaned continually, for the ball had completely shattered the intricate joint of the shoulder.

The passengers, in the meantime, hardly knew what had happened. In half a second the stage had crashed on

its side, and they found themselves cut and stabbed by
the ten thousand pin pricks of the brush into which they
had fallen. William Oliver lay semiconscious, from a heavy
blow on the head. His daughter was equally stunned with
surprise. Lou Thomas crawled from the shrubbery, shriek-
ing loudly, and Desmond Reardon got up like a drunkard
and staggered helplessly to and fro. Old Logan was up,
too, by this time, groaning with each breath, for he had
fallen on his crooked back; and only Chet Ritchie had
come out of the affair unscathed, except for having the
wind knocked out of him for an instant.

He alone had looked on at the second moment of the
holdup, and seen the pair of robbers go down like ninepins
before the gun of the invalid. He had seen the latter dart
into the tangle of horses and loosen it by magic. He had
seen Ford disappear, afterward, into the trees and brush
at the farther margin of the curve. And Ritchie was the
first man to get to the wounded.

He cared less for their wounds than for their masks. He
stripped those away, first of all. The bigger man was a
redheaded fellow with a face now white with fear and
with pain. Yet he kept his jaws locked to force back the
least murmur.

"Turk Henley!" exclaimed Ritchie. "You're the Larry
Lynmouth that's been doing murder and robbery around
here, are you? And who's the Tom Daniels that rides with
you, or is it the real Tom, after all?"

The second mask, torn away, revealed a dark, handsome
face somewhat in the style of Tom Daniels. It was now
contorted in a fury of terror and of agony.

Its owner cursed Chet Ritchie in his first breath, and
begged him for help in the second. He crawled to his
knees, then to his feet.

"Lemme go, Chet!" he breathed. "I got enough to
make you rich. Lemme slip away into the trees and get
to my hoss. It ain't me! It's that yegg, Turk Henley. He's
done it all. He just kind of dragged me along—Chet, lemme slip away. It won't cost you nothin', and I'll make
you rich for it!"

"Aw, back up," said Turk Henley. "Don't you know
Chet and Dick Logan? They'd hang you, if they had a

half chance, and maybe they're gunna have more'n a half chance before we get through!"

Old Dick Logan, hobbling a little, but fierce of face, was the next to get out.

He ran straight past the two robbers and went on to the spot where the young bay leader had fallen dead. He pressed up the eyelids of the gelding, and then raised both his clenched fists against the sky.

"As good a hoss as ever stepped in harness!" he vowed. "And two hydrophobia skunks, two wooden-headed murderin' cur dogs, they done him up while he was still as sound as a piece of steel! You pair of rats, why couldn't you've stopped the team by dropping that no-good gray in the off lead, or that balky fool of a pinto in the near swing? I gotta mind to brain the two of you!"

Every one was out, now; Kate and her father in the rear, holding each other by the hands, and still looking at one another with desperate fear of what might have happened to each. She began to laugh, half hysterically. And he, putting his arm around her, brought her straight up to the place where the dead horse and the injured men lay. For the smaller of the two had sunk down again in his despair and his suffering.

Said the banker:

"Help with those two, Kate, if you can stand the sight. I'll do what I can. Nothing matters now except that they are in frightful pain and losing blood every instant."

"I can stand it," she replied. "Just at this moment, I could stand anything!"

She went gently about her work, and yet with a sort of quiet courage that was almost exultation. Her father, helping as he could to cut away clothes, wondered at her. He had only suggested the task in the hope of keeping her from a hysterical reaction after the accident; but she accepted the post with eagerness and skill. Desmond Reardon, his eyes still big, clumsily filled in where he could, for all the work of the bandaging and cleansing of the wounds fell to the three of them.

Lou Thomas, sitting on the bank, was rocking back and forward, with her face between her hands, or else throwing up her arms to heaven. Then she would look down at her torn dress and burst into hysterical laughter, and again she was moaning over a twisted wrist.

As for Logan and Chet Ritchie, they saw that all was well on the field of battle, and went first into the brush to try to discover the horses of the robbers.

One they found. There was plain sign of the spot where a second had bitten away the tender bark of the sapling to which it had been tied, and where it had stamped a hole in the soft surface ground with its forefeet.

"Where's it now? Who took it?" asked Logan.

Chet Ritchie did not answer at once.

Instead, he went hastily down the slope a little distance, bent far over and studied the ground.

"Here he went," said he. "He turned here around this old rotten stump. The hoss stepped here. Then it went down that slope. There's where it slid—and yonder, by the jumpin' Jiminy, there he goes, lickety-split, with his dog-gone old linen duster flyin' out behind him like the tail of a magpie! D'you see him, Logan?"

The old driver came to his side and stared in turn.

"There he goes. He's a ridin' fool, old son."

"He's a ridin' fool," said Chet Ritchie explosively.

"No more of an invalid than me," said the old stage driver.

"No more of an invalid than a catamount, you dog-gone ol' fool," said the guard.

"I ain't so old, neither," said the driver. "I ain't so old as to be brittle, anyways! A fightin' fool that gent is, Ritchie!"

"The out-fightin'est fool that ever I seen," said the guard. "Did you watch that shootin'?"

"I seen a kind of a blur of it," answered Logan, "because I only had about half of an eye to look with, just then, I was that busy gettin' my wind back! A slick hand it would take to down Turk Henley, and that poison rat, Sid Walsh, in one little scrap like this."

"And then he dived right on into the hosses and sliced the traces and let 'em get free. You'd've had your team turned into jam in another five seconds, Dick."

"Would I? I reckon I would. Who was it, Ritchie?"

"I dunno."

"What made him run after he done this?"

"Why, you fool, he wanted to get away from a lot of thanks and hand-shakin', I reckon."

"Likely hè didn't want to waste no time in sendin' up a fresh hoss and some medicine for the two crooks that he dropped."

"Likely he didn't," said the other. "Which I reckon that we had a man along with us in that stagecoach today, you old mangy mossback, you!"

"Why, you ol' wall-eyed, lantern-jawed slab-sided, spavined has-been," said the other cheerfully, "I don't reckon nothin' but what we had!"

They went back, leading the captured horse with them. The harness taken from the dead leader was fitted upon it. The cut traces were repaired as strongly as possible with ever-ready baling wire, and the team was worked back into its proper place.

By that time, the two wounded men had been bandaged. They were propped against the bank, and William Oliver stood over them rather grimly. He put his questions to the older of the two, and the taller, Turk Henley. Walsh was still trembling with fear, which even a powerful dram from a whisky flask could not diminish.

But Henley, perfectly composed, was willing to answer.

"Only, shut up the yappin' of Lou Thomas," he said. "Hullo, Lou! Catch hold of yourself. This ain't quite the same as dancin' together in Paradise, is it?"

At this, Lou burst into fresh hysterics.

"Where'll I do my next dancin', I wonder?" said the robber composedly. "Now, whacha want, Oliver? I ain't the man to let you die from thirstin' after information."

"What made you pick out this particular stage for your holdup?" asked the banker.

"Twenty thousand dollars in the boot. That was what made me," replied the robber.

"Who told you about that?"

"Aw, I guessed," said Henley. "Look here, Oliver. I don't mind tellin' you enough to hang me and the runt, here, because I know that we gotta hang, anyway. But I ain't gunna pull in nobody else into the mud by the flap of his ear!"

"You won't tell me which one of my clerks let you know? I think that I can guess anyway."

"Yeah. Maybe you can, but I won't help you. The hound didn't tell me that he was gunna be along with you, though."

"Who?"

"Why, him!" said the robber impatiently. "Him, of course."

He jerked a thumb over his shoulder toward the distant mountains. Every one had gathered close, now.

"I don't know who you mean," said the banker.

"Why, your extra gent is what I mean, the one you embalmed in the linen duster. The one that you faked up in half of a mustache. Your hired piece of chain lightnin'. Your pet that makes a gun talk three languages at once—all of them understood perfect in the place that he's sent plenty to. Larry Lynmouth. Who else?"

30
TURK HENLEY TALKS

WITH a stout young pole of a sapling as a lever, the men rocked the overturned stage back upon its wheels, and found that its tough hickory had stood the strain wonderfully well. There was only a little splintered wood.

They decided to return to Crooked Horn. In Paradise there was a doctor, but not a jail, and both were absolute requirements for Sid Walsh and Turk Henley. Besides, if one set of rascals knew about the shipment of gold coin, others might know also, and a second attempt might very well be made. So they turned the cumbersome vehicle by hand, hitched on the horses, and went back to Crooked Horn.

It was the longest trip that most of the passengers ever had taken, except for Kate Oliver. Chet and Dick, on the driver's seat, were hungry to spread the tidings of the holdup among the townsmen. Desmond Reardon was desperately anxious to learn where he and the outlaw stood in the judgment of Kate. The banker feverishly turned and returned his thoughts as he pondered the uncertain future which might be extending before his daughter.

Finally he said softly to her:

"Kate, did you know from the first that that fellow was Larry Lynmouth?"

She shook her head.

"Did you know before Henley told us?"

"I knew," she said, "the instant that he caught me up and threw me safely clear of the stage." She looked firmly at her father. "I would have been caught under the stage when it fell," she pointed out, "except for what he did."

"Yes," admitted Oliver, who always tried to be fair. "I forgot about you and jumped. I wish to Heaven that girl would be still!"

But Lou Thomas could not be still. She hoped that the accident would not give her a nervous breakdown. She hoped that the robbers would be hanged. She hoped that Larry Lynmouth would receive a pension from the government. It appeared that she always had liked Larry. She had an innate respect for him. Something told her that he never had done the things of which he was accused by brutes and fools. For her own part, she felt that he was a great man, a good man, and, of course, a startling hero!

This chatter hardly ended all the way to Crooked Horn.

Oliver opened a running fire of questions upon the two captured robbers.

"You might tell us if all the recent jobs have been your work," said he.

"Why should we tell you?" snarled Sid Walsh.

"Shut up, Sid," said Turk Henley. "Don't be a fool. Mr. Oliver will see that we get a square deal, maybe."

"We'll never get a square deal. We're framed!" said Sid Walsh.

"I'll tell you, Mr. Oliver," said Turk, who lay couched in sacks and blankets at the bottom of the stage, suffering misery with every jolt and jar over that mountain road. "I'll tell you. No two men could have done all the things that have been laid to Daniels and Lynmouth lately."

"What's your proof of that, Turk?"

"There was the Jackson Ford job, a couple or three days ago. That same night, Flank Thomas was stuck up by another pair of riders at Wolf-eye. How could the same pair've rode fifty miles in four hours?"

"That's been done, I believe, a good many times."

"Sure it has. But mostly in books. No, sir, there's more'n one couple've been livin' on the danger and trouble that Lynmouth has fell into!"

"And how long have you been on the road this way, the pair of you?"

"You wanta know that?"

"Yes, that's what I'm asking."

"Today is our first day."

"Do you expect me to believe that, Turk?"

"No," answered the wounded man with his surprising way, "I don't expect you to, of course. You'd be a fool if you did."

"I'm afraid," said Oliver, "that you're coming to a hard end, because of this affair, Henley."

"Sure I am," nodded Turk Henley. "Aw, I know that."

"So help me gosh." Sid Walsh suddenly screamed, "every word that Turk is sayin' is the truth!"

"Shut up, shut up!" exclaimed Turk Henley. "Maybe you think that he'll believe you when he won't believe me?"

"Most of these crimes around here will be put on your shoulders, Henley," said the banker, curiously probing the mind of the wounded robber.

"Yeah, I know that," said Henley. "I know that they'll hang us pretty pronto. And we don't deserve no better—playin' the skunk and tryin' to live on another man's hard luck. Lynmouth's, I mean!"

The banker suddenly looked up and found the calm eye of his daughter upon him. He could not help flushing a little, and looking hastily back to Henley.

"How many of these recent crimes do you attribute to Larry Lynmouth?" asked Oliver bluntly.

He was irritated by the quiet triumph in the eye of his daughter Kate.

"Not one," came the amazing response of Turk Henley.

"What?" exclaimed Oliver. "You're going to let him and Daniels off from everything?"

"I can't help it. You'll see through it yourself, in another minute or two, I reckon."

"See through what?"

"This case of poor Lynmouth. Lookit what he done today."

Oliver hesitated, but he was a just man, and had to give credit where it was due.

"I hope," he said slowly, "that Lynmouth was not on this stage for the same purpose of robbery that put the two of you in ambush there at the curve of the road. I hope that he did not have his own plans spoiled by the appearance of you two!"

"You hope that, do you?" asked Henley, with a faint sneer. "Well, maybe you'll tell me what would've kept him back. He dropped the pair of us—*whang, bang!* Then he turns around and sees the rest of you gents spilled out in the brush like Mexican laundry. What would've stopped him from linin' you up and shootin' out the eye-teeth of them that looked crooked or tried to pull a gun? He had the chance, and he had the time. Or maybe you don't think that he can shoot straight enough?"

He showed his teeth as he smiled at his own last remark.

"Yes," confessed Oliver. "He can shoot straight enough. He's brave enough—but to let him off scot-free for all the other crimes which have been attributed to him around here—"

"You wouldn't do that?" asked Henley, the same faintly critical sneer reappearing on his lips.

"I wish to be fair," muttered the banker.

But he began to doubt his own fairness for the first time. Frankly, he was enormously afraid of Larry Lynmouth for the sake of Kate.

"Whacha think?" said Henley, who in this argument seemed to forget his own pain to some degree. "Whacha think put Lynmouth in this here stage?"

Oliver bit his lips and glanced aside sharply at his

daughter. Her head was high. Her hands lay loosely folded in her lap. Her smile was directed calmly to the far-off mountains. For the first time in many days he saw again in her face the mysterious and beautiful aloofness which always had baffled him and troubled him with wonder. Lynmouth was in her mind, he knew; and she was content again.

"I don't exactly know," said the banker.

"Why," said the robber, "he was tired of having every murder and stickup job laid to him and young Daniels. He couldn't write to a paper and deny that he'd done the work. He just come down and got wind of this frame and stepped in and busted it up. He broke the window, but it looks like you won't let in the light and air. Besides, Mr. Oliver," he added in a slightly lower voice, "would he have any reason to want to save you twenty thousand dollars—and other trouble?"

He glanced quickly at Kate as he said this.

Oliver's face pinched with pain. "I don't know," he said honestly. "You would give Lynmouth a clean bill of health, Henley?"

"Yeah. I would."

"And Daniels?"

"I dunno. Tom went with Larry Lynmouth to help, if he could, I suppose; and ever since then, I take it that Larry has been tryin' to keep the kid out of trouble and with clean hands."

"Have you any reason for being so easy with Larry Lynmouth?" asked Oliver suddenly.

The other looked down to his bandaged legs.

"That could've just as well been through the head instead of the legs," he answered.

This, for some reason, made Oliver silent. He returned on a different track.

"You managed that holdup to roll the stage over the edge of the cliff, Henley," he accused.

"Yeah. It looks that way. I told the kid, here, that it was likely to be a bad place. But he figgered that with the stage doin' down hill and takin' a sudden swing, like that, nobody would be ready for trouble. He was right. But—"

He cast a sour glance at Sid Walsh, and the latter

turned a ghastly white. Beads of perspiration stood out on his forehead.

"Mind you," said Henley hastily, "I ain't crawlin' out from under. I'll stand what's comin' my way!"

The banker began to ponder these things slowly, deliberately.

"Do you believe what Turk Henley is saying?" asked the quiet voice voice of Kate.

William Oliver started. "I don't know," said he.

"Do you believe every solitary syllable that he's said?" she repeated.

Her father stared at her. There was a sort of cold and impersonal inquiry in her eyes that made him understand he himself was now on trial, and for something dearer to him than life. He looked inward.

"Yes," he replied all at once. "I believe everything that has been said by Henley. Every word of it!"

"And so do I," said the girl.

"And so do I!" said Desmond Reardon unexpectedly. His brow was knitted. It seemed apparent that he knew what a sacrifice he was making.

Oliver turned again to Henley.

"If I have the slightest influence in Crooked Horn, I'm going to try to get you a square deal," said he.

He hardly heard the thanks of Turk Henley. He felt that a battle had been fought and won against him, but he could not tell whether to be glad or sad. Bewilderment seized on his mind.

31

FOUR MEN WAITING

But Mr. "Ford," alias Larry Lynmouth, did not make a rapid trip across country. He merely sprinted on the captured mare while he was putting the first distance between him and the stage. Then he went on more slowly, and journeyed at an easy pace to the point where he had cached Fortune.

Taking Henley's horse to the nearest highway, he turned it loose, and saw it trot away on the road toward Crooked Horn as though it knew the right direction home. Then he went off to the nearest good camping ground among the trees and spent a comfortable enough night.

After that, he took the way back to the mountains, and he came onto the trail to the house of old Link Jarvis in the dusk of the day, having purposely delayed until that time. He dared not take chances now, even at such an out-of-the-way place as the shack of the eccentric old trapper.

It was exactly the right moment for maneuvering and cautious approaches, for the light of the day was dying, and the strength of the moon, hanging low in the east, did not yet begin to tell. Yet, dim as the light was, his keen eyes suddenly showed him an outline among the trees to the right of the trail.

He reined back instantly and jerked a gun in time to cover the form of a rider as the latter came out into the open—a small rider, on a small, nervously active horse.

"Larry?" called the voice of Cherry Daniels.

He slid his gun out of sight and rode up to her and took her gloved, small hand in his. There was light enough, when he was very close, to see that her cheeks and eyes were brilliant.

"You're a long way out, Cherry," he told her. "What's brought you here?"

"Squirrels," said the girl. "I've been out hunting for them all day. You know how it is. You pick a squirrel, and then you see another better one farther along. I just happened to wander up here, and along comes Larry Lynmouth. How are you, Larry?"

"I'm just between night and day, Cherry," he answered her. "Have you come to see Tom?"

"No," she said.

He pretended not to hear her.

"We'll go up the trail to the house," said he. "Old Link Jarvis and his wife will set you up a snack. Cherry. I know that you're hungry."

"I am," she said, "but I won't eat at the Jarvis house."

"Why not?"

"For the same reason that you won't."

What's up your sleeve?"

"More than you'd guess. A sheriff and nine of a dozen man hunters with their tongues hangin' out for Larry Lynmouth."

He caught her by the arm.

"Do you mean they've got Tom?"

"Yeah," she nodded. "They've got Tom."

Larry groaned, throwing back his head in an excess of grief and despair.

"They've got Tom! They've got him while I was out fixing my own affairs!" he exclaimed.

"Listen," said the girl, "everything that goes wrong in the world ain't your fault, is it?"

He groaned again. "It makes me dizzy, Cherry. How could they have found him?"

"It was old man Chick Anthony," she answered with wonderful cheerfulness. "He had an idea about you crossing the mountains and not showing up any farther down from them. He had an idea that you were cached away in some hiding place. So he comes up and tried Link's, and there he finds that the big cat's out hunting, and the little one is left home, mighty sick."

"I'll get him away again," Larry said through his teeth. "I'll have him back, Cherry. Wait here, while I—"

It was she who caught his arm this time.

"I think you would," said the girl. "I think that you'd go up there singlehanded and see what you could do. But it's no good, Larry. He's not there."

"D'you mean to say," he exclaimed, grinding his teeth, "that they've carted him off, sick as he is?"

"He's not so mighty sick. He's a lot better," said the girl, "and he's down in the jail in Crooked Horn. He got there about two hours after the Paradise stage pulled out the other morning. They slipped him into town and into the jail mighty quiet, with a mask over his face, and all. They hope that nobody knows. But I got a whisper."

"So you came here for me, and you're right, Cherry. But you wouldn't have to ask me to help him. No asking would make me do more than I'm ready to do right now."

"I didn't come here to ask you to help him," she answered. "I came to tell you that Link Jarvis's house in a trap that's set and poisoned for you. Those fellows up there don't know about the Paradise stage, yet; and maybe they wouldn't care so much, even if they did know."

"What has the Paradise stage to do with this?" he asked her. "Except that it took me away from the place where I should have stayed to guard poor Tom!"

"Yeah," she agreed. "It wasn't much of a job. Just the shootin' of a pair of crooks, and the savin' of twenty thousand bucks, and a few lives besides, likely—of course that ain't much of a job for a fellow like you, Larry. But other people are makin' quite a talk about it."

"Tom!" said he. "I want to know about Tom. How is he now? What are they going to do about him?"

"I don't know," said the girl. "I wasn't there in town long after the stage pulled up in coming back down the Paradise road. Tom is well enough, I think. His fever is down. He's only a little weak. They won't do anything to Tom."

Then she pointed down the trail.

"We'd better get out of here, Larry. I've scouted the house, and they've planted men all around it. They've got old Link Jarvis tied up, and they've even gagged him, because he wouldn't stop swearin' and shoutin' at them. Link, he says that if they harm a hair of your head, he'll slaughter them all. You have a way of making people love you, Larry."

"I won't budge," said Lynmouth, "till you tell me the truth about Tom. You're certainly trying to cover something up."

"What difference does it make?" said the girl. "You've done what you could for him. I know that. But you can't help him now!"

"Do you think so?"

"I mean, he'll get out of the jail in a while. They won't do anything to Tom—"

"Cherry," said Lynmouth, "turn up your face."

"I won't. Why should I?"

She tried to rein back her horse, but he caught her firmly, and tilted her face, his hand beneath her chin.

"You're crying about Tom!" said he.

"I'm not," said the girl.

"Then what's wrong?"

"I'm a little nervous—I'm sort of tired—I don't know why."

"Cherry, it's about Tom. Tell me what's happened!"

"Why, there's nothing about Tom. I've simply come up here to tell you to leave the country. It's too hot for you here, Larry. You never can make good again. There's too much just blind hatin' where you're named. Even after the news of the Paradise stage come in, and every one began to buzz and talk, only about half were for you, and half were against, and the half who are against include the fightin' men. Larry, you've got to leave. Trek back over the mountains and never turn your face this way again!"

He hesitated. There was an apparent truth in all that she said. He felt that he had been fighting a losing battle for a long time, and that the best way now might be a new scene, a new name, and then perhaps a new hope in life. He looked toward the mountains.

The rose of the sunset was quite gone, and the pure cold light of the moon grew every moment upon the topmost snows.

"I can't go," said he to himself, and yet aloud.

He turned back to the girl.

"You must go!" said she.

"I want the truth about Tom."

"I tell you, no matter what the truth is, you couldn't help him."

Her voice rose high, then broke in a faint wail.

"What is the truth? Or do I have to go clear to Crooked Horn to find out?"

She stammered at him suddenly:

"I should have known that I couldn't handle you. But this is the truth. The Jarvis shack is one trap for you. The Crooked Horn jail is the other!"

"A trap?"

"They've fair lined it with fighting men—and Jay Cress!"

Lynmouth sighed a little. "I have to meet Jay Cress," he said slowly. "Why not there?"

"Because he's not alone! Because he's not alone! It's

a hopeless thing. Don't you see? Tom is only the bait. They're holding him there in the hope that you'll come in and try to rescue him! It isn't Jay Cress alone. He has four others!"

"What four?" Larry asked tersely.

"You could easily name them," said Cherry.

"No. I haven't heard. Has he hired four men to take care of him?"

"I don't know why he has them—except that they're to help him against you. That's pretty clear! They sit there, waiting, like five watchdogs. They know that you'll try anything, and the more impossible it is, the more sure you are to try. The Paradise stage showed that!"

"Well," Larry said, "I'd like to hear the names of the four."

"You can name them. Who are the worst, hardest, cruelest set that you know about?"

"Why, there's no set. I'd put Happy Joe and that cat, Harrison Riley, somewhere near the top of the list."

"You've named two of them! Now try again!"

"Are they both there?" exclaimed Larry, with a start. "Not both Joe and Riley?"

"Yes, both. Now try some more!"

"Who else? There's that brute with the face of a bear. That one-legged murderer, Peg Leg Sam Dean. I never saw a worse face, and I never met a worse man."

"He's the third."

Lynmouth sighed.

"Who else, Larry?"

"I don't know a fourth to go with them."

"What about little Jud Ogden?"

"Aye," said Lynmouth. "I forgot that bloodthirsty ferret of a man. Not all four of them, Cherry!"

"Yes. All four! You see that it's hopeless?"

32

JUDGE BORE SPEAKS HIS MIND

WHEN William Oliver returned to Crooked Horn on that eventful stage ride, the first thing that he learned, after the astonishment attendant on the arrival of the party had died down, was that Tom Daniels was in jail, and that Mr. Jay Cress had been asked to help protect the prisoner from the rescue which, as all men were willing to swear, Larry Lynmouth was sure to attempt.

Crooked Horn rarely took itself seriously as a political unit, but now a meeting was called by Rancher Bore, who was also Judge Bore.

The judge was one of the best men in the world. He was the best neighbor, the truest friend, the most cheerful companion, the bravest fighter, the most faithful husband, the most devoted father. He ran his ranch with liberality, and yet with success. He had every Western virtue of uttermost hospitality; and it was said that Judge Bore would go ten miles to pat a sick dog on the head.

But he had two weaknesses. One was for the law. One was for speechmaking.

Whether he stretched himself on his legs and looked down his nose at a long Thanksgiving or Christmas dinner table; or whether he stood on a platform beside a table on which to rest his hand and a pitcher of water; or sat behind his official and judicial desk, with an ear wisely canted, listening to testimony, and ready to pronounce sentence, Mr. Bore dearly loved to hear the sound of his own voice whenever the occasion rose.

If the occasion did not rise, he was apt to help it to its feet. As for the law, he knew that his understanding of it was limited, but he was always able to make up his mind before the testimony was so much as opened in the court, so that it hardly mattered to him what was said by the witnesses or the opposing attorneys. To these people he maintained an attitude as polite as possible, but it was plain that he saw through everything to the heart, and in all his career, there never had been a jury which had disobeyed his orders. Instructions they could not be called.

This day was important for several reasons.

In the first place, Tom Daniels had been brought in a captive by several of Sheriff Anthony's deputies.

In the second place, the Paradise stage had returned, literally dripping with red.

In the third place, the judge felt his very heart yearning toward a speech.

A speech came upon him as a poem comes upon the poet, rather as a swelling of the heart and a lighting of the mind than as an actual idea. He felt the emotion before he saw the words, but old experience taught him that the words would not fail to come. Therefore, he called a meeting.

The children were happily turned out of the schoolhouse, and the greater part of the population of Crooked Horn was turned in. They sat in the little desks with cramped knees, and with stern faces, and with hearts ready to be entertained. There were more than the room was able to seat. The men got up and said:

"Here you are, Mrs. Smith. I done enough sittin' already to last me a lifetime." Or, "Hullo, Minnie. C'mon and sit down here. I wanta stretch."

The ladies were seated. In Crooked Horn, they took a large share in the public life. It was a sign that the town was progressive.

Of course, Judge Bore was presiding at the teacher's desk. And he felt as much at home as though he were in his own dining room or courtroom. Joy swelled in him. But he forced himself to be grave. His pleasure showed itself in those kind smiles which made people love him, as he looked from one friendly face to another.

Everything began with a speech. Bore, of course, made it. He began on a minor note:

"My dear fellow citizens, or let me put it more directly —my dear neighbors and my dear friends, for friends and neighbors we all are, two important events caused this meeting to be called."

He drew his breath. Then he lowered his voice, an effect which he loved to produce saying:

"My dear friends, scoundrels have dishonored Crooked Horn, robbed her citizens, blocked her roads, broken her jails, and murdered her men. Only one of them has been captured. One of them is still at large!"

He said this with such a soft impressiveness that some of the ladies looked apprehensively over their shoulders toward the open windows, hoping that the dangerous open air would not hear these things. The men forgot the cramps in their knees. They leaned forward and set their teeth. They would show the scoundrels! Only—who were they?

"I refer," said Judge Bore, "to the highwayman and thief, the cheat and traitor, the robber and man slayer, Larry Lynmouth!"

People drew in their breaths.

The judge went on, feeling them all in the hollow of his hand:

"The brave man when it comes to weaklings and children, the coward when he meets his match!

As he said this, he rose from his chair and pointed.

All heads turned. There was a flash of white and a glitter of eyes toward a place where a small, pale man leaned against the wall.

It was Jay Cress!

There was a murmur of interest and applause.

Jay Cress looked down and cleared his throat. He was embarrassed. Some people swore that he blushed, but this was an exaggeration. But they all looked at him with an affectionate familiarity and fondness, somewhat as freshmen look upon their college hero who won the big game of last year with a ninety-yard run in the last ten seconds of play. To be merely in the room with him was enough.

The ladies had tears in their eyes, for ladies love men who are slightly wicked, or even more than slightly. And Jay Cress was a gambler! It was said that fortunes had passed through his hands. Nerves of steel, unperturbed as millions flowed and ebbed on the gaming table! They thought of him, too, as a matter of course, as the great hero, standing small but terrible before that formidable name and face—Larry Lynmouth.

In this manner that group looked upon the gambler, and well the gambler knew it. But he was able to bow his head, and not call up a blush. Fame had ceased to be an ambition to him. It had become a necessity, like his daily bread.

When Judge Bore saw that he had made a crashing point, he went on with the main thread of his speech. That is to say, he went on with the main current of his words, for a connected thread rarely appeared in his discourses. It was true that he had a certain number of "whereases," but the "therefores" usually did not appear.

He said that the time had come when Crooked Horn was no longer to be disgraced among the cities of the fair West. He said something about the noble eagle spreading its wings in the sunset of something or other, and the terrible song of her battle cry shrilling forth something or other else. In one fist it appeared that the eagle of America, the bald-headed glory, was holding the dastardly robber, Tom Daniels. In the other set of claws they, the citizens of the good town of Crooked Horn, would forthwith place the other evildoer, the chief miscreant, the wretch whose name haunted the minds of all men, et cetera, et cetera, Larry Lynmouth!

If this should not happen, it further appeared from the moving discourse of Mr. Bore that no man could sleep peacefully in his bed, and no man could quietly sit down to enjoy the fruits of his daily labor. Furthermore, little children dared not venture innocently forth on their way to school, nor must they loiter by the roadside to pick the daisies on their way home. Not only was this true, but shame would sit in every bosom, and a stinging taunt of cowardice, and inefficiency, and treason, would be hurled in the face of poor, suffering Crooked Horn by all its smug-faced neighbors.

On the other hand, if Larry Lynmouth were brought back "loaded with chains and opprobrium, as of right he should be," then all would be well. It seemed that, in this case, the land would pour forth its fruits with unstinted hand, and the children would gambol off to school like jolly sheep, and every one would be good, happy, and virtuous. Even the before-mentioned eagle would be appeased, and, rising through the golden and crimson clouds of its glorious sky, would wheel on enormous circling pinions above the happy homes of the free and the brave, et cetera, et cetera.

It was a stirring peroration.

Judge Bore got himself into a good, healthy perspiration sawing the air about it. It was truly a stirring sight to see him land upon the thin air of wickedness all manner of right crosses, full-arm swings, lifting uppercuts, overhand crushers, side-slashers, jolts, and jars. He tore evil apart and trampled it underfoot, and if the stock of Larry Lynmouth had been par when that speech began, shares in him would have been exchanged for a stick of peppermint candy when the good judge had ended.

He waited a little, panting, and he got his applause in a roar. He raised a hand for silence. They roared still louder. He raised both hands. They whooped and yelled.

He said "No, no!" with his rather fat lips several times, and appeared annoyed, and was so—as much as any actor taking curtain calls.

At last he had a chance to speak, but he had hardly declared, "If the assembly is in general agreement with me as to how—" when Rancher Tom Calkins broke out loudly:

"Look at here, Bore—that was the outstandin'est speech that I ever heard you make!"

The applause broke out again, while Judge Bore vainly, bitterly protested, and waved both hands in the air and shook his head until his plump cheeks quivered.

No matter what came of this, it was a personal triumph for him. The House of Representatives seemed to Judge Bore, at that moment, no further away than the stoop of the school house; and the United States Senate was by no means an unattainable goal!

After this, he gradually managed to get silence restored, although a good many of the ladies were still smiling shaking their heads and looking at the judge through actual tears of admiration. But finally the business of the meeting could be resumed, when Hackett, the assistant district attorney—more assistant than attorney, some one had once rudely said—got up and made a matter-of-fact talk, in which he seconded all of the proposals of the judge. He floated a while on the shining wake of the speech of Bore. Then he stated that they ought to do two things—authorize the sheriff to comb the whole countryside with a fine-toothed comb for the purpose of securing the person of the desired malefactor, and place ample funds in his hands for the hiring of extensive posses; on the other hand, they should place the prisoner, Tom Daniels, partner of the chief criminal, in the capable care of that celebrated and popular supporter of the law.

Hackett was learning from the judge.

He made a point now almost as good as that of the judge by extending his hand toward Jay Cress, and refraining from naming him. There was a great deal of applause again. People enjoyed turning to Cress and nodding and smiling at him, while they smote their hands together.

A wave of silence began to extend from around a form newly risen from one of the school benches. That silence was rather icy. It froze out applause and turned smiles to marble. It was William Oliver who stood there, waiting for a chance to speak.

33

THUMBS DOWN!

THOSE people knew Oliver, and respected him.

They did not exactly love him because bankers are not often loved in big cities, and are even apt to be hated in small ones. For there is no pleasure in borrowing to be compared with the pain of repaying—with interest. William Oliver was as fair and true and straightforward as steel. He was also on occasion just as hard. He had an edge that had cut certain men to the heart. He had had five bullets fired at him point-blank. He bore the scars of two of them. Mutterers at such places as the veranda in front of the hotel, and loungers in the bars of the town, were apt to shake their heads darkly when the name of the banker was presented to their attention. It is always easy to appear to know more than one cares to speak. There were quantities of people who were ready to adopt that attitude toward the subject of William Oliver. Nevertheless, as before said, he was respected, and even the most reluctant had to admit that he was a good and open-handed citizen, and worth almost any ten others to Crooked Horn. His unboasted and unpublished charities, for one thing, gradually were becoming known. So they listened to him now.

He said: "May I ask a few questions?"

Debaters love questions; orators hate them. Judge Bore was an orator, still panting from his peroration. But he had to say that of course he would be glad to have questions put, and would answer them as well as he could.

"Larry Lynmouth has broken jail in this town," said the banker. "Will you tell me what other crimes he has committed?"

"The detestable crime of attempted manslaughter, for which he was accused, tried by process of law, and convicted," said Judge Bore, "is one."

He was proud of that sentence.

"That crime," said the banker, "is denied by Lew Daniels, the so-called victim of the fight. He and his father and mother and his sister are filling the town paper in Jackson Ford with demands for the reopening of the trial. They declare that they have good evidence to produce."

"What sort of evidence?" asked the judge, with a beetling frown.

He began to wish the banker never had entered that room.

"Evidence on their own oath that Lew Daniels came here seeking the fight, and forced it on Lynmouth. Evidence that Cherry Daniels went to Larry Lynmouth and begged him to let her brother off lightly. And that in return he actually consented to leave the town and avoid the fight."

The judge looked around the room and blinked. He searched for sympathy, and he found it. To the crowd, it was not a matter of right or wrong of Larry Lynmouth.

It was a debate between Bore and the banker, and there was no doubt as to which was the more popular man. Feverishly they waited for the judge's answer. They leaned toward him, and they stared with frowning hostility toward Oliver.

"This is saying a great deal, Mr. Oliver," said the judge.

The crowd sighed with relief. They had not exactly seen how the judge would answer things that were rather generally guessed to be true. This answer had dignity and restraint, even though it did not reply to much. The thrust had been dodged, if not parried.

The banker went on in the same quiet and logical, unemotional manner.

He said: "Aside from the presumed guilt of this man in the Daniels affair, what other crimes are charged against him?"

"His whole life has been one long crime!" thundered the judge.

It was a point—a veritable point! The crowd burst into tumultuous applause, and then waited breathless for the rejoinder of Oliver.

To their surprise, he did not seem at all upset.

He merely said: "He has received legal pardons for every wrongdoing up to the date on which he met Daniels. Does any one deny it?"

The judge was at a loss. So was every one else.

Said Judge Bore: "Are you retained by Larry Lynmouth to defend him here, sir?"

A good, heavy question, felt the listeners, and nodded their heads.

"I am here," said the banker in his usual unmoved tone, "to defend our public decency and good sense. I'm here to prevent a wrong, if I can."

"What wrong, sir, what wrong?" thundered the judge.

It was useless to thunder at Oliver. Other men had thundered at him before—with guns, even.

"The wrong of persecuting a man who may be trying to live a decent life."

Judge Bore had a gift almost as great as his power of eloquence. He had laughter at command, and he commanded it now. A good, throat-filling laughter that rang and rerang through the room, and in which the crowd spontaneously joined. An ocean of mirth roared against the ceiling, burst out the windows.

"A decent life, indeed!" said the judge, and wiped his eyes.

Then he rapped his knuckles on the desk, as though partly calling for order and partly asking Oliver to talk sense.

"There are at least fifty men who will swear that they have been robbed, assaulted, victimized, within the past few weeks by that arch-scoundrel, Lynmouth, and the poor boy whom he has corrupted—Tom Daniels!"

Every one murmured. There was an impatient stir. How long was Oliver to take up their good time with his follies?

"I suppose," said Oliver, as calmly as ever, "that at least twenty-five of the fifty are now in this room."

This caused a good deal of craning about and nodding, here and there.

"Is there one man among those witnesses who definitely saw the face or recognized the voice of either Tom Daniels or Larry Lynmouth?" asked William Oliver.

"In the law——" began the judge.

Oliver raised his hand, and even Bore was silent.

"I am not asking you that question," said Oliver, "because I don't believe that you claim to have been hurt in your own pocketbook by Lynmouth. I'm asking what other man dares to say that he identified Larry Lynmouth?"

That "dares to say" had the weight of a blow and the sting of a whiplash. It took away the breath. Certain faces grew crimson. They were the faces of men who had accused Lynmouth and Daniels. Then spoke the nasal, drawling voice of Lynn Hopkins.

"I never said nothin' except that I was robbed by a couple of gents, and one was bigger than the other, and they kind of had the cut of Lynmouth and Daniels. That's all I said. Everybody knew they was on the road!"

People murmured contentedly. Honest Lynn Hopkins! His very drawl was a testimonial in his favor.

"Everybody suspected; but what did any one know?" asked Oliver.

He turned his head slowly. He surveyed all those faces.

"I was in the Paradise coach, today," said he. "We were stopped, as you know, by two masked men. They even had two horses, we learned, of the general appearance of Lynmouth's famous mare, Fortune, and Tom Daniels' mount. Every man and woman in that stage would have been willing to swear—and I include myself—that we were stopped and nearly tipped over the cliff by the two arch-ruffians, Lynmouth and Daniels."

People listened breathlessly. The judge looked down and chewed his lip, searching for an answer to what he knew was coming. He wished to appear bland. He merely appeared blank.

"We all would have sworn that our lives had been endangered by the pair. But it happened that one of the passengers was not quite what he seemed. He was a hunted man. He was a man loaded down with opprobrium against which he could not defend himself. He had seen rascals slipping out onto the road and masquerading as himself and his friend. This friend was now a very sick lad. And the hunted man left him, as he thought, in a secure place, and came out to unmask the scoundrelism of which he had become the victim. He put himself in imminent danger. He rode with us to the scene of the holdup. He saw us stretched helpless in the brush."

Here, although not an orator, Mr. Oliver paused, but no one interrupted him. He continued in his grave, quiet way:

"Then our extra passenger jumped into action, and it was such action as I wish you could have been present to see, Judge Bore."

The judge stiffened suddenly. He interlocked his fingers, and twirled the thumbs. He pulled back his head until his first and second double chins disappeared behind his collar. He was being judicially attentive, fair, but a little dubious.

"Our extra passenger was encumbered by a long linen duster," continued Oliver. "But he stepped a little faster than a frightened cat. He shot down the two bandits. Yes he did not shoot to kill. There was no murder in him, Judge Bore. He was simply trying to defend his injured reputation, you see. He risked his life again, in order to put those fellows down without killing them. He saved the horses, which were in a murderous tangle. And then, instead of waiting for thanks, he went off on the horse of one of the masqueraders."

Still Oliver was not done. He finished:

"This notorious thief and villain then turned loose the horse of the bandit, and I believe that the animal has just come into town.

"Now, then, Judge Bore, I have pointed out one definite and true fact which will be to the credit of Mr. Lynmouth. I want to know what man, woman, or child can point out a single other fact against him, in order to justify the tiger hunt and slaughter with which you are proposing to sweep the country at the present moment? That is all I have to say."

But he remained on his feet, turning gradually, slowly, from face to face, and receiving not a sign of an answer.

Instead, he found all eyes fixed upon the judge, expecting him to be their champion.

"Gentlemen, and my dear Mr. Oliver," said the judge, desperately cornered, but suddenly equipped with a thought, "there is such a thing as public opinion. I thank Heaven. It is above evidence. Public opinion did not wait to be logical. It rose in its instinctive might and freed the thirteen young colonies from the vicious grasp of the mother country. Public opinion is the great instrument which organized our liberty, created our law, maintained our Union, banished slavery and chains, and to this moment supports and strengthens the hands of the law. Without public opinion what is law? It is tyranny! With it, the law marches forward in a brilliant light.

"You ask me for an answer, Mr. Oliver! Here are my answers!"

At this, he stretched out both his hands toward the eager faces in the crowd.

"The honest women and the brave men who have met here today," said he, "because they feel that Larry Lynmouth is a public danger, a public disgrace—they are my answer to you, Mr. Oliver! Do you find enough of them? Do you find any fault with them?"

Mr. Oliver surveyed them without either conviction or

admiration in his eye. Then he turned on his heel and left the schoolroom.

Thunderous applause for the judge followed.

But it left Judge Bore a little retrospective. He knew that he had won, but the doors of the United States Senate seemed to be in the more shadowy distance just now. He felt that it might be a costly victory.

34

DARK AND FAIR

As William Oliver had striven to the utmost of his strength against public opinion and Judge Bore for the sake of the outcast, his daughter endured a trial in the same cause, lost as it was. She had lain down in her room behind drawn, dusky shutters. But she did not relax. With her arms thrown wide, and her hands gripped hard, she looked up at the ceiling and felt again the iron grip which had lifted her from her seat to safety. And again she saw the bowed and swaying form of the invalid in the linen duster.

She answered a tapping at her door and a Mexican house *moza* came in with word that a certain Señorita Daniels was waiting below to see her. That name went through the brain of Kate Oliver with an electric thrill of pain.

People were saying strange things about the Daniels family and their devotion to gun-fighting Larry Lynmouth. They said that Tom Daniels was as willing to die as to go to prison for the sake of the outlaw. They said that Cherry Daniels herself rode out in whatever way she could to help the hunted man. Cherry was young and pretty, moreover, said the same flying rumors. She would not believe it. She had her own opinion of creatures who would throw themselves without shame in the path of a man. She sat straight up on her bed.

"Tell her that I'm not home—that I can't see her!" she exclaimed.

The *moza* drew the door shut.

Then Kate Oliver leaped from the bed and raced to throw the door open. The pulse of its breath fanned her face and lifted the hair along her shoulders.

The servant stood immediately before her. She had not stirred a step, and her smoky eyes looked with somber interest upon her young mistress.

It was almost as though she knew that she would be recalled before she had time to begin the delivery of her message. Kate Oliver felt half shamed, but her excitement still held her.

"Tell Miss Daniels that I'll be down at once," she said. "No, no—ask her to come up here at once."

She closed the door, amazed at herself. There was a fierce pulse in her temples. She felt that her face was hot, and glancing at herself in the mirror, she hardly recognized her flushed cheeks and her gleaming eyes.

She slid her arms into a dressing gown. She gathered her bright hair into one massive, carelessly twisted coil, and then the door was opened for Cherry Daniels, just as Kate Oliver was pushing the shutters wide.

In came a thrust of sunshine that set dancing ten million dusty motes. Half the room blazed; half was left in dusk; and in the flame of the sun stood Cherry Daniels.

Kate Oliver, gathering her gown at the breast, and staring, felt that the stranger could stand the full brilliance of the sun. She was made for it, to endure and thrive in its heat. Her rich olive skin would not shrivel or darken in the hottest August day on the desert. Her black eye would not grow dusty with fatigue in no matter how many miles of wild riding. She looked like a young Indian, with the smile of the wilderness still on her lips and freedom in her eyes. She was shorter and even slighter than Kate Oliver, but in the poise of her head and the tilt of the chin there was something that made the banker's daughter feel slight and frail.

Cherry Daniels closed the door behind her and, like a man, took the broad-brimmed hat from her head. The red mark of the heavy band crossed her brow.

"I'm Cherry Daniels," said she, and then struck straight

home. "I've come here to talk to you a little about Larry Lynmouth."

To Kate Oliver there was something brutally crude and harsh about this direct statement. At the same moment, it weakened her knees and took her breath. She managed to offer a chair, and to take the hat of the girl. Cherry Daniels sat down, slim, erect, her dark eyes steadily upon the face of Kate Oliver.

"Or maybe you guessed right off that I'd come about him," she went on.

"I didn't know," said Kate foolishly. "I only—that is—"

"Don't get yourself all tangled up," said the other. "The way of this is that Larry's in hot water. I want to help him. Do you?"

Once again it was a bludgeon stroke of frankness from which Kate winced.

"Yes," she said. "I do."

She sat down, but gingerly, watching this lithe, brown-faced youngster as though in terror of fire.

Pretty?

She would have been glad if she could have dismissed the face of Cherry with such a weak word. But no. There was rare charm, beauty. She tried, suddenly, to imagine a man who might not find this wild girl enchanting; but all the world of men seemed empty.

"You want to help him," said Cherry. "That's a good start. But how much do you want to help?"

"Yesterday he saved my life," answered the girl. "My father's life, too."

"Yeah," said Cherry Daniels, with slangy indifference. "I know about the stagecoach. You'd never turn him away on a cold night if he come and battered at your door. That what you mean? Or d'you mean that you'd do something for him?"

Kate Oliver said nothing. There was a tremor in her throat. She dared not trust the steadiness of her voice.

"I mean to say," went on Cherry, "that I've been trying to figger out why Larry should stick so close to Crooked Horn. He's never had a square deal, here. All they want to give him here is a rope around the neck. He's got no old friends in this town. They want his hide here, and that's all. Am I wrong?"

Still Kate did not answer. And still, for an unknown reason, she grew more and more afraid of this terribly direct girl.

"Of course I hit on the answer," went on Cherry Daniels. "It's you. Am I wrong?" She did not wait. She said simply: "Does he mean a lot to you?"

Her hostess could merely stammer. And, to put her at her ease, Cherry continued:

"I ask because he's about all that I can see inside the rim of any one sky at a time. He's the tallest and the straightest that I've ever seen, the squarest shooter, and the best pal. I'd give a hand to get a smile from him; but all I could ever get out of him was politeness."

She smiled again, but Kate Oliver could guess that there was profound meaning under her light manner of speech.

"I've tried to get him away from Crooked Horn," said Cherry. "And if he'd turn, I'd go barefoot to keep him company. I've tried to let him see that, too. But a man can sure be blind when he don't want to see."

Breathlessly, Kate Oliver listened.

Cherry Daniels had, as the gamblers' saying is, laid her cards upon the table, and now Kate saw that something of the same kind was expected of her. The position was made clearer and clearer.

"I know," said the other girl, "where Larry will be this evenin', near to Crooked Horn. Would you go there and meet him and try to turn him away?"

"If I could influence him—" began Kate, and stuck there. Her terror had grown. She felt that she was beyond her depth—that the water was closing above her lips.

"I dunno," said the visitor. "Maybe you couldn't. But he might turn away if you'd go with him."

"What do you mean?"

Cherry leaned forward and studied Kate Oliver.

"Yeah, you know what I mean," she said. "I don't mean to go as far as a minister's with him, and then leave him in the lurch. I mean, to go and keep right on riding with him, whether he goes up or down. I've talked to you straight; will you talk straight to me?"

"How can I tell that I would influence him at all?" asked Kate.

"I can tell," said Cherry, nodding critically. "Black hair and black eyes don't go as far as the yellow and blue. Can't be seen as well. Don't light up as well. The blondes are the ones that make the little boys open their eyes, and the big boys, too. I've been half a minute from bleachin' my hair ten times in my life. But never so near as I am while I sit here and look at you."

The flattery in this speech fell almost unheeded upon the ears of Kate Oliver. She felt a profound respect for this girl, and a pity for her, too; because she could guess that she was hearing the truth, and that the cause of poor Cherry Daniels was lost indeed. But her own problem was taking her by the throat.

Now who saw not poor Cherry Daniels, but as through the screen of the front door, the face of Larry Lynmouth, when she had confronted him and denied him in a horror of shame.

Cherry seemed to mistake this silence.

"It's the Jay Cress business that stops you," she said. "Well, it never would stop me. I can't explain it. I don't have to have it explained. Can't you feel that way, too?"

Kate tried to find words, but she could not.

"If there never was a thing before, in his life," said Cherry Daniels, "he's done enough since to show what he'd made of. He's tied all of Crooked Horn into knots. He's met my brother and dropped him—shot the guns out of his hands. Did that take nerve? I think it did! Could Jay Cress show the same? I don't think he could. What happened to Larry when he met Cress? Well, I don't know. Hypnotism. I've thought of that. Have you?"

"No," said Kate faintly. "Not till this moment!"

Cherry Daniels stood up.

"I've got no right to press you for any answer," she said. "I don't suppose that I've got any right to persuade you. But I know that if you don't do something, nothing else can ever make Larry turn back from Crooked Horn."

"Why is he coming?"

"He's coming to set my poor brother Tom free. Account of Lew, he's been outlawed again. Account of Tom, he'll get himself shot to pieces—"

Her voice trembled away to silence. She blinked, and then she continued with a wonderful steadiness:

"I'm going to wait for you on the rim of the town, beyond the sheriff's house. You know the poplars there?"

"Yes," said Kate faintly.

The darkness of the trees in prospect possessed her with fear once more.

"I'll wait for you there along about sunset, or a shade after. That'll be the best time. Will you come along with me? No, don't you answer me now. Wait till you're alone. I reckon that before long, you'll be holdin' your breath and dead anxious for that sunset to come. If you ain't—then Heaven help Larry Lynmouth!"

35

TWO GIRLS RIDE

ALL in one rush the rest of the day went by for Kate Oliver.

It was a fierce debate in which she prayed for more and more time, so that she could find the proper answer, all the while knowing that time alone would not answer it, for the inevitable darkness was coming, and the broad sun was rolling down toward the western horizon like a great wheel. It bulged. It turned crimson. It magnified in size, and still she was walking hurriedly up and down in her room, debating.

If she went, could she dare to tell him that she loved him, and that she would really follow him to the ends of the world?

She remembered, again, the sick horror with which she had heard the ghastly tale of Jay Cress and the humiliation of her lover. The same sick wave swept over her again and left her cold. For she had loved him as a master of men, and she had denied him as a weakling and a traitor to his fame.

Then she thought of Cherry Daniels, and her bright, resolute eyes. She, at least, never would be untrue to a great devotion. She was rather one to nail the colors to the mast and go down with the ship. This comparison shamed the girl.

Then she remembered her father, and, sitting down suddenly by the window, she told herself that she would never be able to go. At that very moment she heard his footstep coming up the walk to the front door, and she ran down to meet him.

She found him coldly reserved, drawn into the heart of some inward trouble

Then he said to her:

"They're organizing Crooked Horn like an army to capture Larry Lynmouth."

She said nothing, but drew back a little into the shadow near the door. The sun was almost down.

"You cared about him once, Kate," said the father. "Are you really made of ice, my dear? I've tried to talk to them. That bull-faced idiot, Bore, was in a speechmaking humor, and all he could think about was Lynmouth's crimes. What crimes? They won't listen to reason. I tell you, ten good men in a group can be as evil and as cruel as any one criminal! But you don't care," he added, almost bitterly, as she stood silent, still. "Oh, you women are made of stone! It takes brass buttons and a brass band to melt your hearts!"

He strode into the house and let the screen door slam with a metallic jingle behind him.

But Kate remained outside, head bent, looking down the avenue of trees, now thinly flooded with the dusk of the evening.

She tried to think. She tried to ask a question of her heart, but all remained a blur and a jumble, except the thought of Cherry Daniels waiting there among the darkening poplars beyond the sheriff's house. So her own life, it seemed to Kate, was darkening.

Death would come to Larry Lynmouth. Or else, having achieved that romantic and impossible deed of freeing Tom Daniels from the law, he would be off into the wilderness with beautiful Cherry Daniels.

Beautiful Cherry—and how beautiful she was, how loyal and how brave, without a selfish thought, with the courage of a man, and the great heart of a child!

Now, as the eyes of Kate grew dim with tears, from the kitchen window she heard a shrill whistle piping, and the theme of it pierced her ears and reached her heart.

> "What made the ball so fine?
>   Robin Adair!
> What made the assembly shine?
>   Robin Adair!"

She listened with bated breath.

And then all her heart rushed out to Larry Lynmouth. Her doubts were scattered suddenly. She turned into the house, and, hurrying to her room, she changed quickly into a riding dress, and went out hatless to the stable.

There she saddled her fastest, although not her surest, horse. The result was five minutes of frantic pitching, which she barely managed to sit out. Yet at last the bucking ceased, and, avoiding the drive past the front of the house, she headed across the pasture trail.

A loud, distant voice called after her:

"Kate, Kate! Where are you going?"

With the speed of her gallop that voice was blurred and faded behind her, but a guilty shudder passed through her body. For she knew that it had been her father who had called after her.

She went on at high speed. She jumped the fence, waded the creek, labored up the slope, and made the standing horse jump the fence on the farther side.

As she went on, she knew that she had done a thing which she never would have ventured on in the sanity of daylight. But now it seemed nothing. She judged; she did not feel the danger.

She was galloping across a wide field. The smell of tarweed was rank and pungent; it swished like water around the sweeping hoofs of the good horse. Then trees rushed like wind around her, and out under the red-stained sky she broke again.

She could see a light to her left. That was the sheriff's house, of course. Chick Anthony was an old acquaintance—a friend, even. But he was not her friend on this night, because she was riding outside the law. At the thought of this, and of his wife's pinched, tiresome face, she felt a new sense of wonder.

For it was she, Kate Oliver, who was doing this thing!

She could remember whispers that had buzzed not too softly around her. Other girls were wild and did wild things. But safe Kate Oliver, gentle Kate Oliver, sweet Kate Oliver, kind and good Kate Oliver—she could be trusted as safely as the rising of the sun and the setting thereof.

She felt that her old self was whirling away on either hand with the flying trees and melting into a blown smoke behind her. She went on, riding with a good pull, because the horse felt his oats and came strongly on the bit. He ran nervously, enjoying his own speed, but afraid of the night. But there was no fear in him like the fear that came up in the girl when she saw before her the poplar trees standing closely together, shoulder to shoulder, and in the last daylight their leaves winking like dull steel.

She took a pull and brought the horse back to a slow gallop, back to a lope. She could realize then how fast she had been flying. Her face burned from the friction of the air.

She was almost on the verge of the trees when she saw a dark form on a dark horse, motionless beneath the shadow. Instinctively she drew aslant from that point. For it did not seem that any woman could have the courage to wait there under the wing of the shadow, with the grim night thickening, and stealthy danger whispering through the evening air.

Then she saw that the rider was small, and the horse small also. Suddenly she knew that it was Cherry Daniels, and swung in toward her.

She felt a new wonder, then.

Cherry Daniels, brisk, keen, fresh, and vital, was there to lead a rival out to find the man she loved. Cherry Daniel's giving her heart away for the sake of a selfish affection. It made Kate look inward not for the first time, but for the first time with a glance that went to the core of her heart. She saw herself against a horizon of blazing light as a dim, misty creature, never very bad, never capable of badness; never very good, cither, because incapable of goodness.

Then she drew up beside her guide.

"I'm late!" she gasped.

"You?" said Cherry, calmly surprised. "No, you're right on the dot."

"Let's hurry on," said Kate.

"What's the hurry?"

"I'll have to get back."

"Maybe you'll never get back."

Kate checked her horse to a full stop. "Never go back?" she asked.

"No, maybe not. Are you afraid of that?"

"Never go back!" gasped Kate.

"You gotta throw your hat in the ring and go in after it, tonight," said Cherry. "There ain't such a thing as being halfway, if you're to deal with Larry Lynmouth."

"No," said Kate. "No—I see. Otherwise, I'd never persuade him."

"He's as crafty as a fox. He's likely to read your mind, anyway," said Cherry.

"Let's go on," breathed Kate.

"Take it easy," suggested Cherry. "Take it easy and make up your mind. You got your lines ready?"

"What lines?"

"Why, it'll have to be like a play. You think that just appearing will be enough. No, it won't. You'll have to talk. He's got a head on him, and you'll have to talk to that."

"I can say—"

"Sure," said Cherry, filling in the pause generously. "You can say that you can't live without him, but you'll have to talk about Tom. You'll have to talk about my brother. I've tried. But I'm Tom's sister, and don't count, anyway. You'll have to point out that there ain't any proof against Tom, and he'll be sure to get off at his trial, anyway, and that taking him out of the jail is only making him sure to get to prison, or a lead diet, pretty soon. You'll have to talk about Tom. Maybe he'll listen to you if you talk hard and fast enough. I don't know. You'll have to think up the ways of persuadin', and they'll have to be good ways, if you're to turn him back from Crooked Horn."

"I'll try to think—I—my head's swimming, Cherry."

"Well, you start off by having no father, no mother, no home, no nothing except Larry Lynmouth. If you can look at him and tell yourself that he's heaven, and life, and a happy home, all wrapped up in one man, for you— then you might be able to persuade him. Is he those things to you?"

"I don't know. I seem to be a new person tonight, and I'm not sure of myself."

"He's sure of himself," said Cherry. "He's as cold and as hard as steel, right now. You make up your mind. He's down there in that old deserted shack in the hollow, there, where Bud Newton and Paul Bright used to live. You can see it from here."

Kate could, very dimly, for the sky was darkening fast, and the moon was not yet up. Then it seemed to the girl that the pungent fragrance of the tarweed was speaking to her, and the whisper in the evening wind. Doubt left her. She saw her lover with more than the light of day.

But was he still her lover?

"You're not stopping, Cherry?" she said. "Must I go all alone?"

"Yeah," drawled Cherry Daniels. "I reckon that I won't be much use, after this far. I'm only good to show you the way."

She laughed, softly, and the laughter broke off on a note that wrenched the heart of Kate Oliver. Yet she had judgment enough to say no more, but let the horse follow its own lead, and it went with cautiously pricking ears straight toward the little hut that was located in the hollow, blind as it was with darkness.

36

FAILURE

As KATE came nearer, the shack grew larger to her eye. She could see the sag of the roof line, and the crooked twist of the stovepipe, but she was very close before she made out a horse cropping the grass near by, with an empty saddle on its back.

Her own mount went slower and slower, picking up its feet cautiously, as though it were treading upon marshland. Then a low voice called from the shadows:

"Is that you, Cherry?"

She found that she could not answer. Her horse halted with a jerk, trembled, and stiffened its muscles for a spring away. It seemed to instantly recognize danger, and fear, certainly, was in her also.

A form detached itself from the dark of the shack and came toward Kate. It reached the head of her horse and stretched a hand out. Suddenly the horse relaxed and was still.

"Kate!" said Larry Lynmouth.

She tried to find the words which Cherry Daniels had told her to rehearse, but they were lost in a spinning mist. She heard him asking her why she had come, and found still that her tongue was lost. He became silent in turn. For an eternity of some seconds she remained there in the saddle, looking down at the black silhouette of his head and strong shoulders, seeing no feature of his face, but, nevertheless, looking into him as she never had done before. She thought that now she could see in him the wildness of a child, the folly of a child also.

But that was not all. He was to other men as a thoroughbred to plow horses; and for that very reason, no doubt, they hated him. She saw him again as he had been at the dance, long ago, laughing, loving danger.

Other men would have kept on talking, to make it easier for her, but Lynmouth was waiting still.

She slipped from the saddle. The darkness, then, seemed to sweep up from the ground and swallow her; the head and shoulders of the outlaw towered above her.

"Cherry brought you here?" asked Lynmouth.

"Yes," she answered, and even with the speaking of that one word, she felt easier. Speech became possible.

"What on earth possessed her?" asked he.

"She thought I might persuade you to go home with me."

"What do you mean, Kate? To your home?"

"No," she replied. "To our home."

"Do you mean that you're coming to me, Kate?"

"Yes, if you'll have me."

She grew tense, as she said it, for the other Larry Lynmouth would, at that, have had her instantly in his arms; but this new man merely made a pause before he answered:

"It's a fine, brave thing, to come out to me like this. I suppose I understand it, too. It's to keep me from trying to help Tom—to keep me out of the trap, you'd say?"

"You wouldn't be helping him," she explained. "You never could reach him—not even you!"

"Are you sure of that?"

"Yes, yes, sure! They've raised the town, Larry dear. They've got together the fighting men. Jay Cress is there—"

Her voice caught.

"That's all right," replied Lynmouth calmly. "His name is no terror to me. Jay Cress and his four, I suppose?"

"Yes. Such men as I've never seen before. And Chick Anthony is back again, furious because he wasn't able to catch you at the Jarvis place. You see, they all understand that you'll risk anything to get Tom Daniels free. And knowing that you'll try even the impossible, they're steady and prepared for your coming—they expect you this very night!"

"I knew most of that before," said he.

"And still you came on?"

"You see that I'm here."

"Will you tell me what Tom Daniels can gain, Larry? They have no proof against him, and they'll set him free at his trial."

"They had no proof against me," answered Lynmouth. "But they were ready with their prison sentence."

"They hated you. They don't hate Tom Daniels."

"I would trust the law," said the robber, "as I'd trust a pack of dogs. They're safe when they've eaten themselves fat. The law has to eat men, and just now there's an appetite in Crooked Horn for the Daniels-Lynmouth brand."

"If he's taken out, he's outlawed," she said.

"If he's left in, he'll be put in the penitentiary."

"And even if he were, for a little while, he's young."

"It isn't the time; it's the poison of the penitentiary that counts," said he.

Kate felt herself half beaten before her argument had well begun. Tears came into her eyes.

"Will you please let me talk to you on my own account, Larry?" she asked him.

She heard him sigh. "Let me tell you what you're going to say," he suggested. Then he went on, taking her pause as permission:

"You're going to say that you and I should be married. Is that it, Kate?"

"Yes," she murmured.

"Then we should gallop off together, it hardly matters where?"

"Yes, yes," said the girl. And she moved a little closer to him.

The level, steady voice stopped her again.

"The trouble is, that there has to be an ending to every journey, Kate. That's the curse of being young and trying to be happy. That is, of trying to be free and happy. There's no freedom. I begin to see that. One man can be free for a little while, but if he's free, he's bound to be lonely. Even friendship is a bondage, in a sense. And people living in their towns and cities, they hate the outsider who dares to pretend to be happy by himself. But they're right. There's no real happiness except in company with other folks. Finally, a man has to marry, have children. And how can he raise them in a desert? They have a right to belong to the herd if they care to. And if they stay away too long, they'll be misjudged when they try to return, as I was misjudged by every one—even by your father and by you."

"We've repented, Larry," said she. "My father is trying with all his might to change the opinion of people about you. And I've come here to ask you to forgive me, Larry, and to take me if you will." He threw out his hands until his arms were almost about her, and she could hear a faint groan of eagerness rising and checked in his throat.

But he stepped back suddenly.

"I've answered you before," he said, his voice harsh with pain. "I don't question that you mean what you say. I don't argue that most of this is pity, and a feeling that you must repay me for having done something for you on the stage the other day. But even if you mean what your coming here seems to mean, I couldn't take you, Kate. If you and I are willing, the world isn't willing. And we're slaves, all of us, to the world and in the world. We can't escape. Go back to your father's house. It's the only right thing."

"There's something else," she said, half choked with grief and with fear of this new man who spoke with the voice of Larry Lynmouth.

"There is something else," said Lynmouth. "I'll tell you what it is, and you'll despise me for it. I've seen enough of the mob in Crooked Horn to detest them. They've licked my hand; and then they've bitten me. I think that I detest them, and yet I can't die happy until I've tried to prove to them that I'm a man."

"By letting yourself be murdered by numbers? Is that a proof?" asked the girl, trembling.

"I must reach Jay Cress," said the outlaw. "He knows that I'm coming for him, and he's prepared. He has his four gunmen to help him. But I must get at him through them. If I once reach him—and I'll have to pass him to get to Tom Daniels, I know—then he goes down and my name goes up, or else I go down and end the misery that I'm in now. I tell you, Kate, that I've been able to keep my head up all my life, until I met Jay Cress, and he bought me. I tried to tell your father that, and even he smiled."

"But he won't smile now, Larry!"

"Other people do. They won't when I've met Cress man to man. Guns or hands—"

His voice rose and rang. He checked himself with an effort.

"You really must go back, Kate," said he.

She saw that it was a hopeless task that she had undertaken. She turned in passive obedience, and he helped her strongly onto the horse.

It was the only time that he touched her. He did not even linger beside her or take her hand, but stepped back instantly. She tried to speak some farewell, but her voice was too broken, and Lynmouth made not even the effort.

She rode slowly up the slope of the hollow.

Beside the next trees, a horseman swung up to her. It was Cherry Daniels, but Cherry did not pause. She merely slowed her mount to a lope, and then darted past, as though the fallen head of the other girl had told her a story eloquent enough.

But Kate Oliver went back to her father's house slowly, keeping to the roundabout roads.

She found the whole establishment frantic with excitement over her prolonged absence. She was an hour late for dinner!

She put up her horse in the stable, dodged questions, and with hanging head she went up to her room.

There her father found her stretched on the bed, face down. He sat beside her and stroked her head gently.

When she was able to speak she said:

"It was Larry. I went to meet him."

He did not answer or comment. He simply let his hand rest lightly on her head and waited.

"He's comming into Crooked Horn this night," said Kate Oliver. "He's going to let himself be killed trying to get Tom Daniels out! I wanted to stop him. I offered to go away with him."

Her father started, but still he said nothing.

"Is it true?" she asked suddenly. "Is it true he tried

ɔ tell you that Jay Cress had bought him to do that
hameful thing?"

"Yes. He tried to tell me."

"And that you smiled?"

"Yes."

"Because of that, he'll let himself be killed tonight, I
hink!"

"Aye," said Oliver, "it very well may be!"

He went to the window and looked out into the dark-
ess. All the windows gleamed with lamplight; the wind
vent through the trees with a rustle like crumpling silk;
nd the stars shone thin and far beyond them.

"Aye," said the banker, "disbelief and doubt make a
•ad profession. I've handled money too long to handle
ien now. Guns kill their tens, and sneers kill their thou-
.nds."

GOOD ADVICE

HEY rode together, side by side, to the verge of
rooked Horn, and there Lynmouth said good-by to
herry Daniels. He held both her slim hands in his. They
1ade it perfectly casual.

"I'll be seeing you again before long, Cherry," said he.

"Of course you will," said she. "Good luck to you, Lar-
y."

That was all, except that her grip clung to him des-
erately for a moment longer. Then her hands fell away.
ortune carried him down the street. He turned once in
1e saddle and waved back to the girl, and she waved in
eply. Then he turned the corner and was gone.

Neither of them expected to find one another again in
1at world.

But in front of Larry Lynmouth, as the lights began

to twinkle on either hand, there appeared a huddled form on the back of a long-legged mule.

The mule rider halted and raised a hand. Lynmouth, amazed at this early misfortune, nevertheless halted also. He was very glad that there was far from enough light to make him recognizable.

"Well, stranger?" he said.

"Am I a stranger to you, señor?" said the unexpected voice of Brother Juan, the Franciscan.

"Were you waiting for me here?" asked Lynmouth.

"Yes."

"You knew that I'd come in this way?"

"Yes."

"How did you know that? I didn't know which way I'd come myself until the last moment."

"It wasn't hard to guess that you would come by the openest and most dangerous road. They are watching every alley mouth and every winding lane, but, of course, they are not watching the main street. Only a madman would ride in this way."

"And you thought that I was mad, Brother Juan?"

"I knew you were desperate, so I waited here, just beyond the reach of the lights."

"Just why have you come here, Juan?"

"To waste a little moment of your time."

"Very well," said Lynmouth. "I'd trust you with a year, why not with five minutes? What is it that you wish to say?"

"First, that this is very dangerous, though you know it already."

"I can guess that it is, Brother Juan. I don't think you've come here only to tell me this."

"No, but for something else. To tell you the names of the men who are guarding the jail to which you are bound."

"Tell them, then."

"Cress, Dean, Happy Joe, Ogden, and Harrison Riley."

"I've heard of Cress and his hired men."

"Then there are the sheriff, Chick Anthony, and the new jail keeper."

"That makes seven."

"Yes, seven men, well armed. The jail is like an arsenal. It is filled with weapons. They have revolvers, rifles, short-barreled carbines, pump guns, riot guns. They are at every hand. They could sweep a regiment from the street."

"You've been inside, Juan?"

"Yes. I've been inside."

"How many ways are there into the jail?"

"There are two windows on the main floor. There is a cellar door, and a cellar window beneath; and in the attic there are two more small windows, which are barely large enough to admit a man."

"Tell me, Juan. Are they guarding Tom Daniels, or are they guarding the jail?"

"What do you mean?"

"I mean, are they sitting on guard around Daniels, or are they watching the possible entrances?"

"They are watching the entrances, Señor Lynmouth."

"Ha!" cried Larry Lynmouth with sudden exultation. "Then by the gods, I have half a chance, after all. They're guarding the jail?"

"Yes."

"And it has six windows and doors, besides the main front door?"

"Yes."

"That will require six men, I suppose?"

"Yes, I suppose so."

"Which leaves only one man free?"

"Exactly so, señor. But to enter into a small building occupied by seven fighting men, armed to the teeth—"

"Two in the cellar, brother, and two in the attic, and one man roaming here and there—that means that no more than three can be at a time on the main floor of the jail."

"Yes, perhaps it means that. But to attempt to break in—even a child should be able to keep you out if you try to force your way through."

"Aye, if I tried to force my way with my hands, or even with guns."

"Are you going to melt through the strong, thick walls, señor?"

"I am thinking of a way to go through. Juan, is that all you have to say?"

"I have much more, señor, but it will be of little use. I came to persuade you. But I see that I can neither persuade nor stop you."

"No, Juan, you cannot."

"At least I can give you comfort, then."

"Well, I don't know. What sort of comfort? We're not of the same religion, Juan."

"No," said the friar, "but you and I are working for the same goal."

"What is that, Juan?"

"We are trying to be good."

Lynmouth laughed, but his laughter was faint.

"Am I trying to be good, Juan?"

"Yes. You are trying to save your friend, and to make yourself respected. I think that you are choosing the wrong way, a suicidal way. You will achieve nothing but your own death, but I wish to give you some comfort before the end."

"Well, Juan," said the gunman, "what sort of comfort can you give to me?"

"There is a man at Los Verdes who has a wife and five children. This man, señor, was badly hurt in a fall from a horse a year ago. Since then he could not work, and worry was killing him. His children were starving. His wife was half mad. Today, he is in comfort; his children are well fed; he is confident of the future, and his confidence gives him strength."

"What of that?"

"It is your work, señor!"

"Ah, the money I gave you, you mean?"

"Yes. Seven souls pray for you, though they do not know your name."

"Juan," said Lynmouth, greatly moved, in spite of himself, "I am glad of that."

"Furthermore, not three miles from Crooked Horn, there is an old man who has worked for sixty years, and he is now too feeble to work any longer. He was too proud to beg. This man, señor, I have saved."

"Do you mean old Sam Rogers?"

"That is he."

"But he's a Protestant, Brother Juan."

"Protestants," said the friar, and dimly through the darkness the robber could see the friar's smile, "Protestants can be as hungry as the best Catholics in the world. Besides these people, there is a ten-year-old boy with a twisted leg and a crooked back. His life could be made normal and his body strong by an operation, but there was no money to send him off to the great doctor in New York. He is already on the train, señor, with his mother. She weeps as she rides, I am sure, and thinks of the unknown man who has helped her."

"She owes me no thanks," said Lynmouth. "I did not give you the money because I was swelling with any pity for humanity, or any desire to do it good. I gave the money because it was a tainted profit, and I did not want to keep it in my hands."

"For whatever reasons you gave it to me," said the friar, "I wish you to know the good that you have done."

"That you have done," said Lynmouth. "Look on that money as something that you picked out of the dust."

"Let me tell you of others, also," went on the friar. "There is up the creek a small house where—"

"Hush!" said Lynmouth.

At this, the friar thumped the sides of Alicia with his heels and forced her nearer. He laid his hand upon the arm of the robber.

"Ah, my son," said Brother Juan, "how much and what great good you could accomplish, and you have accomplished! Instead of dying here at the gratings of a jail window in a hopeless and lost cause, come with me and I will show you death for your name and life for yourself while you are still on earth. I will show you dangers which cannot be faced with weapons. I will show you such adventures as mountain climbers, robbers, warriors, never have encountered. Crooked Horn is large enough for you to be buried in, but it is not big enough for you to die in, my son!"

Lynmouth caught the hand of the good man in a crushing grip.

"Juan," said he, "if I waited here another two minutes, you'd persuade me. Good-by."

"Good-by," said Juan, "and may Heaven have mercy on your soul!"

He attempted no other word of persuasion, and Lynmouth went slowly on down the street.

38
A FREAK OF FATE

To BE deliberate was Lynmouth's plan of action, everything without haste, every movement casual. In this manner he hoped to advance to the center of the town without being noticed. If he went at full gallop, the fastest horse in the world would not have speed enough to escape from the bullets which were sure to be showered at him.

When he had come to this conclusion, he kept to a steady pace. Sometimes he allowed Fortune to walk, but usually he kept her jogging at the dogtrot which all Western horses learn, and prefer. At a walk, at a trot, at a canter, the striking beauty of her gait would like a light illuminate her body, and he did not want eyes to be directed too closely upon her. Yet he wanted her with him if ever there were a chance for him to get young Daniels and bolt away for freedom. Nothing but blinding speed could serve him then!

The dogtrot brought down her head. It made her in the night, only streaked at random by lamplight from door and window, appear like any of ten thousand cattle ponies—with a touch of good blood qualifying the old mustang strain. He had used red clay to stain the white spots that were her characteristic markings. This was the only disguise that he used.

For himself, he had not done even this much. He merely wore an old black slouch hat with a brim wide and loose, so that it fell down over his forehead and obscured his eyes, those telltales in any face. With loose rein, slumping in the saddle, he went.

There were no signs that the town was on the alert. He saw no armed men. It was only curious that at this time of the day, when usually men from near-by ranches were starting homeward in a rush on horses or in buckboards, there was not a horseman on the street but himself. Whoever was in Crooked Horn wished to remain there for the party!

There was a party, moreover!

No matter what might be expected in the way of excitement, Judge Bore would not allow the festival of his daughter's birthday to be interrupted or postponed. The men of Crooked Horn would take care of the outlaw and his schemes! Let the children go on with their party! So his house was lighted fore and aft like a ship on a gala day in port.

The judge spent little of his time on his ranch during these days. The little shack was too small to house so important a man. And though Crooked Horn was not large, yet he looked upon it as the firm base from which his political name and fame must grow.

Therefore, he had bought the old Chester place in the town.

Chester had been a cattle king of the very old days. He had freighted in quantities of sawed timbers and boards, and built a good big house with wooden carving on the front, and a pair of turrets in the pseudo-Gothic style. Naturally, the judge had wanted this place, and he got it cheap, because it was too big for the other townsmen, or else too pretentious, for such a man as William Oliver, say.

He renovated the house. The towers were staggering. So he tore them down and rebuilt them—a good deal taller!

Now, from the little mangy garden to the tips of these turrets the old house was gleaming with lights, for the judge's eleven-year-old daughter, Alice, was celebrating her birthday. Alice had cross-eyes and a stutter. She was knock-kneed, sandy-headed, and built like the figure eleven. Therefore, the judge was all the more careful to surround her with attention. If she could not charm the mind, she must command the eye of the world, he felt. And such an occasion as a birthday was not to be overlooked.

From the open windows of this house, young Larry Lynmouth could hear the shrill cries and then the pealing shouts of laughter as the party began. Most of the youth of Crooked Horn was invited. For the judge knew that he was in a diplomatic part of the country. Not that he counted votes in whatever he planned, but, after all, the business of a politician is politics. In other words, it is his actual duty to win admiration, and a politician should be ashamed of standing anywhere except in the center of the stage. Otherwise, he has wronged himself, and his career, and his party. In fact, his country suffers. And every good politician loves his country.

Larry Lynmouth allowed a faint, stern smile to touch his lips as he stared at the house of the judge. That man was written down in his book of the mind, and written in red, moreover. The day might not be far away when Judge Bore would be called to an accounting, and no mercy would be shown.

In the meantime, Lynmouth almost forgot his own danger as he eyed the Japanese lanterns in the garden, like self-luminous butterflies that glimmered here and there among the trees. And through the windows he could see twists of colored paper strung across the rooms, and more gayly masked lanterns everywhere, so that the place was a great swirl of color.

Here Fortune swerved suddenly from a flutter of paper in the center of the street, and a sharp cry was knocked into silence under her feet. Lynmouth was out of the saddle instantly, his heart in his throat, and picked up the limp form of a boy of ten or so.

He was covered with dust, but when Lynmouth pressed his ear to the breast of the youngster, he heard the heart beating steadily and strongly.

That instant the youngster opened his eyes with a gasp. "Jiminy—I seemed to run right into— Hello—where am I?"

He struggled to his feet. He was swaying a little, but he made no sound. "Are you hurt, son?" asked Lynmouth.

"Not a bit," said the boy stoutly. He was unsteady enough on his legs to make the rider disbelieve this.

"How did it happen that the mare hit you?"

"I was late for the party. I was hoofin' it along, sort of." He chuckled. He seemed at ease. But Lynmouth knew that he had been badly shaken up. Of such stuff as this is a man made.

"Are you going on to the party?" asked Lynmouth.

"Why, yeah, I guess so."

"You'd better go back home and lie down."

"You think so? Maybe I better, at that. But I wanta be around and up tonight. You can't tell—maybe Lynmouth—"

The saying of this word, as though it cast a light, suddenly made the boy start and stiffen. He stared at Larry Lynmouth by the dull glimmer of light that came from the houses to the street. And suddenly Lynmouth remembered how on a day he had dashed out of Crooked Horn and seen a boy bouncing up and down in excitement, and shouting to a comrade.

"You're Lynmouth!" gasped the boy.

It was too unaccountably cruel a stroke of fortune that he should be recognized in this fashion, and by a chance encounter with a child. His grip instinctively hardened on the lad. He heard a quick intake of breath. It was not a groan, but he knew by it that his iron fingers were hurting the youngster.

"I'm Lynmouth," he admitted, loosening his grasp.

A sense of utter defeat and shame and bafflement swept over him. He had been struck by a force which he could not resist, he could not fight back. A sheer child had worsted him!

"You're Lynmouth," said the boy. "What're you gunna do with me?"

"I'm going to trust you," said Lynmouth.

"Trust me not to tell you're here?"

"Yes."

"Jiminy," said the boy, his breath coming in with a gasp again. "Are you really gunna do that?"

"Can you keep a secret?"

"Well, I've tried to, before. I can't say that I'm anything extra special at it, but I can try. You betcha that I can try!"

"Try now," said Lynmouth. "I'm going on down the street. But if you say a word, you can wreck me. You understand that, of course?"

"Mr. Lynmouth," said the boy, who was beginning to tremble violently, "I would sure like to know what you're gunna do."

"Whatever," said Larry, "luck puts in my mind to do when I get to the jail."

"Will you tell me one thing?"

"I will if I can."

"Are you sure enough gunna meet Jay Cress?"

"Yes," said Lynmouth, with a curious change of voice. "I'm going to try to meet Jay Cress."

"And you're gunna fight with him?"

"Yes," said Lynmouth, "I'm going to fight with Jay Cress."

"Oh," cried the boy, though beneath his breath, "if ever you pull a gun on him, you'll kill him sure!"

"Yes," said Lynmouth, his teeth coming together so hard that it put a pain in the hinges of his jaw, "if ever I pull a gun on him, I'll surely kill him!"

The youngster stepped back half a pace.

"Go on, Larry!" said he. "I'd rather be burned to a crisp than ever to tell a gent that I'd seen you here. You try to believe me there, will you? You just try to believe me, and I'll never let you down."

"I do believe you," said Larry Lynmouth.

"Could I foller along toward the jail?"

"I wish you wouldn't. I'm in such danger, son, that even the weight of an eye might tip me over a cliff a mile high."

The boy sighed. "I reckon I understand, but I terrible wish that I could be there!"

"You'll go?"

"No, sir, I won't go a step."

"You're a good lad," said Lynmouth. "Will you tell me your name?"

"Sure. My name is Tommy Anthony. I'm Chick Anthony's son."

"You're—you're the sheriff's son?"

It staggered Larry Lynmouth.

"Yeah. That's why I'd sort of like to go to see what happens around the jail."

"You're the son of the sheriff, and you're not going to give the alarm against me?"

"Does that sound funny to you? I tell you what, Mr. Lynmouth, they's seven of them inside of the jail, everybody says, and they's only the one of you. Why, I'd wish pretty nigh everything for you—except the hurting of dad!"

Once more the very brain of Lynmouth reeled at what the child was saying. He could not help being honest.

"Do you realize, Tommy," asked he, "that if ever I get into the jail, your father is a fighting man, and so am I?"

"Yes," said the boy. "Pop, he'd never quit fightin' while he could pull a gun."

"And if bullets are flying, one of them might kill him?"

The boy shuddered violently. Then he doubled his fists hard.

"He's gotta take his chance," said he. "He's got about ten or twenty chances to your one. He's gotta take his chances, same as you're takin' yours. Only—"

"Aye," said Lynmouth, his voice lowered, "if there'a a way to be easy on him in the fight—supposing ever I get into the jail—I'll try to remember you, Tommy."

"Thanks," said Tommy Anthony. "I'm wishin' you all the luck that I can, except for what I've gotta wish my dad. Nobody in the world never tried nothin' like what you're tryin' now, I guess, Mr. Lynmouth."

"Good-by, and thanks for your wishes."

They shook hands. Lynmouth sprang into the saddle, and as he rode off he felt the eyes of the lad following and turning after him, and reaching him like a friendly hand on his back through the obscurity of the village night.

This meeting had more significance than he wanted to give to it. It proved, above all, that even in children there is a possibility of loyalty and truth.

How dared he, then, deny such virtues to the fathers? How dared he feel that the world was a desert of treachery and hate and meanness, when there walked in it such creatures as Cherry Daniels, Brother Juan, and little Tommy? A woman, a man, and a child, they shone upon his mind with their own peculiar lights.

In the meantime, the mare was taking him at her steady dogtrot down through the heart of the town, when in the distance, from the verge of Crooked Horn to the south, there was a crackling of musketry. Fully twenty shots must have been fired in rapid succession, and here and there doors slammed and Lynmouth heard people running down steps into the street. They were wondering if that meant the death of famous Larry Lynmouth— that salvo of firing.

No, he was there among them, jogging past on a down-headed horse.

39
"OPEN, SESAME!"

HE CAME out into the little plaza around which stood the jail, the courthouse where Judge Bore made the most eminent figure, and the post office that had been Crooked Horn's pride until the bill for its construction had to be paid.

It was a naked, dusty square. The wind was forever forming little whirlpools of dust in the air, and wisking them away over the plaza. Along one side ran a board walk. The other three sides were furnished with plain dust in the summer, and plain mud in the winter. There were a few umbrella trees, also, but their meager heads and slender trunks offered no shelter for loiterers.

No, it was an open, naked square. There would be no way of avoiding a sweep of rifle bullets, as Lynmouth came into it, except by the chance that he might go unrecognized. And now all Crooked Horn was trembling on edge in the hopes of seeing him.

He wondered what shifting of shadows, what unlucky cow wandering among the bushes, had been mistaken for

Larry Lynmouth on the southern edge of the town and forthwith riddled with bullets?

In this wonder he remained, but let the mare go straight forward across the square toward the squat, low, ugly, blind face of the jail building!

He had made his plan beforehand. There was so much that was like insanity in it that he dared not repeat it to himself, even. He could merely wish to commit himself to the course of action, and then trust to what chance might offer him.

He arrived at the hitching rack in front of the jail. Here there stood eight horses, and every one of them was a chosen mount, as he could guess. Eight horses, and all of them with the long legs of speedsters. They were saddled and bridled. He saw the loaded rifle holsters of several. They were, in fact, apparently as well equipped as cavalry troopers would be.

As he came up, from either end of the line stood forth a man equipped with a rifle.

"Who's there?" snapped one of them.

"Aw, shut up," said Lynmouth, and rode the mare straight into the middle of the rank.

"We got no orders about nine hosses, in here!" exclaimed one of the men, the more aggressive of the pair, it appeared.

He came hurrying up, and found that Lynmouth had already dismounted, and that he was tying the reins in what seemed a secure knot, though, as a matter of fact, it was a slip which would come loose at the slightest touch.

There was no need to tie Fortune securely.

"You, there!" said the guard. "Who in heck are you and whacha want here? Back up, will you?"

"You talk like you had on long trousers, boy," said Lynmouth. "Back up yourself and rest your chin on your chest, will you?"

"I dunno. Who's askin' me? Big talk never knocked me out, stranger. You don't look so dang old yourself!"

"Are you huntin' for a fight?" asked Lynmouth, putting a snarl in his voice.

"I ain't dodgin' it," said the man instantly. "Are you?"

"Get that hoss out of the line," now insisted the other guard.

"You ask the sheriff about that," replied Lynmouth. "My business is with him, it ain't to stay out here yappin' with the pair of you!"

This was telling the truth fairly enough, though something less than all of the truth. But he turned his back upon the two guards, and went straight on toward the front door of the jail.

That door, studded with heavy iron bolts, he had seen before, and he knew it well, and could recall the sound of it as it struck heavily home behind those who entered.

"We better stop that gazebo," said one of the two men outside, looking fiercely after Lynmouth, who heard the words clearly.

"Aw, leave him be," said the other. "Likely he's some scrapper that the sheriff has sent for."

"Yeah, but it's our duty to question everybody that fools around here."

"Well," said his companion, "he ain't gunna gain much by leavin' his hoss in our hands, is he?"

"I dunno, but I'm gunna go up and have another look at him, and it seems like I've seen the cut of that head and shoulders before."

"Go ahead," said the other, with a chuckle. "Maybe you'll find out that it's Larry Lynmouth!"

At this good joke, both of the men could not refrain from laughter. It appeased the angry curiosity of the more efficient of the pair.

In the meantime, arriving at the head of the steps, Lynmouth clenched his fists and gave the door a heavy blow. Then he turned, sauntered back a pace, and made a cigarette.

It assured the two men below that the newcomer was indeed an expected man at the jail.

And as he lighted his smoke, Lynmouth, looking across the plaza, saw the figure of a small boy dart around a corner and then shinny like a cat up the narrow, smooth trunk of an umbrella tree.

One part of his promise, Tommy had not had the will power to keep. But now he would see something worth while from among the branches of the little tree.

There was a step, and then a muffled voice inside the door.

"What's that?"

There are two ways of disguising a voice simply. One is to speak softly, and the other is to speak loud

And now Lynmouth answered in a huge voice: "Hullo, is that you, Chick?"

"Yeah," said the sheriff, behind the door. "This is me. Who are you?"

"'S me," replied Lynmouth ungrammatically. "Open up the door."

"Yeah," said the sheriff, "it's likely that I'll open up the door, ain't it? Whacha want?"

"You ol' blockhead," said Lynmouth. "I mean to say that I've got news for you."

"What kinds news?"

"Bad news."

"Yeah? What kinda bad?"

"Mighty bad."

"Bad about what?"

"About the kid?"

"Who? Jessie?"

"Nope. About Tommy."

He hated to use that word and that name, but he had to have the door opened. After all, the sheriff had not scrupled to use extra-legal means against him. Now he would be justified in retorting with an equal cruelty.

"Tommy!" exclaimed the sheriff.

Then, as there was a sound of slipping bolts, Lynmouth could hear the poor sheriff asking again, loudly:

"What's happened to him? What's wrong with him? Has the tough little kid got into a fight with a greaser and got himself all sliced up?"

Then the door was jerked half open.

A sudden dizzy, almost sick joy swept over Lynmouth.

They expected him at the cellar window and door, or through the attic, or through the bars of the main-floor windows, penetrating mysteriously, as it were, through the good, tough steel bars.

And here was the front door of the jail, opening to him under the sheriff's own hand. And, as the door swung open, the edge of it flicked with a clashing sound against the bundle of keys at his belt.

Reliable Sheriff Anthony! He had not trusted any other person with the keys on this night of nights! He carried them upon his own person. Let him see who would take them away from him!

"Who are you?" demanded the sheriff. "What's happened to Tommy, for Heaven's sake?"

"He's been run over," said Lynmouth, and stepped into the dimness of the jail interior.

"Run over!" groaned the sheriff, in horror.

"Yes. run over."

"By what? A wagon?"

"No, by a hoss," said Lynmouth, reaching in his coat's inner pocket, it appeared.

"By a hoss? Rode down by some drunken fool of a puncher—busted to pieces— O stranger, tell me what happened to my kid!"

"Chick," said Lynmouth slowly. "I'm mighty sorry for you. The boy's all right. He's just shaken up a little. But you're a lot worse off than he is."

"How d'you mean?" demanded the sheriff, bewildered.

"I mean in this way," said Lynmouth.

So saying. and thrusting the door to with the weight of his shoulder, he quickly removed his hand from beneath his coat.

The sheriff, in a fever of anxiety, frantic, half extending a hand as though to receive a doctor's written report, suddenly looked underneath the shadowy brim of the stranger's hat, and there he saw what he would not and could not believe.

It was Larry Lynmouth.

The next moment Sheriff Chick Anthony and all his reputation were struck a stunning blow. For as the hand of the robber reappeared from beneath his coat, it bore a long and heavy Colt, the barrel of which thudded with a faintly metallic ring against the tough skull of Chick Anthony.

Down he went, slumping his shoulders against the door of the jail, the keys clashing softly against the floor, with a tinkling note of complaint.

Lynmouth leaned to detach the bunch, and as he did

so, he heard the lips of the unconscious sheriff murmur the last thought that had been in his mind before that club stroke of doom landed on him.

"Larry Lynmouth!"

It startled Lynmouth to hear the name said in this barely audible whisper.

Then he stood erect. The whisper told him two things, that he had been recognized, and that even this crushing blow had not killed the stout sheriff. He was glad of both things, and of both for the sake of Tommy, the son.

His way was clear now. The main aisle between the cells opened here before him, and he sauntered down it, rather dismayed to find that there were several new occupants in the jail room.

The larger the crowd, the more intensely difficult his work would be. He felt, now, that he was halfway through his labors. Only halfway!

And, if he opened the door of the cell of the prisoner and found the man in irons, then would not all his work be in vain?

He went on, forcing himself to saunter, swinging the keys in his hand.

"Hey, Anthony!" called a sudden voice from the window to the south. "Hey, Chick Anthony!"

And there was no answer except the soft step of the stranger, passing down the aisle of the cells.

40
FREE!

AT LAST, Lynmouth reached the cell of young Tom Daniels. It was the same one which he himself had been placed in, in the far corner of the room, with a new door, of course, to secure it.

There were two things to be grateful for. One was that

there was no prisoner in the next cell. The other was that there were no irons on Tom Daniels.

Now Larry could only pray that he might find the correct key quickly. The first he tried would not even enter the lock!

Tom Daniels stood up from his couch—then he sat down again quickly, and Lynmouth knew that it was because he understood. Key after key entered the slot of the lock and failed to turn it. Perspiration broke out on the face of Lynmouth. He trembled. Every second passed him like a soul on the wing, for there was death or life in each moment of delay.

He heard the guard at the southern window bawling out again: "Hey, Anthony, Anthony!"

"Aw, shut up, you," answered one from the north.

"I want Chick."

"He's busy, you chump. Leave him be!"

In spite of himself, a smile twitched at the lips of Larry Lynmouth.

"There's the sheriff now, in front of Daniels's cell."

It was one of the other prisoners speaking, a man who stood grasping the bars of his cell.

"A good place for him," answered the guard on the north, and he from the south broke in:

"Where? In the aisle? I have to speak to him."

"Well, he can hear you, where he is."

"Hello—Chick!"

Lynmouth tried to summon the voice of the sheriff into his throat. Suddenly, as he heard footfalls, he roared:

"Shut up!"

Silence followed this rude command, and then a small pulse of laughter from the guard on the north.

"I told you!" said he. "Leave Chick alone. He's busy."

Yes, very busy, indeed!

Then, from behind him, from the cell across the aisle, a small, guarded voice struck cold into the heart of the intruder, for it said:

"Lynmouth! Larry Lynmouth!"

He turned his head, at that moment quickly fitting a new key into the obdurate lock.

"Larry," said the whispering voice, "can you gimme a

chance to get out, too? I'll fight through the outside lines with you. I'm not quitter. I'm Tuck Mason!"

"Stay where you are, Tuck," said Lynmouth. "You're not in for enough to make a jail break worth while. Stay where you are!"

"Larry, for pity's sake, gimme a chance, will you?"

The voice had risen in great excitement; and before Lynmouth could answer, the key turned in the lock, the door sagged open.

And Tom Daniels made his first step toward freedom!

Some one down the aisle cried out sharply: "What's that? Is that Anthony letting Daniels out?"

Now, up to that moment the interior of the jail had seemed very much like a dusty twilight, so dim was it, or like the light which passes through deep water to the lower rocks, and the forms of sea life, strange and wavering. But at the sound of this challenge the entire interior brightened in a flash. It became to the startled eye of Lynmouth like the brightness of noonday.

He handed a revolver to young Tom Daniels, the boy whispering something in a voice choked with exultation.

"Lynmouth, Lynmouth!" exclaimed the man across the aisle, excited beyond control of his speaking tones. "Take me with you!"

Tom Daniels had stepped out from the door of his cell.

To him, speaking rapidly, Lynmouth was saying:

"Now we move fast. Break straight for the door. If there's any one in the way, shoot low, shoot low. Don't shoot to kill except at the murderers that Cress has hired. Outside, there is a string of horses. Two guards. If they stand for us, then shoot as straight as you can. Grab the nearest horse, and we're away!"

He spun around as he said this, and at the same time there was a deep, muffled voice that sounded from near the front door of the jail, calling:

"Help! Help! Lynmouth—"

It was like the booming of a muffled alarm bell. It seemed that every man in the jail, prisoner or guard, began to shout at the same instant with all his might, a babel of sounds in which one word predominated.

"Lynmouth! Lynmouth!" bellowed out in rage, and in fear, and in wonder.

But Larry Lynmouth was running down the central aisle at full speed and straight toward the door by which he had entered. He heard another door slammed heavily at the side of the cell room. And then a shrill voice cut knifelike through the clamor, yelling:

"Peg Leg, Riley, Joe, Ogden—he's here!"

It seemed a whole company of footfalls were answering that shout, but the one who yelled the signal was the one in whom Lynmouth was interested, for he had recognized the voice of Jay Cress, different among the others as the yelping of a coyote among dogs.

Both barrels of a riot gun roared from the side, where the guard of the northern window had opened fire. The loud report was followed by a tingling sound as the slugs rushed among the bars of the cells, and then a prisoner was reard shouting:

"You've hit me! You've hit me! You've killed me! Oh, dang you!"

But Lynmouth held his fire.

He could see, before him, at the front door, the staggering form of the sheriff, still only half conscious, but on his feet with both hands pressed against his head, reeling uncertainly, drunk with pain and with stupor, and like a chant repeating:

"Help! Larry Lynmouth!"

The fellow on the left, who had fired the sawed-off shotgun with such unlucky results, had flung himself down on the floor out of sight, to avoid a return bullet. Also from the left that other door had slammed, and through it he saw a swarm coming, with shouts, and with ready guns.

Lynmouth had expected that all the forces in the jail would be scattered, and slow to collect. He had felt, when he passed the sheriff at the door, that half of his work was done. But like wasps these fighters were all responding at the first sound of the alarm. He could hardly believe it. It was as though this were a trap exactly prepared to catch him in just such a maneuver as he was attempting.

The revolver of young Tom Daniels clanged behind him, like a pair of gigantic hands clapped under his ear. One of the group that ran toward them staggered suddenly to the side and went down in a peculiarly reeling fashion, with arms outstretched like a rope dancer recovering an almost lost balance. Down he went, cursing. That was Peg Leg, the bear and brute.

Three more remained. Lynmouth distinguished the tall, graceful form of Harrison Riley, that cat of a man, now shooting as he ran. And beside him were two others, with a smaller form behind.

The smaller form was without doubt Jay Cress, now so famous.

"Make the door—get to the door!" barked Lynmouth over his shoulder to the boy; and as he gave the command, and Tom Daniels darted ahead, Lynmouth checked his own speed abruptly, and wheeled to face the charge.

That halt saved his life for a moment, at the least. Some three or four bullets hummed through the space just ahead, where he should have been.

"Cress!" shouted Larry Lynmouth. "Cress!"

The rage and the shame of all that he had endured since that day they met in the saloon, when he had sold his honor, now rose and rang in the cry of Lynmouth. There seemed a special and almost miraculous force in it.

Riley, Dean, and Ogden turned right and left. Behind them was their paymaster, Jay Cress; and the little man, as the living screen parted before him, was seen on his knee with a rifle steadied against his shoulder, drawing a steady bead.

Lynmouth fired for the head, and knew that life had ended as he pressed the trigger. Jay Cress, strangely enough, seemed to be driven both backward and up by the force of the impact. He came to his feet. The rifle exploded aimlessly from his hands, and Lynmouth saw the gambler clutch at the air and fall back.

He saw that as he swerved for the door, already dragged open by Tom Daniels. And the iron-bossed face of the door itself, swinging wide, was the shield against which the bullets of Cress's hired men spent themselves in vain.

At the heels of Daniels, Lynmouth, giving the door a strong drag, leaped through to the open, and straight into the arms of the two guards who had been placed over the horses. The roar of the guns had brought them to the danger point, but they had no chance against this sudden eruption of two strong men into their very faces.

The weight of Daniels knocked one of them head over heels down the steps, so that he lay a twisted, helpless form before the hitching rack.

The other received the driving fist of Lynmouth and collapsed on the very threshold of the jail.

The noise which had been begun in the jail had spread by magic over the entire town. People were shouting in the streets. Doors were slamming. The alarm bell began a mad, rapid clanging. And beyond the housetops Lynmouth saw an arm of red raised, lowered, raised again. A second arm went up beside it.

The towers of Bore's house were covered with flame! And as Lynmouth flung himself on the back of Fortune, he remembered the butterfly gaudiness of the Japanese lanterns in the garden and in the house.

Inside the jail, but at a vague distance, he heard men cursing at the door. But the latch had caught, and they did not know the trick of opening it—would not until the jailer himself came or the brain of the sheriff cleared.

Beside Lynmouth, young Tom Daniels had vaulted into the saddle of a tall, rakish-looking gelding. They twisted their horses at the same moment out of the line at the hitching rack and into the street.

"After me!" called Lynmouth with excitement, and sent Fortune racing down the street.

A fierce pleasure burned in him. In one moment his two worst enemies had been struck down—Cress, the pretender, who had attempted to buy another man's reputation, and Bore, who had ventured to judge him. But he decided to go close to the fire. Even a prison break would hardly draw the crowd away from the red spectacle of the flames.

There he would be least looked for, but if he and Daniels strove to break out from the town headlong, probably they would find every exit blocked by watchful men, posted for that purpose in strategic places. In the heart of the town was less danger, so he drew Fortune back to a jog and let Daniels come up beside him.

41
FLAMES AND FANCIES

THERE was an outburst of riot as they whirled about the corner. Behind them, the raging men inside the jail had burst open its outer door, and the guards were spilling out into the street, half stifled, and entirely maddened with rage.

For the impossible had been accomplished, and one man had deliberately walked into the Crooked Horn jail and taken from it a prisoner. He had done it though his coming was expected. By this very deliberation he had stunned the guards at that jail. And, so long as they lived, they would be remembered as the men through whose fingers Lynmouth had come and gone.

He, in the meantime, had pulled up in the throat of an alley that wound between two houses—an old, dusty cow-path, still weaving from side to side as in the old days before lots were laid out in Crooked Horn. Brush grew along its edges. As they entered behind this screen, a comparative solitude and quiet received them.

On one side, they could hear the wild voices of the guards from the jail. On the other side there was a deep, hoarse roar of excitement from the direction of Judge Bore's house, near by.

Tom Daniels hurried up to the side of his leader.

"Nobody else in the world ever so much as heard of a thing like you've done tonight, Larry!" said he. "But why go so slow? We need to hurry. They're so hungry for us that they'd eat us raw!"

"Wait a moment," said Larry Lynmouth. "There's

something else to think about. They're still guarding the exits, and the ends of the streets, I suppose. It'll be a while before the sight of the fire calls them in. And, when that happens, we can slide out of Crooked Horn without any danger whatever. Besides, I want to scout as near the fire as I can. I imagine that they're blaming it on me —because they know that I have reason to hate the judge."

"Scouting?" said Daniels, trembling with excitement and with wonder. "Scouting near Bore's house? Man, man, don't you realize that they'd throw you into the fire if they saw you there?"

"There's more curiosity in me," said Lynmouth, "than there is fire in Crooked Horn. I'm going on. You wait here in the brush for me."

"No, I'll stick with you, Larry."

"Hush," said Lynmouth. "You're still weak and half sick. Stay here and keep the horses—keep Fortune for me. Now, if anything should happen to me, it will happen within half an hour. If I'm not back in that time, get on Fortune, leave the other horse behind, and bolt out of town. They'll have drawn in the guards by that time, and Chick Anthony will be riding with a sore head and a posse all over the face of the county."

He dismounted and was instantly gone into the brush, leaving young Daniels bewildered behind him.

But Lynmouth, as he had said, was drawn on by a curiosity which was partly a savage eagerness to see this blow dealt to the judge, and partly he wished to learn if the fire were attributed to his malice.

He went through several back yards, and eventually found himself close under the burning house.

There was a crowd before him. The greater part of Crooked Horn had come there to witness the burning of the biggest house in the village. It was the passing of a monument, an historical landmark, a pride to the entire county. And Crooked Horn stood about with raised faces on which poured the fierce red light of the flames.

The eastern side of the house was already shooting flames high into the air, the tower on that side standing up like a great torch. The lower floor of the building was thoroughly ignited now, dusty billows of flame appearing behind the windows, sometimes thrusting out huge, lazy, red tongues. The upper story was packed with fumes, every window appearing stuffed with cotton white, yet even here the fire itself was coming, for now and then a red flicker of lightning crossed the apertures.

The bucket line had been abandoned almost before it was formed. The old, dry timber of the house was going up like matchwood. In the brief time from the moment when Lynmouth passed the house, to this instant, the fire had broken out, gathered head, and was now eating the building rapidly. Instead of trying to save the house, the volunteers rushed to save its contents.

Even this they only partially accomplished, but they had piled on the ground among the trees of the garden great heaps of clothes, beds, chairs, books, even kitchen utensils, family photographs, which had long smiled dimly from the walls of the Bore house, and a thousand useless articles.

This work of rescue had to be interrupted. The fumes were too stifling, and the fire was running too wild, licking down the whole length of a hall at a single stroke. So now the crowd stood about to gape, wonder, shake heads, and really enjoy the spectacle enormously.

The judge was revealed to the left, a picturesque figure with his wife weeping on his shoulder, and the hand of his younger daughter clasped in his.

Well the judge knew that picture and its value! He understood how tall and strong he seemed, how rugged, how strongly based as a rock, with the slender little woman leaning on his breast, and the child in his other hand; while behind him, fortunately rather out of sight, stood poor Alice, with her long, spindling shanks and her crossed eyes, and the pink party ribbon knotted high on her tow head like a foolish pair of wings.

She, in this manner, was obscured, and the noble family group remained bathed in the ruddy glow of their own flaming house. It was costing the judge fifteen thousand dollars, but he had no doubt that he would get a return from it of at least that value in votes. Strong, calm, cheerful, he endured this catastrophe in such a manner that any reasonably intelligent voter must have seen at a glance that this was exactly the sort of a man to send off to Washington to represent a district—aye, or a whole State!

The fire which hurt his pocketbook would, the judge felt, be another rung in the ladder up which he was mounting to glory. Nebulous language formed in the brain of Judge Bore. Metaphors which concerned the phoenix which rises newly resplendent from the ashes of the old life—and then the purging of carnal desires and carnal objects—these and many other images flowed through his mind until, in a measure he felt the invigorating atmosphere of the platform in the presence of his own burning house.

He began to wonder at himself. He was astonished to find how he was divided into two parts, each of which gaped at the other. In fact, the judge had been in politics so long that his emotions rarely ran higher than headlines or deeper than a column of type.

Other people were looking at him, now, and admiring his truly fine presence. The judge could hardly have been more inspiring if he had been leading a cavalry charge. And, if he had led such a charge, he would have died without feeling the bullet that struck him down, had he been so admired as he was now!

Larry Lynmouth, lurking in the background, with people passing him and repassing—blinded to his face by the redness of the light and their interest in the spectacle—presently heard what he had hoped to learn, one way or the other.

For a man near him broke out:

"This'll be the end of Lynmouth. Men'll stand murder, but they ain't gunna stand for arson!"

"Well, they got no proof!"

"No? What kinda proof d'you want? He comes to the town, and the same evening, Bore's house busts into fire."

"I heard that it was one of the kids that dropped a Japanese lantern and set fire to a curtain—"

"Listen! You rear a lot of rot! It was Lynmouth. That gent is no good. He never was no good, and he's worse than ever now. Since Jay Cress fixed him and put him down—"

"Jay Cress is a dyin' man, now, over in the jail. And who put him down?"

"You'd argue for the sake of arguing, wouldn't you?" said the first speaker.

"Aw, I guess that Lynmouth's no good, all right. But I never heard of nothin' like what he done tonight!"

"You never did?"

"No."

"Then you dunno much."

"Whacha mean?"

"Why, I mean that he done it by knowin' where to spend his money."

"Hey?"

"That's what I said."

"You got no proof of that!"

"You want proof, do you? Then I ask how one man could handle seven? With money. That's how he done it. And I bet that one of the other crooks was hired to take the pot shot at poor Jay Cress! Lynmouth never would've had the nerve to face him again."

"He would. And he done it."

"Aw, in the dark jail, anybody might've done it."

"I talked to Harry Riley—"

"Riley's a liar, anyways."

"Yeah, maybe he is. Well, you're right about one thing. I guess that Lynmouth is no good."

"He sure ain't. Hey, lookit this!"

For suddenly the tone of that gathering changed from suspense to pity and horror.

42
PERIL'S PATH

OVER the crackling and the increasing roar of the fire, there broke out now a shrill noise of barking that seemed to come from the central sky; but, looking up, Lynmouth saw a small dog almost at the top of the western tower. A small ornamental balcony skirted the head of that structure, and on this balcony a little fox terrier ran up and down, yipping in a voice as piercing as a needle.

It brought a groan from the entire crowd. From a grand spectacle the fire turned instantly into a horror. Some women turned away in haste. Others remained, fascinated by the sight.

Some one suggested that a rug be spread and the dog would jump into it, while four men held the corners. But though the terrier came to the verge, he shrank from the jump. In the meantime, the tower windows swirled with smoke, flame lighted now and then, and the blaze roared up more and more violently from the other side of the building. The heat of it was driving the crowd farther back.

So closely was attention focused on the poor dog that no one noticed Alice Bore.

But Jimmy belonged to her. Jimmy was her special own property. She had raised him from three weeks, first with a bottle and then with the most careful of hand feeding. She had trained, whipped, scolded, petted, and loved Jimmy with all her heart. He had slept on the foot of her bed on a little rug on his own. He had walked with her, played tag with her, fetched and carried. He would even bring her slippers from the closet, though he chewed them a good deal on the way.

And now Alice saw her dog on a very island of peril.

It did not occur to her to ask for help. She had always handled Jimmy before, and instinctively she rushed to him now. She merely gave one half-stifled little gasp and ran for the tower door; and not a soul in that crowd, gaping upward as they were at that moment, saw the girl dart into the smokey atmosphere of the tower.

She hastened up the winding stairs.

It was very hot. She choked with smoke and fumes. She was startled by crawling, glimmering streaks of flame. The whole floor of the second story was quivering with lines and waves of blue and of red fire.

But she scampered across this, went up the remaining stairs, and reached the little window that opened upon the balcony just as the sagging of the entire house brought weight upon the beams that held up the second-story floor of the tower. That floor went down with a roar and a rush. Sparks and flames belched out through the windows and shot up into the night air.

And, the next moment, the crowd saw Alice Bore climb out of the balcony window and take the puppy in her arms.

There was no ladder to reach her. There were no stairs by which a man could climb to her inside the building. She was lost as completely as the little dog had been before!

A wild, hoarse shout that had a groan in it went up from the watchers. Mrs. Bore fainted. Judge Bore forgot pictures, self, and politics. He ran wildly toward the tower door, and three men seized him and dragged him raving back from sure death.

He stood on the ground near the tower, with the sparks showering about him. He threw up his arms to Alice on the balcony high above. But she was as far from him as a hawk in the sky, to all intents and purposes, it seemed!

Larry Lynmouth had few nerves, and they were as hard as steel. This very night he had been as close to death as a man well can come. But now he turned his head, sick at heart, from the spectacle of the child on the balcony so far above them, only half seen, now and then, through the swiftly rising cloud of smoke. He turned from her and looked to the big pine tree which stood a good twenty feet from the side of the tower.

The idea leaped in his mind. Twice he tried to shut it away. This was not his business. Crooked Horn might save her if it could.

He grasped the shoulder of a cow-puncher standing near by.

"Look, partner," said Lynmouth. "There's a good rope on the ground. There's the tree to climb. You can get up there and noose that rope over one of the little turrets, tie it around the trunk of the tree, and make a bridge to the girl—"

"Yeah?" said the puncher, without even turning his head. "Look at that tree. It's smokin' already, and in another minute it'll bust into flame. I'm gunna be dead soon enough, stranger!"

Lynmouth stepped back, with a groan, and then,

through the roar of the fire, he heard the pitiful cry of the child.

At that, his reason snapped. He lurched forward, caught up the rope, and throwing the coil of it over one shoulder, he swarmed up the big pine tree as agile as a sailor.

Below him, the man to whom he had spoken stared at him, and after him. Then he drew the attention of those near him to the smoking tips of the branches nearest to the burning tower, and to the man struggling up toward the top of the tree.

And a yell of excited admiration came out of the throats of the spectators. A yell with hope in it, amazement, and delight.

Not a man there but felt better because there was such heroism in any human being. For the pine tree fumed and smoked, and once fire touched it, so much as a spark, they well knew that the whole resinous tree would explode into terrible fire.

Through the screen of the branches, they now could see Lynmouth working out on a big bough, opening his noose, then flinging the rope toward the tower.

It missed the little ornamental turret at which he had aimed, and as though in answer, a red arm of flame darted out of a window just below and made a fleeting wall between him and the child.

To Lynmouth, that seemed the end.

He looked down, half expecting to see the fuming branches of the pine trembling with blue fire; but still the tree had not caught.

Hastily he regathered the rope. He was like one walking the deck of a flaming ship, with a powder magazine beneath his feet. And as he remade the coil and opened the noose once more, he saw through the branches the upturned faces and the tossing arms of the crowd.

He cast again, and this time the noose fell true and sure over the little turret. He pulled it taut with all his might, then knotted the other end of the lariat around the trunk of the tree.

The child was eleven years old. Could she support her weight and swing across that line? He saw her come to it, reach out to it, and then, shrinking away, she clasped the terrier closer to her breast.

That was enough for Lynmouth.

He was one of those men who, having commited themselves to a course of action, cannot hold back, but are swept away with a current. And he himself, swinging clear from the tree, went hand over hand across the line.

It was while he dangled there in midair, with the wild light of the fire sweeping over him, that the staring crowd recognized him, and the sound of his own name roaring up from all those throats beat against his ears like the sound of a surf.

He reached the balcony's edge and heaved himself lightly up onto it.

And there he found himself face to face with little cross-eyed Alice Bore, her crooked eyes fixed upon him in a strange calm.

"You're Larry Lynmouth," said she, "and yet you're going to try to do this for me?"

It sounded so grown-up, so composed, so full of meaning, that Lynmouth was fairly staggered. But the upward flight of a wall of flame past them covered whatever amazement he felt.

He examined the rope carefully. It had been singed by that flight of fire, but he judged that the heart of it still was strong. He tested it with the force of both arms.

Then he looked down toward the crowd for one instant, like a man peering from one world into another. They were swarming here and there, trying to get a better view of him at his work. He saw Mrs. Bore in the distance, kneeling and praying with her hands raised. He saw Bore himself turned to stone, standing straight and still. Yonder was William Oliver, and Kate Oliver standing beside Cherry Daniels. There was Lew Daniels, too, on his crutch; and Sheriff Chick Anthony, with a red smear on his face; and Harrison Riley beside him.

These faces he saw in one second, while he waited for his arms to rest a little from their first labor. Then he turned to the girl.

"Hold close around my neck, but not tight enough to choke me. Hang perfectly still. Keep your heart up, and don't be afraid. It will soon be over. Will Jimmy stay on my shoulder?"

"Are you going to take Jimmy, too?" asked the child.

And then her calm deserted her. She began to cry. In pity of the virtue of the bandit, Larry Lynmouth!

He shook her rudely.

"No tears!" he commanded. "Help me or I can't help you. Now are you ready?"

"Ready," she said, setting her teeth.

"I'll let myself swing down on the rope," he told her. "Then you lower yourself over my shoulders and hang from my neck. Call to Jimmy and make him jump to me. Then we'll cross."

He lowered himself at once, and as he did so, he heard a cry from the crowd in which there was the booming of men's voices and the wild cries of hysterical women.

But all that he thought of then was the little Franciscan, Brother Juan, who performed not one good deed in a lifetime, but every moment of whose existence was noble.

Then a column of flame shot up, covering Lynmouth. His clothes, his hair scorched. A section of that side of the tower had fallen out, and allowed the fire free play. That explosion of flame had been the result. Gasping, choking, he looked up toward the girl, and saw her through the smoke that enveloped them, prepared to make the venture.

She climbed as he had directed, over his shoulders, and hung about his neck. She called, and the weight of Jimmy landed like a shot on the shoulders of Lynmouth.

His lungs were bursting, now. And the weight of the two figures, small in themselves, worked the narrow rope hard into his fingers.

He swung out, hand over hand, yet not venturing to take long-arm hauls, but short shifts, pulling outward.

He felt that his lungs would surely explode. Breathe he must, and the heavy smoke cloud still clung about him, enveloped, and shrouded him.

Breathe he did, and at once his lungs were on fire, as though flame itself had entered his body.

He could see nothing. Red-lit darkness swirled before his eyes. Then behind him he heard a great crash. The rope jerked in his grasp, and grew trembling taut, so that he felt the vibrating of it growing tense.

Yet still it held, while he heard the roar of upward-shooting masses of fire, smoke, and sparks. Heat worse than that of an oven seared him. His arms were tired, but breath was what he needed, breath was what he must have.

He looked down in his agony to the child on his breast, and she looked back in utter pity, in utter trust. That gave him strength. He had hung motionless, pendulous, for an instant, but now he went on.

Jimmy, on his shoulder, began to whimper, and lick his face, while little by little Lynmouth worked on along the rope.

He heard a wild shout of joy as he swung out of the screening smoke, and for the first time could draw in a breath of sweet, pure air. Yet it seemed to do him only partial good. His lungs were burning and choking still.

He went on. The tree was before him like a green heaven, but fuming along every branch.

Other men had swarmed into it, daring this danger at last, when another man had dared so much more.

The triumphal shouting died, turning to a great cry of terror. Lynmouth turned his head, and behind him he saw fire shooting from the top of the tower, bathing the very turret around which the rope was looped.

So, in desperation, he put forth all his strength. The tips of the pine branches brushed him. Then hands caught at him. The weight was loosed from around his neck.

And then he was fumbling his way to the ground, and staggering away into the open. The last man was not away from the pine before it caught from head to foot, and sent a pouring mass of flames roaring and hurtling high into the black vault of the sky.

43

ALL THAT MATTERS

THE fugitives found shelter in the house of William Oliver. There was Bore, his wife, his two children, and there, also, was Larry Lynmouth.

Chick Anthony, stubborn as a bulldog and true to his duty, insisted on arresting Lynmouth, but the crowd would not have it. They threatened to let the good sheriff taste the strength of their united hands, and Chick Anthony desisted. He had done very much to place this dangerous man in safekeeping; but, after all, he was a servant of the public will, and had to stoop to it.

He contented himself with sending a long telegram to the State capital. Then he went back to the jail to sit beside the dying man, Jay Cress.

No matter what good deeds had been done by Lynmouth, how were they to avoid the consequences of the killing of Cress? That would have to go down as murder, of course. Yet the sheriff hesitated to begin proceedings against this newly crowned hero whom Crooked Horn was worshipping with its whole might.

Anthony had a very sound idea that if he jailed Lynmouth again, Crooked Horn would tear the jail down with its bare hands.

Two hours later, his doubts dissolved, and he sent a telegram to the same quarters, stating:

Cress dead. Confessed killing of Kinkaid in El Paso three years ago and murder of Thomason in Phoenix.

Hang the outlaw for killing the gambler? No, rather heap rewards upon his head!

But the information which he sent in the telegram

was not the most important news that the sheriff got from the dying man.

He had sat there with wondering eyes while he drank in the speech of poor Jay Cress, as that man lay plucking at the blanket which covered his shivering body, and, staring at the ceiling, rehearsed the grisly story of his life up to the moment when he had met with famous Larry Lynmouth.

Behind the chair was the jailer, a silent witness, and in the corner of the room a deputy also listened. They heard the strange tale of how the gambler had bought Lynmouth's reputation, and how Jay Cress had taken advantage of that "frame."

And on the heels of this groaning testimony, Jay Cress closed his eyes to end a bad life, and died without a sigh. In his last moments he had made what reparation he could.

That news spilled instantly out of the jail and spread through Crooked Horn.

It was the dawn of the day, and as the tidings went from kitchen to kitchen and from field to field, it was picked up and swelled by the wings of rumor. If Lynmouth was reinstated by the heroism of that feat at the Bore house, he was redoubly established now that the mystery of his shame was exposed.

Everywhere the tidings went, and as it passed, smiles followed after.

But the sheriff himself rode wearily out to the house of William Oliver in the first freshness of the day to tell what he had heard and to put all things as right as might be.

He met Cherry Daniels on the way. She was coming in toward the center of town, riding hard, but she checked her horse when she saw the sheriff.

"What is it, Chick?" she asked.

He told her briefly, and she nodded, a flash of joy in her eyes; though they instantly went grave again.

"That makes everything as easy as sliding down hill, for Larry," she declared.

"You look white, Cherry," said the sheriff. "What's wrong with you?"

At this, she hesitated for a moment.

"I'll tell you, Chick," she said at last. "I've been play-ing a game in which the stakes were pretty big. I've been playing and hoping for a good draw. There was a while when I thought that I was going to have the luck; but then everything went wrong, and now I'm pulling out. I've checked out and I'm going home."

Chick Anthony stared at her.

He understood perfectly what she meant, for gossip in Crooked Horn was more exact than any telescope for finding out the minds and motives of people.

"All right, Cherry," said he. "You listen to me, though. There ain't anything such as losin' when you've played the game straight!"

"Do you think so?" said she wistfully.

"I know so," he answered. "Go back to Jackson Ford —and wait. There's always more than one good hand in a pack!"

She smiled again, faintly, but no color came back to her cheeks.

Then, with a wave of her hand, she went galloping off down the road and away forever, he knew, from the life of Larry Lynmouth.

He went on, more slowly, with some of the pleasure taken from his mind. For, as a matter of fact, he was aware that all the world of that vicinity would be focus-ing toward the same point. He was only an extra messen-ger in this play of happiness!

At the gate of the Oliver house he was stopped by a strange warden—little Brother Juan, who held up his hand.

"My friend," said Juan, "are you a bringer of good news or of bad news?"

"Good news," said the sheriff.

"Enter, then," said the friar. "I am a sentry here to keep out the other kind."

"From Lynmouth?" asked the sheriff curiously.

"Aye," said the friar.

"Tell me," said Anthony, "what makes you such a friend to him, Juan?"

"Brother," said the friar, "when you see in a circus a man walking a tight wire, you wish for his safety."

"Aye," said the sheriff, "and Lynmouth, he's had his

share of close shaves. His neck had been next to busted more times than one!"

"I was speaking of his soul," said the friar, smiling faintly. "But today, good news cannot harm him. By the grace of Heaven, after this day he never can come to harm."

The sheriff went on, more slowly still, and coming to the house, he dismounted and met the banker, William Oliver, pacing up and down. He greeted the sheriff with a certain amount of constraint and apprehension. The latter dispelled this gloom at once. He told the story of the deathbed.

"Judge!" called Oliver.

Judge Bore came instantly from the house. He looked pale. His plump face sagged, and his eyes were tired; but he wore the smile of one who has seen something worse than death and lived through it.

"Judge," said the banker, "we have the dying words of Cress that he bribed Lynmouth to go through that horrible business in the saloon. Bribed him with money that he had won with a crooked gambling trick—a double-faced pair of coins, d'you see? And Lynmouth, it's plain, willing to stake his soul in order to have money enough to start life with Kate. A confession, too, that admits a pair of cold-blooded murders. I think that frees our minds concerning poor Larry, judge?"

The judge sighed with prodigious relief.

"I've sat on the bench for the last time, Oliver," said he. "I've made my last speech, and sat in the public sun for the last time. Hereafter, I have a ranch and a family, and no more. And the only wish that I have, outside of this, is that Larry Lynmouth may be happy. Where is he now?"

"Yes," said the sheriff, "he'll have to hear this from me, right pronto."

"I don't think he'd hear you," answered Oliver. "Listen!"

He raised his hand, but they did not need any perfect silence in order to hear the gay music of a girl's laughter inside the house.

"And the laughter of a man joined it in a deeply ringing note.

"She's supposed to be reading to him," said Oliver, smiling. "A lot they'll find in any book, today."

"Whose horse is that?" asked the sheriff suddenly, pointing.

"Why, that's Fortune, of course! Tom Daniels just brought her in. You won't be wanting Tom, sheriff?"

"No," said Anthony, "I want nothin' of any friend of Larry's. The town wouldn't let me hold 'em. Like you once said, judge, there's a good deal in public opinion."

"Aye," said the judge. He sighed, remembering the glory of that day in the schoolhouse. Then he shrugged. "Public opinion," said he, "it's usually right, but sometimes it takes a long time coming round! I've tried to lead it, Oliver, when I was blind, walking in the dark!"

A dog barked sharply from within the house.

"That's Jimmy!" said the judge, with a happy smile. "He ain't left Lynmouth. He wants to pull the bandages off of his face."

"Is he badly burned?" asked the sheriff.

"Singed," said Judge Bore. "Just pretty much singed. But if his whole face was burned away, what difference would it make? We know the heart of him now, and that's all that's worth seeing."